ALSO BY TOM LEVEEN

HELLV

HELLWORLD

TOM
LEVEEN

SIMON PULSE

New York   London   Toronto   Sydney   New Delhi

SIMON PULSE

An imprint of Simon & Schuster Children's Publishing Division

1230 Avenue of the Americas, New York, New York 10020

First Simon Pulse hardcover edition March 2017

Text copyright © 2017 by Tom Leveen

Jacket photograph copyright © 2017 by Arcangel/Rekha Garton

All rights reserved, including the right of reproduction in whole or in part in any form.

SIMON PULSE and colophon are registered trademarks of Simon & Schuster, Inc.

For information about special discounts for bulk purchases, please contact Simon & Schuster Special Sales at 1-866-506-1949 or business@simonandschuster.com.

The Simon & Schuster Speakers Bureau can bring authors to your live event.

For more information or to book an event contact the Simon & Schuster Speakers Bureau at 1-866-248-3049 or visit our website at www.simonspeakers.com.

Jacket designed by Jessica Handelman

Interior designed by Mike Rosamilia

The text of this book was set in Minion Pro.

Manufactured in the United States of America

2 4 6 8 10 9 7 5 3 1

This book has been cataloged with the Library of Congress.

ISBN 978-1-4814-6633-2 (hc)

ISBN 978-1-4814-6635-6 (eBook)

For Dianne, Michelle, Joy, and Alecia,
who drove into the darkness together

And for Bob,
who should be here

There exists a darkness so deep, so profoundly absent any light or hope, it causes dizziness and nausea. In this cave, with no source of light and the bodies of the dead surrounding us, there are already plenty of reasons to experience both.

I think we are in Hell.

What have I done?

Charlie's voice drifts to me through the black. "Abby?"

His breath comes out ragged, as if from between strips of flesh. I shut my eyes against the image. Open them. At least when I blink, I can feel my eyelids moving. That's something. But there is no difference between open and closed.

"Yeah?" I whisper. The sound goes only as far as my lips. It feels like being in the deep end of a pool, blindfolded, all sensation muffled.

"Selby?" Charlie says, but hesitantly.

Why did he ask for me first, when Selby's supposed to be his girlfriend? Because I had a better chance of being alive.

No response from Selby.

I listen hard, straining as best I can, trying to ignore the sound of my own heart attempting to fight its way out of my chest. Rocks and pebbles grind into my palms and knees. Finally, to my left, a miniscule whimper needlepricks my ears.

"Selby, say something," I whisper.

Another whimper—louder, but only by degrees.

"Charlie, she's here. She's alive."

"Okay," Charlie says. "Okay. I'm going to try to make my way over to you."

"My stomach . . . ," Selby moans.

I try to resist a memory of the knife plunging into her. "Don't move," I say. "Just don't move—we'll come to you."

Panic whirlpools in my torso, twisting every organ inside me to the south. I discover that teeth really do chatter if you're scared enough. Mine clack rapidly as ice water replaces the blood in my veins. Selby's bleeding, we're all effectively blinded, and we're trapped in here. Trapped, with what remains of *them* . . .

No, I tell myself. *No, Abigail. You can't lose it. Work the problem. You lose it now, in here, and you die.*

Death in here would not be a good way to go. Less painful than crucifixion or being drawn and quartered, sure, but the darkness . . .

Every moment we swim in it, I feel myself getting closer to terror and insanity. Buried alive. We'd likely die from dehydration. That would be the official cause. Not that anyone would ever find us. Dying of thirst will take two or three days. Two or three days to die.

But the darkness.

The hope that somehow, miraculously, we can inch our way in the pitch-black to find the cave entrance, the way we came in, and be free . . . but that hope is the worst part. Outside, we'd still die from lack of water, but we'd die with the sun or stars overhead, and fresh air in our lungs.

But the darkness . . .

"Stay where you are," Charlie says from some nebulous place in the black. "Keep talking. I'll make my way to you."

"The pit," I stutter through my quaking teeth. "You'll fall in."

"I'll go slow."

We can't have been in this chamber of the cave for very long, yet an eternity has passed since we found them.

Them . . . still in here with us . . .

Stop, stop, stop, I tell myself. *They're destroyed, they're dead, they can't hurt you.*

But they were dead before we got here, and that didn't stop them. They're still in here with us, still close enough to reach out, grab an ankle, a wrist, a throat . . .

No! Stay calm, Abby. Stay calm. Work the problem. Work the—

"The camera," I say.

I hear Charlie stop his slow slide across the gravel floor. "Huh?"

"Do you have it? Is it working?"

Selby whispers, "I wanna go home."

I ignore her. I hate to do it, but have to. "The viewfinder. If the camera's working, open the viewfinder. It'll be light. Not much, but something."

Charlie makes a sound in the darkness, like a sigh of realization. I hear more scuffling.

"Go slow," I say.

"Right."

Time goes blank again. Now that I've oriented my ears toward Selby, I can hear her breathing. Shallow, rapid, and very much like my own.

But I haven't been stabbed in the gut.

"Hang in there, Sells," I say. Then I realize I've used Alex's nickname for her, and hold my breath. Will it push Selby over the edge? *Is* there an edge for us anymore, after what we've seen? What we've *done*?

"Got it," Charlie says with a relieved, exultant note in his voice. In the underwater muffle of the darkness, I feel more than hear the electronic whine of the camera booting up.

Please, I beg, unaware that perhaps I might actually be praying and not caring if it's ironic or not. *Please just let it work. Just that tiny blue square of light, please, please, without light I will go crazy, I will go insane if I'm not already, because insanity pales in comparison to this all being real.*

Gray-blue light appears, no more than ten feet from me; tiny and pathetic in the black, yet offering hope like the sun.

"Thank you," I say softly, but not to Charlie. The taut skin of his face glows in the light. He was so handsome two days ago. Confident and relaxed. Now fear draws tight lines down his features, distorting his good looks.

Charlie slowly slides toward me, pointing the viewfinder at the cave floor to make sure he doesn't slip into the pit in the center of the cavern. I don't know how long it takes; maybe a minute, maybe a year. Maybe eternity. When he reaches me, he sets the camera down carefully before surrounding me with his arms. I can feel by the strength and weakness in his embrace that he is as grateful for the contact as I am. Warm, living, human flesh. We bury our heads into each other's shoulders, trembling.

"Okay," Charlie breathes. "I have to get Selby."

"I'm coming with you."

Staying close, we tell Selby to start talking so we can get to her.

"Selby, come on," I urge. "Please, you have to talk so we—"

"Hydrogen," Selby says at last. "Helium. Lithium. Beryllium."

Charlie and I look at each other, and seem to realize at the same time what she's reciting: the periodic table of elements, by order of atomic weight. Selby and I are both sixteen, yet she sounds infinitely younger right then. Or maybe I just feel immeasurably older.

We slide toward the sound of her voice. "Boron. Carbon. Nitrogen."

"We're coming, Sells."

"Oxygen. Fluorine. Neon."

"Almost there," Charlie says. "We're almost there; keep talking."

"Sodium. Magnesium. Aluminum."

"I hear you. We're getting closer."

"Silicon. Phosphorus. Sulfur . . ."

Finally, we see her. Selby sits against one of the cavern walls, curled into an upright ball, squeezing her knees to her chest and shivering, both hands pressed against her side. A far cry from the militant teen scientist I met two days ago.

Selby reaches out as we near, and the three of us huddle close together. Maybe crying, I don't know. I hope not. We need to retain the water.

"Wanna go home," Selby says into our cluster. "I wanna go home."

"We are," I say, sounding much more confident than I would have thought possible. "Let's get to the bags, see what we've still got left, and we'll work our way out of here. Okay?"

I think Selby nods, but can't tell in the grim, cold light from the viewfinder.

"How's your stomach?" I ask.

"Uh, *stabbed*, thanks."

I take her tone as a good sign. "Okay. Do you have your lighter?"

I can still smell cigarette smoke on her clothes from before we entered the cave. How long ago? How long now?

Selby pulls a small pink cigarette lighter from her hip

pocket. She winces as she does it, keeping her other hand pressed against her side where the blade went in.

"How much battery in the camera?" I ask Charlie. Now that we're together and have at least a few square inches of light, the urge to run hard and fast from the cavern is overwhelming.

"There's one bar. So not much."

"We better hurry, then. But careful."

Selby's lighter and the dim glow from the camera don't offer much light, and neither will last too long anyway. I don't honestly think we'll have sufficient illumination for enough time to navigate our way back out of this godforsaken labyrinth. Yet we can't rush, either. Rushing might get us killed. We've already lost one person on this trip. One, and so many more.

Which brings up a question. "What about . . . *them*?"

Charlie and Selby both give me shocked looks. Charlie says, "We can't . . . We're not bringing them out. No."

"Okay. Just wanted to make sure we agreed on that. Let's go."

We scoot back the way we had come, toward our equipment bags.

The news isn't good when we reach them, but could be worse. Some of our stuff fell in the pit when it opened up. Left over in the camera bag, we find two full batteries for the camera, Charlie's iPhone with about half its life left, and three bottles of water. Since we didn't have to do much climbing into the cave—we never even needed ropes—this might be enough light and water to get us out. It just might.

It also just might not. If we lose all sources of light between here and the entrance to the cave, we won't find our way out. We will not. That's the math.

We spent almost eight hours hiking to get this far, to get to where the pit opened up. We had flashlights and headlamps, moving at a careful pace with breaks and food. To find our way out with a viewfinder, a cell phone, and a lighter will take much, much longer.

Not to mention whatever will be waiting for us outside if we even make it.

The three of us stand together, with me helping Selby up. We stare up the steep incline that will take us to the first leg of our escape.

"What if they're waiting for us?" Selby whispers. "What if those things are just waiting for us to show up?"

"We don't have any choice," I say. "We can't stay here."

Instinctively, I cast a nervous glance over my shoulder, waiting for the dead to spring back to life.

Again.

But they don't. Everything is silent.

"Okay," Charlie says, adjusting the bag over his shoulder. "Nice and easy."

He takes one last glance behind us in the darkness, as if he can spy Alex. Even though he can't possibly see him, Charlie whispers, "I'm sorry, man. Love ya."

I consider saying something too, but the darkness is too oppressive, and I can't think. We start hiking up the incline, needing to use our hands as much as our feet, not knowing what the world will be like if we find the entrance. We may wish we'd stayed in the dark and died.

Part of me wants to run through the cave. I'm able to shove the instinct down, but it's not easy. Another part of me wants to crawl, because it would be so much safer. We end up splitting the difference, staying on our feet, walking close together, supporting each other over dry gravel that's as slippery as water.

I noticed the dryness of the cave as soon as we entered. Even as we went deeper and farther into the labyrinth, following the signs and symbols in Charlie's dad's book, we found no water. Now, as we shuffle along the floor of the cave using the dim light from the viewfinder, I start wishing for a distant dripping sound. Something other than the sound of our breathing, our shoes in the dirt, the thunder of our hearts. Hearts that I'm sure can't take much more stress.

"Oh, God," Charlie says softly.

My impulse is to ask, *What?* but I figure it out almost as soon as he says it.

At our feet, off to one side, a boulder has been crushed. Crushed to powder and pebbles, like nothing more than chalk. I remember passing the round rock about as tall as a coffee table, right before we'd reached the slope we'd just hiked. It would take a team of men with sledgehammers and jackhammers to put that rock into its current pulverized state.

"It was stepped on," I say.

We don't stop to examine it.

Without discussing, we start to move faster. I try not to imagine we are being followed by anything alive or dead.

God, what have I done. . . .

THEN—THREE WEEKS AGO

Dad declared Mom dead two years ago. I had to talk him into doing it, because we needed the life insurance money so badly. I never realized how quickly cash in the bank can get used up when there's only one parent working—and then only sometimes, and never for very much money. When you're little and don't know about things like banks and savings accounts and IRAs, you just assume your parents will take care of you. But they don't, not always. Sometimes it's the other way around.

When I got home from my shift at Arby's a few weeks ago and saw Dad's ten-year-old Toyota in the driveway parked next to where Mom's Jeep used to sit, I knew what had happened. I cursed out loud and stopped in the middle of the sidewalk to prepare myself for what would be waiting inside the house.

Our house looked about the same as the other houses lining our street: single-story, small front lawn or gravel yard, concrete driveway, one- or two-car garage. The very model of middle-class Henderson, Nevada, named one of the safest cities in the country just a few years ago. Safe on the outside, maybe. As for inside, one could never tell by the pale look-alike walls of each home.

Mrs. Brower, our next-door neighbor, must've seen me standing out there. I thought of her as being between ninety and nine hundred years old and, in some ways, one of my best friends. I didn't get out much. My fast-food coworkers were mostly the sex-and-drugs crowd, two things about which I had little knowledge. Plus, I had to keep an eye on Dad so often, it didn't matter if anyone invited me to partake in either one.

"Oh, Abby!" Mrs. Brower called from behind her white security door. "I'm so glad I caught you."

I pulled on my Happy Abby mask and walked up to her front door. She muscled it open with her elbows, clad in an emerald cable-knit sweater. Her blue jeans looked about as scuffed as the pair at home I desperately wanted to change into, leaving the impression that she was cursed to be a teenager in an old lady's body.

"Here, I've got it," I said, pulling the door the rest of the way open.

"Oh, thank you, this thing is so hefty," Mrs. Brower said as she passed me a blue pot with a glass lid.

I took it by the handles, feeling waves of warmth like a grandmother's hug radiating from the sides.

"I made too much of this pasta," Mrs. Brower said. "I thought you and your dad might like to have the rest."

"Thank you so much. That sounds great."

"Oh, hold on, hold on," Mrs. Brower chirped and shuffled deeper into the house. Her hips were not in the best of shape. I'd never seen the bottoms of her feet off the floor.

She came right back with a loaf of French bread still intact and in its crinkly brown paper grocery wrap, which reminded me of her skin. "I'll never finish this whole thing," she said, snuggling the loaf under my arm. "You two have it. Maybe I'll sneak by for a bite before it's all gone."

My facial muscles strained as I fought to maintain my expression. "Sure, please do. Thank you so much for this."

"I'm making some peanut blossom cookies later," she went on, winking. "I might be able to lug my old bones over to share one or two."

The vast majority of people should not wink, in my opinion. But Mrs. Brower's felt different. Authentic.

"You don't have to do that," I tried to say, but, as always, I could not change Mrs. Brower's mind.

"I'll just stop by real quick," she said, leaning her short body against the doorframe with her fingers in her hip pockets. The pose reminded me of a movie star. James Dean, I think, or someone cool like that from the fifties. I wondered if Mrs. Brower had been *a real dish* at my age. Probably. I could see it. I hoped I looked as good as she did when I got to be whatever her age was.

"Thanks," I said, and wondered how many times I'd said *thank you* in the past three minutes. Too many. I hate charity. Even when they're charity *cookies*.

"Well, here," she said, standing up straight. "Get on home, I'm keeping you. There's sausage in the pasta, by the way. Really good hot Italian. *I* could sure use a really good hot Italian!"

When I laughed for real that time, I could've sworn I felt rust flaking off my vocal cords.

"Mrs. Brower! My virgin ears."

My ears weren't the only virgin part of me, but my innocence wasn't exactly under any immediate threat these days. I elected not to mention that to Mrs. Brower. We were friends, but not *that* kind.

She cackled delightfully. "Oh, I can't help it. It keeps me young. No rush on getting the dishes back, take your time. I *do* know where you live."

"Fair enough."

Mrs. Brower reached out and gently squeezed my elbow. "I'm praying for you, sweetie. All right?"

"Thank you." How many was that now? Five times? Six? I never knew how else to respond when she said that. *No, please stop—prayer is for delusional people who think a magical sky fairy grants wishes that are patently impossible?*

Even though that's what I tended to think, I would never say it to Mrs. Brower. Or anyone else, really. If she wanted to believe in that sort of thing, she had that prerogative. Just like I had the prerogative to know it was a waste of time.

"Take care," Mrs. Brower said.

"I will—you too. Thanks again." I walked across her drive-way, through the decorative river rocks dividing our proper-ties, and to my front door. We'd had grass in the front yard once. Now our yard boasted only dirt and yellow weeds. We were starting to get complaints.

I let my happy mask drop as I pushed the door open. It felt like entering a cavern: everything dark and cold. Our front blinds were closed tight, and the only light came from the tele-vision ahead of me in the living room, making my father look like a corpse.

Dad sat on our couch, eyes half-lidded, gazing at the TV. Reruns of *M*A*S*H*. I'd had to cancel our cable months ago after Dad lost his previous job, so all we got now were about seven antenna channels.

I said nothing as I shut the front door, blocking out the afternoon sun. As if Dad were a vampire who would burst into flame if exposed for too long. Without a word, I walked past him to the kitchen, set the pasta on the stove and turned the burner on low, then tossed the bread into the microwave to seal it from the air. I moved to stand in the arch between the living room and kitchen. Needle-legged spiders had woven a home high in one corner of the archway.

"Mrs. Brower made us dinner." I struggled not to add the word "again."

"Mmm," Dad said.

I leaned against the wall, digging my hands into my black

uniform pants pockets, feeling less cool than Mrs. Brower had looked. "Want to tell me what happened today?"

"No." He wasn't quite looking at the screen, his eyes aimed just a little below it. On TV, B.J. refused to let a soldier die on Christmas.

"Are you going back?"

"No."

"Dad, you have to work."

"I know, I know, Plum. I'm sorry. I'm trying. Jesus, I'm trying."

The words were undead. Rote memorization and recitation. Even throwing in his nickname for me, "Plum," didn't impress me. "Plum" wasn't the greatest nickname of all time, but it was his for me, and that's all that mattered. Usually, secretly, I loved it. Times like this, it just made the ache sharper.

"Okay, well. Look again tomorrow, okay?"

"Mmm."

"You want some spaghetti? There's sausage in it. It's really good."

I knew that from previous experience with Mrs. Brower's dinners. If Dad wasn't going to be working again for awhile, that meant a nauseating amount of take-home Arby's for both of us. That got old after the first two times.

"No," Dad said.

I watched him for a minute. If not for the slow rise and fall of his stomach, he could have been dead there on the couch. The springs and cushioning had given way, creating a Dad-shaped divot conforming to his body.

"Want me to wake you up in the morning?" I asked.

"Sure."

"Sure" was code for *whatever*; or more often, *probably not*; or, *you can try but it won't work; I'll just go right back to bed as soon as you're gone.*

"I'll wake you up, and you can drive down to the library and check out the job sites." I sounded like Mom when she used to tell me I was, in no uncertain terms, going to clean my room, or finish homework, or wash the dishes.

We had no Internet at home anymore, so that meant frequent trips to the library, where Dad could go online to search for jobs. It's also where I went to school now, essentially, in increments of only thirty minutes depending on the length of the line of people waiting to use the computers. I took online classes exclusively these days, trying to get my diploma as fast as possible so I could get better work as fast as possible and with a little luck even get into college . . . as fast as possible. Usually, I came to the library in the midmorning or early afternoon to study, but I always seemed to run into conflicts with my work schedule. Lately, I'd been thinking of just taking my GED tests and getting the whole stupid thing over with.

"Okay," Dad muttered, as sullen as the teenager I should have been.

I took that response as an improvement. "Okay" was code for *I'll at least attempt to do what you said.* I probably wouldn't get any better from him.

Going back into the kitchen, I forked some of Mrs. Brower's

pasta into a bowl. Adding a couple slices of the French bread
to it, I carried my dinner out to the backyard, unable to handle
eating beside Dad in the dark, or even sitting in the kitchen and
overhearing the brave men and women of the 4077 save more
lives in Korea. We needed our own Hawkeye in this place.

Our house had one of the few tall trees in the area: an old,
crusty, yet somehow smarmy pine rising higher than even the
two-story houses that peered over our walls from adjacent
streets. As if apologizing for my childhood outrage that our
house had one *stupid* story instead of two *awesome* stories like
so many of the other places nearby, Dad had built me a tree
house in the pine. The tree house consisted of a single four-by-
eight piece of plywood that formed the floor, with two sides
protected by a railing. Nothing fancy like you'd see on TV,
and I didn't mind. The other two sides were open, and faced
our small patio. It was about fifteen feet up, and accessed by a
wooden ladder nailed into the trunk.

The way the branches fanned out provided enough privacy
for the tree-climbing girl I'd been, but also formed a hole straight
overhead through which I could watch the stars when I'd come
out at night with Mom's desserts. Sometimes, back then, Mom
came up with me and we'd eat while she pointed out stars and
constellations, and told me about how we were all made up of
star stuff, and that the universe was so big there were galaxies we
didn't even know about yet because their light hadn't reached us.

I missed those desserts. I missed being that girl.

I missed Mom.

"How long's it been?" Selby whispers. Her voice is cramped.

"Since we climbed up?" I ask.

She nods, and holds my arm even more tightly.

"Maybe an hour," Charlie answers.

Neither Selby nor I say anything. Charlie's expression, what little we can see of it by the light of the camera screen, gives him away. He has no idea, no more than we do, but we also know not to check the time on his phone. No reason to waste battery, not even for a second.

"Are the bandages holding?" I ask her.

"Think so."

"Let me see if you're still bleeding."

The three of us pause, Charlie swings the camera toward us—then, dark.

Selby squeals, "*Noooooo.*"

"It's okay, it's okay," I say quickly. How much more adrenaline can my body take?

"Don't move," Charlie says. "Just stand exactly where you are."

I force deep breaths through my nose. *Slow, slow*, I tell myself. *Go easy, Abby.*

Having even the small bit of bluish-white light from the camera taken away, battering us back into the blackness of the cave, makes the darkness worse.

Having that glimmer to hang on to, then losing it . . . it makes it worse.

The *hope* makes it worse.

I wonder if this is how Dad feels every day. Every day, wondering if Mom will call, or show up at home. Five years of wishing and waiting.

And hoping.

I need to call him. As soon as we get out of this damn cave, I have to call him, make sure he's okay. Tell him *I'm* okay. He has no idea I'm here. How stupid am I? I should have told him exactly where we were going. But I couldn't, not at the time. It would've just sent him spiraling . . .

No point worrying about it now. The important thing is to get to my phone and check in.

But how can I tell him about Mom? How can I make him understand what we saw?

Charlie fumbles around with the bag. I hear a series of clicks and bumps, then the camera viewfinder blazes back to life.

"The battery died, is all," Charlie says, shouldering the bag again. "This one's full. It'll buy us some time."

"But not much," I say. I hunker down and peel up the hem

of Selby's shirt. A circle of blood the size of a quarter stains the gauze, but I don't think it's any worse. Then again, I'm not a nurse.

"I think it's okay. Let's go."

She nods briskly and straightens her back, lifting her chin defiantly.

Even if it really has been an hour since we crawled out of the cavern where we found the pit, we have no less than seven hours to go. Considering our snail's pace, probably a lot more.

I don't want to die in the dark. There's no "letting your eyes adjust," because there's nothing for them to adjust to. Only the black—a cataclysmic black that would probably fool us into thinking we were dead long before our bodies dried to death.

"Let's go a little faster," I say.

We go a little faster.

"I'm thirsty," Selby says after several minutes of shuffling more quickly along the dusty ground.

Charlie pauses only long enough to hand her a fresh bottle of water. Selby takes it, sips from the top, and holds it back toward him.

"No, drink it," I say. "Sipping won't prevent dehydration. You have to drink."

"Girl Scout," Selby calls me, but tremulously. I appreciate, briefly, her attempt to make a joke. It's a good sign.

Selby takes two big drinks. It may as well be blood leaking from all three of us. Life-giving fluid, now gone. Irreplaceable until and unless we reach the outside.

"The RV will have food and water," I say, mostly to hear myself say it.

"Yeah," Charlie says. His voice is lifeless.

No. Not lifeless. I know now what a truly lifeless voice sounds like. Charlie is still warm and breathing. But I understand his tone. He knows as well as I do that after the creatures that came out of the pit, after seeing what remained of that smashed boulder, the chances of the RV being in any kind of useful condition are slim.

"I don't wanna die down here," Selby says.

"We're not," I say.

"You don't know that."

"No. But I know talking about it isn't going to help."

Selby falls silent. The cavern echoes with our footsteps crunching over gravel. Here and there we spot more crushed rocks and boulders, all victims to the pounding feet of some of the animals we saw escaping the pit. If "animal" is even the right word.

I wait until we creep up another steep, jagged embankment before asking Charlie and Selby both, "What were they? What do you think they were?"

"It doesn't matter," Selby says immediately.

We climb onto a flat stretch of ground, and pick up our pace to a walk rather than a shuffle. The ceiling is tens of feet overhead, so there's no threat of banging into something and knocking ourselves out.

"It *might* matter," I say. "It might matter a lot. We let them out. They shouldn't even exist, but we all saw them. What do you think they were? Come on, you're a scientist."

"I won a science fair."

"Yeah, but you're brilliant. Going to Caltech, remember? So come on. What do you think?"

"Talking about it isn't going to help," Selby says, echoing me with razor clarity.

I glance at Charlie for help. He doesn't say anything. Silenced, I go first over a pile of rocks blocking our path.

Maybe she's right. Maybe talking about what we let loose just doesn't matter.

THEN

When I was about four years old, a new satellite TV network launched called Outasite. As in, "out of sight." As in, "way out there."

Outasite began as a repository of every old, weird, supernatural, and creepy television show that ever aired, plus several that never should have, and with good reason. Most shows were from the 1990s, like *The X-Files*. Some shows dated back to the eighties and even seventies or earlier. *The Twilight Zone*, *The Ray Bradbury Theatre*, *Alfred Hitchcock Presents*, *Unsolved Mysteries*, etcetera. The guy who played Spock on *Star Trek*—the original guy—hosted a seventies-era show called *In Search of . . .* that always talked about Stonehenge and those crystal skulls from Central America.

Any show having anything to do with government conspiracies, cryptids like Bigfoot or Nessie, UFOs, ghosts, legends, myths—you name it, Outasite aired it. On the weekends they played science-fiction and horror movies, mostly B-grade stuff and oldies you can get for free online. *Night of the Living Dead*, for example, or the black-and-white version of *Last Man on Earth*.

They had original programming too.

My mother became a cohost on one of these original shows: *The Spectre Spectrum*. Even I can admit that *TSS* came off as an obvious rip-off of the show *Ghost Hunters*, but *TSS* had actual scientists of varying disciplines, rather than plumbers, going on ghost hunts. Not to badmouth the *GH* guys; they were really cool. I met them a few times, at conventions and stuff, and they were always nice. One of them even guest-starred on a *TSS* ep once in season one.

The Spectre Spectrum wasn't trying to prove or disprove anything. They just wanted the truth. At least, that's what the opening voice-over always said. My mother was originally a crime scene investigator, which was not nearly as glamorous as the TV shows make it seem. Her cohost, Dr. John Prinn, was an anthropologist specializing in world religions and cults. Dr. Prinn also happened to have two sons, Charlie and Stephen, and I think I started crushing on Charlie the moment I met him. I was nine at the time. Mom thought it was cute. Every week, Mom and Dr. Prinn brought in guest hosts, some of whom came back on a regular basis, and others who clearly did not belong on television. They almost got Neil deGrasse Tyson once, which would have been awesome.

The first season of *The Spectre Spectrum* ended on a cliff-hanger in a mansion in Cumberland, Maine, and ratings rocketed. Had Mom and Dr. Prinn stumbled into concrete evidence of the supernatural when one of their cameramen captured the milky image of a woman in an old-fashioned dress roaming this allegedly haunted house? Skeptical fans who'd enjoyed their takedowns of ESP, tarot cards, and hauntings tuned in to see if the show had sold out; true believers tuned in to see if their beliefs would be vindicated. Season two began with Mom and Dr. Prinn admitting they could not prove nor disprove anything supernatural in the film evidence. Internet message boards lit up with fans taking sides and arguing amongst themselves, and the show's following grew.

Mom and John Prinn were into a rhythm by then, and had great on-screen chemistry. I'm old enough now to know that, sure, maybe some sexual tension existed between them. Proximity has that effect. But as far as I know, nothing ever went on. It's also entirely possible they were *acting*. They had a show to do, after all.

"*All* television is entertainment television," Mom said once.

Season two ended strong, with what one reviewer called "a withering, if not blistering, disassembly and utter demolition of medical miracles." *TSS* became Outasite's highest-rated and most-watched show. Dad got to quit his job as a software engineer and just focus on raising me and building golf clubs, this odd hobby he enjoyed. We weren't rich, but Mom did well that year.

Season three of *The Spectre Spectrum* promised to be even

better as the team went to shoot the first episode at an allegedly haunted cave in remote Southern Arizona.

Except the episode was never finished, and *TSS* went off the air.

While shooting that first ep of season three, my mother, Dr. Prinn, and their entire film crew disappeared. No one had heard from them since.

There had been a search for my mom and the film crew, of course. In the cave and the outlying areas. An investigation that went on and on. But Mom and Dr. Prinn, and the six others who were on the shoot, had simply and literally vanished. The belongings of the cast and crew had been left in the TV trucks and vans like they were expecting to come back. No signs of struggle, no signs of violence, nothing missing. Nothing but eight people, anyway. The cave had proven to be too massive to search in its entirety.

Mom's TV show about strange, inexplicable events actually became a TV show about a TV show about strange, inexplicable events. NBC produced *The Mystery of the Spectre Spectrum*, a two-hour documentary on their disappearance. A handful of knockoffs and "special reports" followed on cable and satellite. The web burst with conspiracy theorists who said our parents had found everything from John F. Kennedy alive, to ancient aliens, to a government facility using Americans as laboratory rats. Those were some of the more *reasonable* ideas floated.

Most people believed there'd been an accident in the cave. A massive ceiling collapse, maybe, or unexpected flooding . . . or maybe they just got utterly lost. The unnamed and unexplored cave spidered out into dozens if not hundreds of side tunnels, a colossal labyrinth underground. Despite a month of searching, no trace of them had ever been found. So the accident theory is what Dad eventually accepted. Or, rather, tried to accept.

That's what I tried to believe too. But I couldn't. Not deep down. Not really.

Mom, like John Prinn, was a skeptic. A scientist who had no time for ghosts, cryptids, or miracle resurrections. I asked her about God once, while she was still a CSI, and she hugged me and said, "Abby-dabby, in my line of work, I've seen too much of what humanity can do to one another to think there's anyone out there looking out for us."

That had been pretty sad, but then Mom said, "But I will look out for you, always. No matter what."

And I believed her. Maybe that's why I still held out hope that somehow, someday, they'd be found alive somewhere. Or, more likely, maybe someday we could have solid confirmation they were all dead. Not the happiest thought, but at least maybe then we'd find peace.

I was eleven when we lost Mom, and Dad was coming up on forty. Over the following months, though, Dad turned into an old man and I turned into a grown-up. That's how we managed to deal. He checked out and I stepped up. I made sure the bills got paid, made sure we had food, fed the cat, pushed Dad to get to his doctor appointments . . .

It hadn't been a great five years. We'd even lost the cat.

Sitting alone in my tree house after eating my bowl of Mrs. Brower's pasta, I shook myself out of yet another reverie about Mom. Nothing to gain by moping. Besides, Dad had cornered the market there.

I rested my head against my raised knees and tried taking deep breaths. I didn't want to be angry at Dad, but it had been getting harder lately. Knowing he'd quit yet another job wasn't helping my emotional stamina.

Once my thoughts shifted to my current frustration with Dad, I couldn't switch them off. Trying to get him into this last job had been hell. He'd finally gotten some low-level data-crunching job, or at least that's what he called it, and possibly only because I'd driven him to a Supercuts before the interview so he'd look mildly presentable. The job had lasted two entire months, as of today. His record so far? A whole year. Things had gotten worse again.

You're not supposed to parent your parent. Not when you're eleven or twelve—or sixteen. It wasn't fair. The truth is, I hadn't ever really cried over Mom because I hadn't had time thanks to Dad's depression. Plus, what could I cry over? No body, no casket, no last words. Nothing beyond photos on our old laptop and my DVDs of *The Spectre Spectrum*.

Dad didn't know I still watched them sometimes. Watched Mom's hairstyle and once-stylish blouses slowly drift out of fashion as she stayed the same age year after year, and the rest of the world moved on, like some kind of godforsaken eternal life.

Sometimes, that's what bothered me most. The whole world just moving on, like it didn't care where my mother went or that she wasn't coming back. What kind of world was this? Mom was kind and good and smart and awesome, and it was no wonder Dad tanked when she disappeared. I sort of wished I could have reacted like he did, except I think we would have starved to death.

Once the sun had set, I climbed down from the tree house and went back inside. Dad had fallen asleep, collapsed on the couch with a book-on-CD playing over our antiquated DVD player. The book, called something like *How to Get Off Your Butt and Stop Feeling Sorry for Yourself*, sounded identical to the others he'd tried. I didn't think they'd helped. Probably we should have returned them for a refund, or resold them on Amazon. The cash would help.

I got out of my smelly work uniform and took a long and very hot shower. Once you get french-fry scent in your skin and hair, it's almost impossible to get out. Gone were the days of natural herbal shampoos and frankincense soap bought by the ounce from natural-foods stores. Now we bought the cheapest stuff available at Walmart. And didn't use much of it, at that. We had to conserve.

After dressing in real clothes, I pulled out a Saucony shoe box from beneath my bed, a remnant from when we could afford actual running shoes.

I took out the box sets of seasons one and two of *The Spectre Spectrum*. Mom and John Prinn glared defiantly at me from the back cover, arms crossed, faces set in *Prove it!* scowls.

Where were they now? Thanks to Mom, I had no real belief in any kind of afterlife, but sometimes I imagined I could still feel her watching us, telling us to get up and get on with life. I was trying, or at least I thought I was, but Dad . . .

Restless, I walked back out to the living room. Dad's CD still spun in the player. The stereo dated back to before Mom's disappearance. Just like everything else in this house: clothes, books, movies, electronics. Our relationship.

I sat down on the coffee table, watching him. Dad, out cold, lay with one arm draped over the edge of the couch, his face mashed up against the cushion.

"What can I do?" I whispered to his sleeping form.

He'd been to doctors, but never for long enough. He'd been on meds, when we could afford them. I didn't know a lot about pharmaceuticals, but I felt sure the yo-yoing back and forth between being on and being off couldn't be a good thing for his brain.

My eyes drifted to a family portrait on the wall behind the couch. The three of us, smiling and posed, but also relaxed because when that picture had been snapped, we'd all been laughing at how *unnatural* we looked. "We aren't a formal people," Mom used to say, meaning we didn't have things like "good china" or pointless knickknacks cluttering every free space. Our bookshelves were crammed with science books and ancient magazines that Mom always swore she'd organize someday but never did. Mom and Dad had been both pragmatic and relaxed: urging me to study hard but not above calling out sick for me so we could all go on an impulsive road trip to the science center, a day trip to an observatory, or just a hike around a lake. One advantage to their atheism was their quickness to embrace taking opportunities and chances as they came up, wanting to enjoy life as best as possible.

One disadvantage was it didn't help me know how to live without them—Mom physically and Dad emotionally.

I looked over my shoulder. More books surrounded the TV in the media case. The newest of them, of course, dated back five years. When Dad woke up, they would be the first thing he saw: memories of Mom glaring pointlessly back at him.

For someone who hadn't been seen in half a decade, Mom was everywhere in this house. How could she not be? Her books, the DVDs in my room, her clothes still in the closet and dresser because Dad couldn't bring himself to donate them . . .

Dad mumbled and whined in his sleep. Right then, I made up my mind.

It was time to move on.

The path through the cave, or what passes for it, begins sloping steeply uphill. That's good news, on the one hand, because every step forward and up is another step closer to the entrance of the cave. On the other hand, it's a lot harder to walk.

"Should we rest?" Charlie says. He's breathing a little hard. Not winded, not yet, but it's coming.

My own lungs feel constricted in the darkness, clogged up in the fathomless depths of the cave. How deeply into the earth did we go? Deep enough that it made breathing harder, anyway. Or maybe it's just fear. An entire mountain stands above us, pressing down. Despite not being in any tight spaces, the claustrophobia from just knowing how deep we are is enough to push my panic button again.

We check the time on Charlie's phone. Seventy-eight minutes since we left the pit behind. Not even an hour and a half. A day's walk still ahead of us. A *day*. A day without sun, without fresh air.

"No," Selby says, and her breath *is* strained. I wonder how many cigarettes she usually sucks down, and how much it must be affecting her stamina. "Let's just keep walking, okay?"

"Won't do us any good . . . to collapse," Charlie says, and grunts a little as we hit a steeper part of the embankment.

They're both right, but saying so won't make any difference. I get the feeling they're waiting on me, though. Waiting for me to break the tie.

I say nothing until we breach the ramp and reach somewhat level ground again. All three of us take a natural pause there, hands on hips, breathing hard. Or are we breathing harder? Is it getting worse?

"Let's take a break, but just three minutes or so," I say, knowing the three will likely be five or more.

Selby sits slowly straight down where she is. So Charlie and I follow. He passes around the bottle Selby drank from.

And we finish it.

"Know what?" Selby says, crunching up the plastic bottle between her hands. She chucks the bottle down the slope. I hear it crackling as it tumbles away. Selby peers down the incline, looking smug. "I'm just gonna fucking litter."

I can't say that we laugh, but that ridiculously minor act of defiance somehow cuts through the darkness for just a moment. Maybe it's enough.

Two bottles left.

After a few minutes—we don't count them, though—the three of us stand and keep trudging ahead. We don't talk anymore. Talking only dries out my mouth, which I try to remember to keep closed as we hike. We stop a few times to match up Dr. Prinn's notes in his book with the markings on the cave walls, and get a small rush of exhilaration each time we spot a chalk mark. We made them as we strove deeper into the cave, thinking at the time we were *a pretty gosh-darn bright group of kids!* So much for that.

Six hours pass. Six exhausting hours of walking, hiking, some climbing, resting, and drinking water. That's when the last of Charlie's camera batteries dies. I expect myself to panic as we fall into darkness again, but I don't. Being relegated to blindness once more feels anticlimactic at this point. Plus, we made good progress; there were twelve symbols from the book that we'd followed, and now there are only four left. Four ancient signposts of a sort, leading us out of this place and into a world I can only hope will be recognizable when we reach it.

Now that we've stopped, my thirst comes raging back. In the light of Selby's tiny pink lighter, Charlie weighs the battery in his hand as if he can feel if there is more charge in it.

"These are kind of heavy. I'm trying to think of any reason to lug them out of here with us."

"Leave 'em," Selby says.

I agree with her. Charlie drops the battery to the stone floor. It thunks solidly. He takes the other two out and drops them behind as well.

"Should've thought of that a while ago," he mutters.

"Cell phone next?" I say.

Charlie nods and activates the little flashlight on the back of his phone. It's brighter than the viewfinder glow had been, which is nice. I also wonder how long it will actually last.

"All right," Selby says. "Let's get the flock out of here."

If it's a joke, I don't get it. Selby stuffs her lighter into her pocket and charges ahead, pressing a hand against her side again.

"Selby, slow down," I say.

She makes some noise, the beginning of a comment, before disappearing from sight with a shout.

Charlie and I, not thinking, rush forward as Selby disappears from the light of Charlie's phone. A torrent of rocks and pebbles rains down after her. I can hear her shouting, sliding, scrambling . . . then screaming.

Charlie barks a curse as we reach the steep slope where we'd lost her. He shines the light down. Now that we're here, I remember it from . . . what, almost a day ago? It had been the only access to continue our trek through the cave. Now, from the top, Charlie's light doesn't reach far enough to see Selby.

"Can you see me?" Charlie calls.

"Yes!" Selby shouts back, but it comes with the lisp of clenched teeth. "I think I'm bleeding here."

"We're coming down," I say, rather stupidly, since there's no choice but *to* go down. I sit and slide my legs over the edge. It's not exactly a cliff, but the floor tilts down at more than forty-five degrees, like a natural playground slide. There had been several places like this, sloping upward of course, as we'd

hiked in. Dammit, we should have been paying more attention, anticipating these hazards on the way out.

"Take the light," Charlie says, handing me the phone. "I'll
follow you."

I shine the phone's flashlight down, lean back on my free
hand, and begin inching down. Inching lasts about ten seconds when gravity and loose stone take over, and I'm skidding
down the embankment on my rear, screaming. For a second,
I'm sure I will fall forever, fall in darkness till the universe ends.

Instead, I hit the ground, my back abraded by the rough
stone. The landing rattles my spine, vibrating my skull under
my scalp.

Charlie lands a second or two later, beside me.

"You okay?"

I nod and examine my hands. Scratched up but not awful.
I pick up the cell phone, which I dropped during the trip,
grateful it didn't shatter.

That was close. Way, way too close. Another wrong move
like that could cost us the flashlight in the phone. Then we'd be
done. Our lives now rely on a sixteenth-inch bulb mass produced in China. Not exactly comforting.

"Selby?" I call, shining the light.

I find her sitting on the ground, holding her side. Her teeth
are clenched tight together, and she's trembling.

"Sells?" I say, and scoot closer.

"Pretty sure some shit got broke," she says, not unclenching
her jaw.

"What, like bone?"

"I don't know. . . . Jesus, it hurts."

Charlie and I surround her. Again I pick up her shirt to look at the bandage. There's more blood now. Fresh blood.

"Charlie, do we have anything else?"

"No. The kit got lost in the . . . thing. Here."

Charlie whips off his shirt. And, so help me, Selby and I both steal looks at his torso. For as stupid as it is, maybe it makes a morbid sort of sense. Who knows how much longer we've got? Might as well savor the little things.

Through Selby's grimaces and groans, Charlie ties the shirt around her midsection. "Best I can do."

"It's fine," Selby says, wincing. "Let's just go. Come on, we've got to be close, huh?"

"Clos*er*," I say. That's the best *I* can do.

Charlie takes the cell. We stand up and form a single-file line behind him with Selby between us.

Closer. We are *closer*, I tell myself. And we haven't run into any of the things from the pit. Maybe we'll make it. Maybe we'll really make it.

Then I smell smoke.

Leaving Dad behind on the couch, I went into their—

No. No, I went into *his* bedroom. It wasn't *theirs* anymore; nothing was *theirs*. It was his or mine or ours. But none of it, none of it belonged to Mom anymore, because there *was* no Mom anymore.

I yanked open the closet doors in the master bedroom. Mom's blouses and shirts hung where they always had, neat but in no particular order. I pulled the long sleeve of one shirt up to my nose, and inhaled deeply.

Nothing. Not so much as the barest whiff of any of her Mom scents, scents I'd forgotten years ago. She was gone, really gone, and keeping all this . . . this *shit* here wasn't helping me or Dad. Especially Dad.

He'll be mad, I told myself as I pulled her clothes down and laid them across the unmade bed. *He'll completely freak out.*

Yeah, but then maybe he'll get better. Keeping all of her things obviously hadn't helped, so maybe this would.

I piled the shirts on the bed, then moved to her dresser. I yanked out shorts, socks, everything, barely aware that each handful got flung with greater force until I looked like a dog digging a hole, throwing clothes out behind me. Five years of frustration boiled over until I found myself smacking and punching at the jumble of my mother's clothing. But I didn't make a sound.

Opening the bottom drawer was when I found the book.

Myth of Gods: The Reality of No Higher Powers, by Dr. John Prinn.

I recognized the cover because we had a copy on one of our shelves in the living room. He'd written the book before *The Spectre Spectrum* ever got started. Apparently, it didn't bother Dad that a book of someone so closely associated with Mom and her disappearance sat there staring at him day in and day out. Or maybe it did bother him, and it just went to show that I had the right idea to purge the house of everything associated with Mom and *The Spectre Spectrum*.

The cover of this particular copy of the book had been defaced by a black marker. It wasn't Mom's neat penmanship, so I thought at first that Dad had done it. But it didn't match his handwriting either. Flipping the book open and scanning the pages, I saw more notes—scrawls and drawings, like a junior high textbook defaced.

Was it John Prinn's handwriting? If it wasn't Mom's or Dad's, then who else could have made the marks? Mom had joked more than once about being unable to read his handwritten notes in the outlines for their shows, and the things scrawled in this copy of *Myth of Gods* definitely matched that description.

But why would he draw two thick black lines crossing through the title in an obvious X? And underneath the title of the book, Dr. Prinn—or whomever—had written a word:

Wrong.

I sat on the edge of their . . . of Dad's bed, crossing my knee with my ankle. Mom must've shoved this into her dresser, but why? The book hadn't been a big hit or anything, not to my knowledge. I opened it up to a random page, and felt my face go scrunchy. Dr. Prinn, if it was him, had written so many notes and drawn so many odd-looking symbols that the white margins were totally full.

I turned pages, slowly, then at a flip. More of the same. Almost every page had handwritten notes or drawings. Arrows pointed at certain words or phrases in the text. I expected highlighter marks as well, but all of Prinn's notes were in plain black ink, using underlines and circles to draw attention where he wanted it. It appeared as if he'd written them all in one long brainstorming session with whatever writing utensil he happened to have lying around. Some of the words could have been from ancient Mesopotamia, or something from Tolkien, for all the difference it made; words like "*tebah*" and "*sunteleias*" and "*skotos*."

Tebah = lifesaver, one note read. Another read, *Pains?* and another, *Ask Riley re: Patayan!*

"What on earth," I muttered. The text itself made sense; I hadn't read it when Mom started the show because I'd been too young to really get it. Looking at it now, the book seemed compelling enough. The premise, it seemed, revolved around deconstructing myths from around the world and showing how they all had a common source, back before modern man ruled as the only hominid on Earth, and that the entire concept of God was nothing but an evolutionary meme. Most of it struck me as sort of scholarly, but readable, something I might even enjoy now.

The handwriting, however, looked like something from a crime TV show. The kind of crazy evidence Mom might have studied at a scene when she used to be a CSI. The notes looked insane.

I closed the cover, my thoughts accelerating. Insane...What if something had gone wrong with John Prinn? What if...

What if it wasn't an accident after all, and he'd done something to them?

"Plum?"

Crap. Dad had woken up, and here I sat on a pile of Mom's clothes.

"What're you doing?" He didn't look or sound fully awake yet, standing in the doorway and rubbing his eyes.

I stuffed the book under a mound of shirts so Dad couldn't see it. I didn't know why; instinct, I guess. Something told me he didn't know this copy of the book existed, and I didn't think showing it to him would be a great idea.

"I thought, um . . . I thought maybe I'd clean up a little. You know. Donate some of Mom's stuff?"

I may as well have stabbed him in the gut with a spear. He dropped his hand from his face and didn't make eye contact with me as his face twisted and shoulders hunched.

"Yeah," he whispered. "Okay."

He turned and shuffled back down the hallway. I heard him fall into the couch. A second later he began to cry, the sounds muffled against the couch cushions.

Way to go, Abigail. Way. To. Go.

I put all of Mom's clothes back. John Prinn's book mattered more now, but I couldn't do anything about it until I got to an Internet connection.

I had to tell Charlie what I'd found.

By the time I'd finished with the clothes and went into the living room, Dad had fallen back to sleep. Just as well for what I needed to do. I hid the book in my room and rushed outside, heading over to Mrs. Brower's. I knew she had Internet and would probably let me use her desktop to access it. My phone was a cheap month-to-month, calls and texts only.

Mrs. Brower opened her security door a minute after I rang the bell. "Come in, Abby! What can I do for you? You look like you've seen a ghost."

That struck me as somehow morbid and ironic all at once.

I'd never talked to her directly about Dad's depression, but

I knew Mrs. Brower to be pretty bright. She had been a nurse back when, according to her, women could be nurses, teachers, or mothers, and nothing more. After her husband passed away, she went back to school and got a degree in psychology, which she then used to work at elementary and high schools as a counselor until retiring a few years ago. She probably could've diagnosed Dad just based on how my dad's walk changed, how often he stayed home, how little he weeded our yard. That was another one of my jobs now, and I'd fallen behind again.

I felt sure Mrs. Brower had kept up on Mom's case in the news, maybe even on the crazy quote-unquote documentary TV shows. We'd gotten calls on our landline for a long time, people asking for interviews from all these shows like *Revealed: Top Secret Files* and *Abducted.* Vultures is what they were. Dad eventually ripped the phone jacks out of the walls, and after a few months of past-due notices, I managed to get the line shut off. Ever watch a twelve-year-old girl try to argue with a phone company rep? Good times.

But Mrs. Brower and I had never really talked about the case itself. She'd expressed her condolences, and had been keeping Dad and me in dinners and desserts for a long time. One of the many things I loved about her: a lack of curiosity. Or perhaps an abundance of tact.

"Hi, Mrs. Brower," I said, walking in and shutting the door behind me. "I was actually wondering if it would be too much trouble to use your computer? I need to use the Internet, and the library will be closed before I can—"

Mrs. Brower waved her hand at me. "It's all yours. It's in the spare room, down the hall. There's no password, just hop on. Can I get you something?"

"No, I'm fine. Thank you."

She smiled at me and went into the kitchen. I heard *Jeopardy!* playing on her TV and Mrs. Brower shouting answers at it as I went into her spare room.

The computer predated me, I think, but functioned. I set the book down on the desk and Googled "Charlie Prinn."

It wasn't that I didn't know where he was or what he'd been up to. When taking breaks from homework on the library computers, I'd kept tabs on Charlie. He seemed to have done well for himself. A documentary he'd made won first place at a film festival in Phoenix, making him the youngest person to have done so. He had an IMDB page, most of which consisted of films he'd worked on, with job titles that struck me as behind behind behind the scenes. At least he'd made it into the industry.

It's safe to say Charlie was the first crush I'd ever had. He was eleven then, and I immediately wanted to kiss him. Mostly on the cheek. We met when Dad and I went with Mom to Los Angeles to meet with the executive producer of *The Spectre Spectrum*, a woman named Marcia Trinity. I remembered Charlie being quiet and serious, taking photos of absolutely everything around him with a digital camera. Even back then he'd had thick, dark hair that I wanted to wind around my fingers.

I was the only human being he took a picture of that day. Everything else was "still-life" artsy shots of doorknobs and things like that. I took it as a compliment.

After that first LA trip, we'd see each other every so often, like when his family came over for dinner, or when Dad and I visited the studio where they shot interviews and host segments. He always liked my tree house, and by the time Mom was shooting season three, I'd started imagining that's where we would have our first kiss.

Then the disappearance happened, and I got busy fast with keeping Dad upright and semi-mobile. I'd kept up with Charlie online after randomly searching his name in Google when I was thirteen, but hadn't reached out. What would've been the point? It had been too long by then, and he appeared to have moved on. No reason to drag him into my personal hell. Which sounds almost funny to say now.

It took a few minutes of digging around, but I finally found a phone number. I entered it into my phone, and shut the computer down.

"Thanks, Mrs. Brower," I said as I passed her kitchen doorway.

"Oh, you're welcome, Abby," she said, standing at the counter mixing dough. "Did you find what you needed?"

"I did, thanks." I started to go, then stopped. "Do you remember my mom very much?"

Mrs. Brower stopped mixing, sending me a surprised glance, which she hurried to soften. "Oh, my," she said, as if needing to say something and unsure what. "Yes. Yes, I do. She was lovely. Do you mind if I inquire what makes you ask?"

"Just been thinking about her lately. And what to do about . . . you know. Dad."

She nodded, giving me an understanding smile. "I do know how much she cared about you and your father. And you know what I remember most? That Jeep of hers. That bright yellow thing. You used to love it. I always worried about you sitting in the back there, even in your car seat. It always looked like the two of you were going on an adventure somewhere, but I tell you, she drove that car like a presidential limousine when you were inside."

A hole opened up in my sternum at the thought of the Jeep. I'd gotten Dad to sell it last year, after it'd sat in the driveway gathering dirt and rain and our loathing. The Jeep somehow embodied everything we missed most about Mom, and I wanted it gone. After I'd nagged Dad into submission—we'd needed the money—he'd said, "We'll get her a new one."

As if she'd be home any minute.

"Thank you," I said again, as I always did to Mrs. Brower.

"Abigail . . . if there's ever anything else you need . . ."

"I know. Thanks."

"Of course, dear. Come back anytime."

I said good-bye and went home. Dad still lay on the couch. I found myself veering outside and climbing into my tree house again. With fall starting, the air had already begun to cool, and it helped clear my head. But maybe not enough, because I was still going to make this call and suggest something absurd.

Which made me stop and stare at my phone, where Char-lie's phone number glared up at me, waiting.

"What are you doing?" I whispered, and my tree whispered nothing in return.

My plan, if it could rightly be called that, made no sense whatsoever. I knew that. Yet in the end, I think, I just needed to see Charlie. Even if my plans came to nothing, which was more likely than not, maybe seeing him . . . God, *talking* to him might be enough to get me through this next bout of Dad's depression. I had to try *something*.

My pulse throbbed high in my throat as I hit send. Then, a bit anticlimactically, I got his voice mail. I licked my lips and left a message.

"Hey, Charlie . . . it's um, it's Abby Booth. Hi. So, long time no see, huh? Um . . . so, listen, I found something today that belonged to my mom . . . or maybe your dad. . . . Anyway, it's a copy of his book. Only, he wrote notes in it. And he crossed out the title and wrote the word 'wrong' underneath it. And it got me thinking about them, about the whole disappearance, you know . . . and, um . . . I think I want to go look for them. . . .

"Do you want to help?"

"Do you guys smell that?" I say to Charlie and Selby.

"Fire," Charlie says. "Hold up."

We stop, and he presses the phone to his stomach to douse the flashlight. We plunge into darkness to look for evidence of flames.

"I don't see anything," I say. "What could be on fire in here, anyway? There's nothing to burn."

"Dunno," Charlie says. He brings the phone back up and we keep walking. "Maybe that's a good sign. Maybe it's outside, and we're closer than we thought. That's why we can smell it."

"Perfect," Selby says. Her voice sounds weak. "We get out of this fucking cave and into an inferno. Hallelujah."

The odor gets stronger as we move forward. There's no question something is on fire, but what? And where?

About an hour later, Charlie checks the book against a symbol on the cave wall.

"That's it," he says, like he's trying to keep the excitement out of his voice. "That's twelve, that's the last one."

"So we're almost there," Selby says. "Let's have that water."

Charlie holds our last bottle, and weighs it in his hand for a second. "We don't know what's out there. This might be the last water for a while."

"The RV," I say.

"If the RV is in one piece, sure. We don't know. We just don't. Maybe that's what's on fire."

"Damn," Selby whispers.

"Only one way to find out," I say.

Charlie nods, and we continue our hike. We do not take a drink.

After another hour passes, my throat dry, my legs weak, my eyes bleary . . . we see it. The entrance to the cave. Or rather, what's left of it.

"Holy shit," Selby says.

Despite untold hours in the dark and a day's worth of rock climbing and hiking, not to mention the horrors we'd faced at the pit, we don't rush to the mouth of the cave. Instead, we stop cold and try to comprehend the scene before us.

When we'd first come in, the cave entrance hadn't been more than a long crevice cut into a sheer cliff face, reminding me of a cracked ice cube. We'd had to come in one at a time, and sideways at that, following the crevice along for about ten yards before it opened up into the first chamber.

Now that crevice is gone. Utterly demolished. Standing at the far end of the first chamber, we're looking out a massive hole where the crevice once existed, like being in a miniature stadium.

Boulders and smaller rocks are strewn across the ground, as if the entrance had been dynamited. It's nighttime, and I can see stars glimmering faintly outside . . . but only through smoke.

The desert is aflame. Immediately outside the hole, the ground has been scorched, and charred ruins of bushes and cacti dot the landscape. But farther out, beyond our sight, it's obvious fires are raging, an orange glow on the horizon lighting the sky.

"The RV," Selby says. Her voice is stoic.

Our big van is still there, and apparently in one piece. The driver's side of the vehicle is blackened, as if attacked by a dragon's breath. The surrounding area, for as far as I can see, is as if a wildfire has swept through desert, burning everything to cinders. My nose wrinkles at the scent of smoke and burnt rubber. A greasy taste bathes my tongue, and I close my mouth.

"Take it slow," Charlie says. "Just in case there's . . . if they're out there."

Together, we pick through fallen and broken rocks, scanning in every direction, waiting to be ambushed by any of the things that have flown from the pit. But the desert is silent. We walk around crumbled earth and deep footprints the diameter of truck tires, stamped into the sandy and brittle earth.

"They knew which way to go," I say. "To get out of the cave, I mean. They knew this was the exit."

"Maybe," Charlie says.

We reach the RV's passenger door, which is oddly pristine and unblemished compared to the burnt driver's side.

"If they'd gone down the side tunnels, I think we would have heard them," I say.

Charlie grits his teeth and says nothing. He opens the door carefully, and for one horrible moment, I'm sure some gruesome hand will reach out and grab his entire skull, dragging him screaming into the RV. But no. Still quiet.

Charlie goes inside, and Selby and I follow. I close the door behind us, and lock it, then almost laugh. *Really? Locking it will help?*

Charlie goes to the fridge as Selby and I collapse on the long white couch in the front half of the RV. He pulls out water bottles and deli meats.

"Still cold," he says, and hands us the water bottles. Selby and I tear the caps off and drink, then the three of us shove the food down, trying to go slow but not succeeding. I never knew honey ham and string cheese could taste so good.

As we lean back and breathe, grateful to be out of the cave, hydrated and fed, Selby gets to her feet.

"Think I'm gonna lie down," she says, and totters to the queen-size bed in the back.

"I should check your bandage," I say, except I can't make myself get up. It doesn't matter; Selby waves halfheartedly and flops face-first onto the mattress, her boots sticking past the edge.

I don't remember anything until sunlight shining on my face wakes me up.

Sunrise.

Charlie called me back later that night.

"Abby Booth," he said, and I could hear him smiling. The thought of him smiling at me made my internal organs tickle.

"Hey, hi," I said, quick-stepping outside and climbing into the tree house. "How's it going?"

"Pretty good. You?"

"Well. You know."

"Nope, I don't. Hence the asking."

He's still smiling, I thought. Teasing. That was *great*. Sadly, it was the most fun I'd had in a very long time.

Then the reason for my call smacked me back to reality. "So, I found this copy of your dad's book."

The smile went away from Charlie's voice. "Yeah, tell me about that."

"It's a copy of *Myth of Gods*. But your dad, or someone . . . I assume it was him . . . someone wrote all over it. Notes and drawings and stuff. I'm pretty sure it's his handwriting. I know it's not my mom's."

"Huh," Charlie said.

It wasn't the burst of excitement I'd hoped for.

"It just gave me this idea today that . . . I mean, I haven't really thought it through or anything, but what if . . . just, like, what if we went and looked for ourselves? You know? Went to the cave and just looked around, tried to find something everyone else missed?"

Charlie took his time responding. "Everyone, meaning all the dozens of cops and cavers and rescue teams?"

"Yeah."

Even before I said it, I heard his point, loud and clear. What could I possibly find that all those professionals had missed? And after five years?

"It's an interesting thought," Charlie said, surprising me. "It's crossed my mind before."

"It has? For real?"

"Totally. Maybe not to the point of actually going out there, but yeah. I've always wondered. But what did you see in the book? We don't talk for five years, and out of nowhere you want to go all Indiana Jones? What's going on?"

His tone was serious. Concerned, even. For a second, I wrestled with the guilt of having not tried to contact him before now. I was eleven when Mom disappeared, and Dad and I had our hands full, first with the search, then with each other. Of course I'd thought about Charlie, wanted to talk to him, wanted to hang on to him. But one day led to another, which led to weeks then months, and suddenly trying to talk to him felt stupid. But I never forgot him. Never. Guys at school before I had to switch to online; guys at work, who were way too old and way too *absolutely never*; guys I happened to see when grocery shopping—all of them had to pass the Charlie Test, and none of them came close.

Now, hearing the worry in his voice, everything I'd had to keep to myself over the years came tumbling out before I could stop it.

"It's Dad. He's depressed. I mean, like, clinically. He keeps losing jobs, and I can barely get him off the couch anymore. He's just not doing well at all, and it's because he thinks she's coming home. And she's not, Charlie. You know that, right? You know they're not coming back."

"Yeah," Charlie said softly.

"But *your* dad changed his mind about something. I've been going through these notes tonight and most of it doesn't make any sense, but it's like everything he wrote in the book, he went back and changed his mind. And, I don't know, it just struck me as weird, and I started wondering if maybe there was more to the story than anything we've been told."

Charlie's concerned tone switched suddenly to something sharper. "You think my dad had something to do with them going missing?"

"No, not necessarily," I said quickly. "Just that there was something going on at that cave that we don't know about."

Charlie was silent for a second before saying, "Let me poke around a little, see what I can find out. I'll give you a call in a day or so. Maybe we can meet up."

"Meet up?"

"Sure. You still in Vegas?"

"Henderson, yeah."

"Well, I'm in LA. Not a bad trip. I'd really like to see Dad's book."

"Shouldn't we take it to the police? In case it's, like, evidence or something?"

"No!" Charlie said. "I mean, not yet. If it's my dad's handwriting, it'd be the first new contact I've had with him in a sense. You know? The cops get ahold of it, it might just disappear into evidence forever. I'd like to see it myself before then."

"Oh. Sure, yeah."

"Could you text me some photos?"

Embarrassed, I said, "No, not exactly. My phone's not . . . I mean, I guess I could take it to a CopyMax and have them scan it or something."

"No, no," Charlie said, and my embarrassment deepened as I detected him trying to keep the surprise out of his voice. "It's cool, we'll just make plans to meet up soon. We should do that anyway."

Yes, we should, I thought, but had the sense not to say it. Instead, I opted to be honest and said, "That's great, but we can't meet here."

"Um . . . okay?"

"I mean, at the house, because of Dad," I said. "I don't think it would be good for him to see you. I don't know what it might trigger."

"He's really that bad off?" Charlie said gently.

I rubbed my eyes. "Yeah."

"Okay. No problem. Like I said, let me ask around a little, and I'll get back to you soon, okay? We'll figure something out."

"Okay. Thanks, Charlie."

"You bet. Hey, it's good to hear from you."

My mood improved. "You too. Talk to you soon."

We ended the call and I sat back, looking up through the pine branches at the stars. Whatever else might happen, I thought, at least I talked to Charlie again. And soon, maybe I'd even actually see him.

I didn't think anything terrible could come from that.

Once it got too chilly, I climbed down and went inside. I got Dr. Prinn's book from under my pillow, opened it up, and began to read.

Charlie called not one, not two, but three days later. Considering I'd been expecting at least a week, or possibly even no return call at all, three days was fine with me. It's not like it was after a first date. What were the calling rules after a first date anyway? Mrs. Brower probably knew better than me.

"So we're going to head down there next week," Charlie said after we'd greeted each other.

I was sipping a Coke in the alley behind the restaurant. My big break of the shift—fifteen minutes by the trash Dumpster.

"Down where?"

"Vegas. Then the cave. If that's still cool."

"No, yeah, totally. Who's we?"

"This is going to be fun, in a sense," Charlie said, and I heard the smile in his voice again. "Check it out. So I got my buddy Alex, who did sound for a couple of my shorts. Short films, I mean. He's a good guy. Crazy insane, but totally reliable. And not inconsequentially, his mom was the executive producer on the show."

"Marcia Trinity?"

"Yep."

"She was on the shoot. At the cave."

"And hasn't been seen since, just like our parents. You got it. Turns out Alex has access to an RV, so we're going to go to that damn cave in style."

"So you're really doing this. I mean, we . . . we're really doing it?"

"Well, yeah. I mean, unless you changed your mind. Sorry, I thought you were serious about—"

"I am. Yes. I am. I'm just surprised, is all. I didn't think you'd be so up for it. That's all. No, I'm in."

"Good. So yeah, if it's all right with you, I thought I'd film it. Kind of a documentary, maybe turn it into a sizzle reel, pitch a show or a special."

I only understood about half of what he said, but I got the

gist, and I didn't like it. "You want to turn this into a TV show? After what Outasite did?"

"What did Outasite do?"

"Well, I mean, it's their fault our parents are gone. Don't you think?"

"No . . . not really. Accidents happen. That's not the network's fault."

"But they let them go to that damn cave. . . ."

Even as I said it, it sounded weak. Outasite hadn't put a gun to Mom's head. The entire film crew went willingly. Still, the thought of turning this expedition into a movie of the week made me a little nauseated.

"No, wait, it's not that," I interrupted myself. "Filming the whole thing, it feels disrespectful. Or just . . . weird."

"I can see that," Charlie agreed. "So, would you rather I didn't? I'm just trying to get some kind of small benefit out of what happened, I guess. And leave a record, you know? That we didn't forget about them."

His last comment struck the right chord.

"Okay," I said. "That's a good point. Forget I said anything."

"You sure?"

"Yeah, yeah. I'm just nervous. Or, excited, I mean. Something like that." I sucked at my soda straw.

"I get it. Hey, at worst, we catch up and take a road trip. The four of us'll hang out. Alex could get some beers if we wanted. It'll be a cool little—"

"Four? Who's the fourth?"

"Oh, sorry. Selby. My girlfriend. Selby Lovecraft."

My Coke lost all its sugar. I hadn't read anything about a girlfriend online.

"She's got quite a following," Charlie went on, blissfully unaware of how my heart had just burst apart like a dust bunny. "She writes this blog on science and skepticism, and a lot of people are big fans. We can probably use it to promote the film. I mean, if we end up actually making one."

"Oh."

"So when's good for you? Do you need a weekend, or is during the week better? We're all free right now, so good timing. Whatever works for you."

"I'm pretty free." The word "girlfriend" kept ricocheting between my ears.

"Cool. How about we get there Thursday, and we all head out to the cave on Friday? Come back Monday?"

I tried to imagine Dad on his own for that long. It hadn't happened since Mom disappeared. On the other hand, he wasn't working, so it wasn't like we had some kind of schedule. And Arby's could probably survive without little old me for a few days.

"Let's do it," I said.

"Awesome," Charlie said. "I'll let you know where we're staying when we get to Vegas. All right?"

"Yeah."

"Great. This was a great idea, Abby. Thanks for doing this. Sincerely."

"Um . . . sure."

"Talk to you soon."

We hung up. One of my coworkers poked his head out the back door and shouted at me to get back up front, we had a rush. I threw my soda away and moped inside, effortlessly putting on my happy mask to serve the public.

I worked on autopilot as I tried to picture what Charlie's girlfriend might be like. What the cave would look like inside. What we might or might not find.

It was both the slowest and fastest day at work I'd ever had.

I wake up surrounded by gray and quiet. I'm almost but not quite comfortable. It seems like hours before I can open my eyes, and even then, blinking against the haze in my vision, I can barely believe where I am.

"Charlie . . . ?"

Charlie pops up beside me, gasping. I yelp and shrink back. I might've laughed any other time at the way his hair has gone kerflooey. Slowly, I piece together my situation: I'm on the couch in the RV. Charlie had been asleep on the floor beside me. Leaning a bit, I can see one of Selby's blue boots sticking out from the bedroom.

So we're in the RV.

Does that mean . . .

"Dreaming?" I ask, and barely recognize my own voice.

Charlie runs a hand over his face . . . and shakes his head.

I slide slowly, painfully, off the couch, feeling like every other inch of my body has a bruise. Charlie seems to already be back asleep as I kneel on the cushions and carefully pull apart the blinds over the window.

Charlie had parked the RV about fifty yards from the cave. Or rather, what remains of the cave. Not a dream: The cliff face where we discovered the cave mouth still lies in rubble. Jagged boulders of all sizes lay strewn about the desert floor like an explosion has torn the mountain apart. The entire first chamber now lies open to the sun.

The sun.

Forgetting the cave for a moment, I lift my eyes to the pale blue sky and nearly lose my breath. The sun's shining. *The sun is shining.*

Humanity has forgotten what darkness is really like. We live in cities and towns with ample electricity, our kitchens lit by digital microwave clocks and ambient porch light to keep the bad guys at bay. Our streets and highways are lit every few feet by sprays of orange light. We've forgotten what real darkness is. And because of that, we've forgotten the restorative power of the sun.

I start crying then. After the tangible darkness of the cave, all we've seen, all that happened . . .

My tears dry almost as fast as they form. This thing is far from over. I go to the side door, taking care not to disturb Charlie, and step out.

The sky isn't blue on this side of the vehicle. It's gray. Smoky gray patched by black, with only spots of bright blue poking through the haze.

The desert is still on fire.

It looks like a dust storm. The kind I've seen video of, rolling across Phoenix, swallowing everything in a brown wall of dirt. People die in those storms, trying to drive through them on freeways with zero visibility. Only now, instead of dust, it's smoke. I hadn't seen it from the other side of the van because the wind blew it away from us.

"What the hell?" I say out loud, then suck in a breath. That turn of phrase brings our encounters in the cave back to mind in brutally vivid detail. I start shaking, and can't stop.

"Abby?"

Charlie speaks from behind me, his voice full of dust. I turn to face him and say his name. He's found a clean shirt from his bag, plain white, and has it on. He steps out of the RV and limps over to me, wrapping me in his arms while I quake against him. I don't cry again, but I've never felt so miserable in all my life—some hellish combination of nausea, terror, cold, and heart attack all wrapped into one awful mental and physical torture.

"I know," Charlie whispers above me, though I'm pretty sure I didn't say anything. "I know."

"It happened," I say, teeth chattering though it isn't freezing outside. "It all really happened."

"Yeah."

"What did I do?"

"Don't know yet. And it wasn't just you."

"Everything's on fire."

"Looks like it."

"God, Charlie."

"I know."

We don't say anything after that. Charlie finally coaxes me back into the RV and sits me on the couch. With pain in his face, he creaks over to the fridge and brings the package of ham and a bottle of cold water for each of us. I open the bottle and drink fast, which is a bad idea as it literally hurts my head and chest. I don't care. Nothing on earth has ever felt or tasted so good.

We sit silently for a few minutes, drinking and gingerly nibbling on the lunch meat before the shakes start to dissipate. Charlie leans back, tilts his head, and pours the rest of his water over his face. It creates channels of clean skin down his cheeks, and only then do I realize how grimy he is. I must not look any better.

Charlie turns to look at me. His eyes, previously underlined with sleepless rings, are now nearly hollow. I've heard of the "thousand-yard stare" that soldiers get after being shelled. Now I know what it means.

"They're out there," Charlie says, and his voice comes from beneath a graveyard shroud. "Everything that we were never meant to see, or to live with. Everything God or *the* gods or mighty freaking Zeus ever wanted to get rid of. They're out there now."

He turns away again, chucking the empty bottle and grabbing his head with both hands, squeezing his eyes shut. Still asleep, Selby moans and rustles on top of the bed-spread.

"We need to get her to a doctor," I say.

"Yeah. I just . . . Man, I don't even know where to go."

"Can you find our way back to the road?"

"Sure. We'll just follow the smoke."

"Yeah, what is that? What's causing it?"

"It's them. It has to be. I don't know how they're doing it. Fire-breathing dragons, maybe. It wouldn't surprise me. But then I don't know what *would* surprise me anymore."

I stand up, and it's not easy. "Let's just go. Maybe to Tucson? That's closest. We'll figure it out. I'm just glad we're outside."

"Have you tried your phone?"

"No." I fish through my bag, find my phone, and call Dad. At least I've got a signal, so that's good, but all I get is his automated voice mail reciting his phone number back to me. When the beep sounds, I say, "Dad, it's me. I'm okay. I'm . . ."

Charlie looks up, watching me, waiting to see what I'll say. Great question, because I have no idea.

"I'm still in Arizona, and, yeah, I'm safe. I'm coming home as soon as I can. Please call me when you get this. I love you."

Before I'm even finished, Charlie's trying to reach his brother, but doesn't get through either.

"Try nine-one-one," I say.

"And tell them what?"

"About Alex."

"Yeah, tell them *what* about Alex?"

It's a good point. If we tell the truth, no one will come. If we lie, it won't make us look very good. Then again, it's our fault—

—it's *my* fault what happened to him, and I don't know that we can avoid not looking so good to the police. Anyway, fires are raging in the desert, and no one can change anything in the cave right now.

"Okay," I say. "We'll call them later, then."

Charlie slides himself into the driver's seat. He tries the ignition, and to my surprise, the engine turns over. The RV being mobile is the first good thing that's happened since before we went into the cave.

But instead of driving off, Charlie says to me, "Abby? It's not your fault."

Some vague semblance of a laugh, with no truth to it, pops out of me. "Well, no, I'm pretty sure it is, Charlie."

"Abby—"

"Don't. Please. Not yet. Not now. Let's just get safe first."

Charlie hesitates, but gives me one quick nod. He puts the RV into gear, and we roll into the desert.

"I'll check on Selby," I say, and go back to the bedroom as Charlie turns the RV in the direction of the smoke.

I stumble to the fridge on my way to the bedroom and scan the contents. Staples, mostly: milk, eggs, bottled water, packaged meats and cheeses, that sort of thing. I go through the cabinets next, finding peanut butter, bread, dry cereal, instant oatmeal . . . the three of us could eat well for a week if we needed to, two weeks if we take it slow.

The three of us. Just the three of us now.

I push the thought away and head into the bedroom. I sit on the bed beside Selby, who is still asleep. I'm not sure if that's good or bad. Her black shirt is crusted with old blood, but not a huge amount. I lift up the hem and peek at the wound. Charlie's shirt has untied itself overnight as she rolled around. The rushed, half-assed bandage job I patched together in the cave is saturated purple red, and dried rivulets of blood crackle against her skin, but there's no fresh blood that I can see. All in all, considering it's a stab wound, I figure she got off cheap, at least so far. Who knows what kind of damage happened internally.

I drop Selby's shirt and lay a hand on her forehead. Her skin feels clammy, but not too hot or too cold. Without being a doctor or nurse, I decide she's probably in as good a shape as could be hoped for.

Selby wakes up just as Charlie discovers what we hope is the dirt road that will lead us to the highway. She lets out a groan, rolling onto her back, blinking against the relative brightness of the RV.

"What happened?" Selby mumbles, and then says, "Oh shit, my stomach . . . Oh shit, what happened?"

"We made it. We're out of the cave. Charlie's headed for the highway, we're going to try to get to Tucson, get you to a doctor."

"Oh, God," Selby says, and I can see the playback footage

from the past couple days rampaging through her mind. She pulls herself up to a sitting position, grimacing. "It really happened? It really did?"

"Yeah. It really did."

Selby starts chanting cuss words and chewing nervously on her lip.

"I need you to focus," I say. "All right? You know science. There's got to be a science behind this, when it's all said and done. Right now, you're the defense department."

"But I—I—I don't—"

"There's an explanation for everything, right? Always a scientific explanation?"

She nods, not quite dialed in, but at least she's listening. I don't for a second think she can solve the crisis we're in right now, but I figure getting her thinking about something else will keep her from freaking out. I'm sure trying hard not to.

"Okay," I say as gently as I can. "So we need a theory. A scientific explanation for everything we've seen. Okay? Can you do that? What is going on out there?"

"Um . . . it's . . . um . . ."

"Take your time. Just think. You're a scientist. You have this huge IQ. Work the problem."

The panic slowly leaves her face. She's still panting a bit and looks pale, but less so than the minute before. She lets her eyes dart from place to place, like a machine accessing information.

"Uh . . . sss . . . string . . . string theory," she says after a minute.

Good. She's distracting herself. Whether what she comes up with is going to help us or not, I don't care at the moment. At least she's backing away from the psychological deep end.

"Okay," I say. "Talk to me like a third grader. What's string theory, and what's it got to do with everything we saw?"

"B-basically it has to do with energy and dimensions," Selby says, licking her lips.

I suddenly wish I'd thought to wash her face while she was asleep; God only knows what kind of grossness is on her skin. Come to think of it, none of us have cleaned up yet. I move that item to the top of our to-do list for when Selby's settled down.

"There are our four dimensions," Selby goes on, as if reminding herself. "Three plus time. There's an idea that there's as many as eleven different, um . . . different dimensions. Ten plus time."

"Okay. Keep going."

Charlie cuts in. "Blacktop. We're on the highway." Then he mutters, "Thank you, God."

"Keep talking about the strings," I tell Selby. "Just keep talking. I'll get you some water and something to eat. You've got to be dehydrated."

"I don't know, I don't know," Selby says, but not in response to me. Her expression shows the strain of a student facing a tough test question.

I get her a bottle of water, which she takes and starts sipping. I grab a washcloth from the bathroom, wet it under the faucet, and add some hand soap. Glancing into the mirror, I barely recognize myself.

Selby's mumbling now, scientific stuff I can only barely grasp, things like "nonlocal" and "bosons." I give her the washcloth, gently urge her to clean up, then go back to the bathroom to wash my own face. The water falls down black into the tiny sink.

Just as I'm drying my face and feeling a little more human, Charlie swears and the RV slows down.

I move to the front and hunker beside his seat, about to ask him what is happening—except I see it for myself out the windshield.

On our left, to the east, runs a set of train tracks. They lie parallel to Interstate 10, the highway we're on, the same one we drove in on from Vegas. And on the tracks—or rather, *near* the tracks—lie the remains of a long train of shipping containers, mostly, and at least one engine car. They're scattered around the desert like Lincoln Logs. The train cars are bashed in, giving their sides the appearance of crumpled tinfoil. At first I wonder what kind of tornado or windstorm could have caused that kind of damage, because as Charlie continues slowly down the highway, the destruction just keeps on going. I try to imagine the train going along, and what could possibly have knocked every car off the rails and scattered them dozens of yards away from the tracks.

Then I remember the giant horn I'd seen in the cave, like a mammoth rhino's horn, and how it had crashed up from the pit. Something like that could have bashed in the sides of those train cars. Whatever god-awful head or body that horn was attached to . . .

I pull out my phone, ready to call the police, except surely someone else has done that by now. Other cars heading in either direction have slowed too. Someone's got to be calling. I see lots of people with their cell phones held out of windows, filming the wreckage. I wonder if having a record of all this will really matter.

Instead of calling the police, I call Dad again—and practically scream when he answers.

"Dad!"

"Abigail? Are you okay?"

The desperation in his voice chokes me for a moment. "It's me. I'm fine."

"Did they get you out of Phoenix?"

"No. I mean, yes. Yes, I'm not in Phoenix."

"Good. Did you get out before the accident?"

"What accident?"

"The reactor. The Palo Verde nuclear plant. Are you sure you're okay? Haven't you heard?"

I can't decide what to do. The fact that I'd lied a few days ago about going to Phoenix definitely doesn't seem to matter, but I'm not exactly ready to tell Dad everything that's happened either.

"Heard what? Tell me."

"The power plant blew up," Dad says. "There's a cloud of radiation headed into Phoenix. Where are you?"

"We're going to Tucson." At least it's not a lie.

"That's good," Dad says. "Okay, that's good. You'll be safe there."

I smother the phone against my shoulder. "We need to see the news," I whisper to Charlie, and put the phone back to my ear.

Charlie pulls the RV off to the side of the road and gets his phone out.

"Dad? How are *you*?"

"Fine."

"Dad, I have to tell you . . ."

I shut my eyes against the image of my mother's face. Try to find the words to tell Dad not what had happened for real, but enough that he could let Mom go.

No, I decide. Now just isn't the time. Too much has happened, and too much is currently happening. I need to get home safe and sound, collect my thoughts, and tell him when the time is right.

I start feeling dizzy with it all. "Dad, listen. I don't know when I'll get home exactly, but I will get there as soon as I can, okay? Will you be all right?"

"Mrs. Brower brought blueberry muffins," Dad says. "That should hold me."

"Good, that's great. Tell her I said hi, and not to worry. I'll be home soon. Okay?"

"Okay, Abigail. Please be careful."

"Okay. Bye, Daddy. I love you."

"I love you too."

We hang up. Charlie stares down at his phone screen, eyes wide.

"This isn't going to get better any time soon." He hands me the phone.

I almost drop it when I see the footage. Now I know what that mammoth rhino horn belonged to.

At nine thirty Thursday morning, I borrowed Mrs. Brower's old Chevy pickup to make the drive to the MGM Grand. Mrs. Brower still drove the truck from time to time, but not often. According to an agreement we'd made when I'd gotten my license a few months ago—she'd taken me to the DMV because Dad wouldn't get out of bed—I could use the truck as long as I asked her first, which made sense since she had the keys. I also agreed to run errands for her every so often. Groceries, dry cleaning, things like that. Not a bad deal for not having to make car payments or pay insurance. I did have to fill the gas tank before returning it, which was no big deal, since I never drove very far anyway. I gave myself an allowance from my paychecks when I could, and most of it went to gas. Which, again, was not much.

People of all makes and models wandered around MGM, about as busy as normal for a weekday morning. It wasn't packed like on the weekends, when Mom and Dad had

taken short "staycation" trips here years ago. I self-parked
and walked through the lower-level entrance, past enormous
banners shouting about graying, elderly rock bands who'd be
playing there soon. Is that commitment on their part, or just
stupidity? Or maybe they had debts to pay off from their hey-
day and would take any gig they could. I could understand
that. One minute there's steady income, the next you're working at Arby's.

The glass doors swooshed open automatically, letting me
into a snaking, windowless hallway. I rounded the only corner,
and there he was.

Charlie leaned against a wall, gazing dispassionately at a
magic shop. He saw me coming and straightened up, smiling.

"Hi, Abby."

I swore he hadn't changed, though of course he must have.
I'd turn seventeen next month, so that made him eighteen
now. Spiral-curl black hair hung off his head in tight, crazy
ringlets. His brown eyes had gotten deeper, more thoughtful.

Other than that . . . Charlie had grown up, and grown up
well. He'd kept his adolescent-boy slenderness but had added
some heft to his shoulders: the kind of body a swimmer might
have. I could check out Charlie Prinn for a good long while.

I shouldn't have been totally surprised, since I'd been spy-
ing on him online for years now. He hadn't been difficult to
track down with Google, and the photos I'd uncovered were
flattering to say the least. Charlie Prinn had become quite the
"catch," as Mrs. Brower might say.

"Hi," I said, reeling suddenly from seeing not merely Charlie, but someone so closely associated with Mom. My guts got heavy and a bit nauseated. It was one thing to keep occasional tabs on him online. Seeing him in person was another thing altogether, apparently. I hadn't expected this reaction.

He stepped closer to me. His arms rose, then lowered quickly.

"So, I don't know if we hug here, or what."

"Um . . . yeah, we can hug," I said, feeling stupid.

We sort of closed the distance toward each other and embraced awkwardly. It was over before I wanted it to be. I took a step back and crossed my arms, imagining an October chill tickling through my shirt from outside.

Charlie, I kept thinking, repeating his name over and over like a mantra. *Charlie Prinn. Charles Prinn. Charlie.*

"How are you?" I said.

Charlie put his hands into his back pockets, rocking back and forth on suede Chelsea boots. "Good, I guess. Overall. What about you?"

"Same," I said, not sure if I was lying or not. "How's your mom?"

"I don't know. She took off a few years ago, ran away with a DP from North Hollywood. I've been living with Stephen outside LA."

Stephen was his older brother. "What's a DP?"

"Director of photography. Sorry."

"Oh. Sorry to hear that."

"Thanks, it's okay." Charlie pointed to a pizza place nearby called Project Pie. "Hungry?"

"Sure."

Charlie led the way into the restaurant. "Ever eaten here?"

"No."

"It's pretty tasty," Charlie said, easily dodging a crowd of family tourists. "I've already been here twice since we got in last night. It's like the Chipotle of pizza."

"So, your two . . . um, friends? They're here?"

"Yep. Alex, I think, is gambling away his life savings on roulette, and Selby's up in our room."

Our room. I didn't like the sound of it at all, even knowing—rather, *especially* knowing she was his girlfriend. Good God, I came here to talk about our parents, but I had time enough to spend being petty and jealous over some girl? *Nice, Abigail, very nice.*

I followed Charlie into the restaurant, which sat empty except for the employees, who had only just finished opening up for the day. We both ordered, and I took out my wallet, but Charlie waved a hand over it and muttered something too low to catch. So I let him pay. Why not.

We took seats at a table facing each other. Absurdly, I felt like I was on a first date and that Charlie might work his way into a kiss. I couldn't be so lucky.

"So what've you been up to?" Charlie said.

"What, the last five years? Honestly . . . not much. I sort of have to take care of Dad a lot. You know?"

"Sorry."

"Yeah."

"And it's because of your mom?"

"Yeah."

"That sucks."

"Truly."

Then that was it. We stopped talking for at least a minute. I tried forming some chitchatty question that wouldn't give away that I'd been keeping tabs on him. I didn't need to go sounding like a creeper.

"So, um . . . you've been making movies, huh?"

"More or less. Not like action films or anything. I'm not much of a writer. I've tried it, and I kind of suck. But I'm really good at *finding* stories. And then putting them on-screen. I made this one last year about American Indians on the reservations—"

"And it won a best film award, yeah."

"You heard about that?"

Nice job, Abigail. "I . . . came across it. Somewhere."

I couldn't tell if he believed me or not. I know I wouldn't have.

"Cool," Charlie said. "Yeah, it won best film at a festival down in Phoenix. Last thing I ever expected. But I was able to get some more gigs off it, so that's cool."

"Good for you." I meant it, but also became momentarily maddened with jealousy. His dad goes missing, his mom bails on him, and life's good? Girlfriend and all?

Where the hell had I gone so wrong? When would I get *my* break?

"Well, enough of that catching up stuff, huh?" Charlie said, smiling again just before taking a bite of his pizza—chicken, pesto, red and yellow peppers. He might have done it deliberately, to stall, but I wasn't sure.

When he'd finished the bite, he said, "What do you think happened to them?"

"I don't know. If I did, I wouldn't be sitting here eating pizza with you."

"You haven't tried it yet. You have to try it. Take a bite."

Trying to regain my patience, if I ever had it to begin with, I took a bite.

"Okay," I said after a minute, "so you're right about this: It's awesome."

"I know. I hope that means you'll trust me."

"Why wouldn't I?"

Charlie folded his hands on the table. "Tell me what you think happened. Then I'll tell you everything I've got. See, after you called, I started poking around a bit. But I need to know where you're coming from first."

I used his tactic—I took a big bite and chewed it slowly. Holy cow, it was good. Maybe it was just a year of roast beef and Horsey Sauce being cleansed from my palate. When I'd swallowed and chased it with a drink of water, I folded *my* hands on the table and looked into Charlie's eyes, trying to figure out how much I trusted him. I mean, it had been five years.

The question was, did I care?

I max the volume on Charlie's phone, which I've browsed to a local news channel stream. Grainy footage plays while a newscaster, a guy, speaks over it.

". . . made available just a few moments ago," the newsman is saying, confusion and stress evident in his voice. "It was taken by a smartphone camera just moments after the initial explosion that rocked the Palo Verde nuclear power plant . . . uh . . . we're tracking down some zoological experts right now to aid us in identifying the, uh . . . the animal we're seeing here . . ."

"That's one of them, isn't it," I say to Charlie.

The footage, which the broadcast replays over and over, shows a massive four-legged creature rushing away from an explosion behind it, something straight out of an action movie. I say "massive" because the animal ran past a tanker truck, and this thing stood twice as tall and twice as long. Nothing on this earth—nothing anymore—gets that big. It did look like a rhinoceros for the most part, except it had a long, powerful neck ending in an enormous head. Jaws that could easily wrap around the cab of a trailer truck jutted from the skull, and its snout was topped by a thick horn that must have stretched six feet into the air and tapered to a sharp, black point. It looked to me like some cross between a rhino and a tyrannosaurus.

"We are unsure at this point . . . We are not able to confirm that the animal you see in this amateur video is connected to the explosion at the power plant," the newsman says. "Or that this footage is even necessarily *real* . . ."

"How many do you think are out there?" I ask Charlie. My throat dries as I think about the train cars tossed around. The thing on the news footage could have done that damage. Easily.

"Lots," Charlie says. "A whole lot."

"How'd we not get trampled? In the cave."

"Luck of the draw," Charlie says, staring at his screen. "We came close. But they didn't notice us. We were off to one side, in a divot, this little crater. I think they just wanted out. Or else someone wanted them out."

His expression reveals he's as shocked to hear himself say it as I am to hear it. Some*one*?

A screech of tires makes us both look up. Outside, on the 10, cars come barreling north. There's normal highway speeding, and then there's this: absolute disregard for anyone else. Such disregard that of course it doesn't take long for something to go wrong. A little red car tries to take the shoulder to pass a bigger truck, but the truck has the same idea at the same time to get around a medium gray sedan, and sends the red car squealing into the desert. The truck slams on its brakes, which the driver behind him—rushing to fill the void left by the red car—doesn't see in time. The car behind the truck smashes headlong into the truck's rear bumper, crumpling the car into a flattened mass of steel.

"Whoa," Charlie says "What's—"

I think we see them at the same time: a swarm of enormous flying creatures the likes of which this world had never seen, or which we had never been meant to see.

Two pairs of long iridescent wings, like those of a dragonfly, extend from the backs of the animals. Their bodies have mantis-like angles and joints, their forelimbs bending and flexing as they fly. The sound of their wings hits us, and I recognize it instantly: the deep, bass buzz I heard coming from the pit in the cave. Their drone vibrates the ground beneath us, rattling the windows of the RV.

Charlie leans forward, phone forgotten. I do the opposite, walking slowly backward, deeper into the RV, but keeping my eyes glued to the windshield.

"What's that noise?" I hear Selby asking.

We don't answer. I reach out to steady myself against a cabinet as one of the dragonfly-mantis creatures swoops down toward the escaping vehicles and unleashes a jet of green, gaseous flame. It hits the car full-on. The car swerves left and right, taking out neighboring vehicles before exploding into a ball of emerald fire.

Tires screech behind us. Other cars had been going in our direction too this whole time, but fewer than what was coming north from the direction of Tucson. That trend now comes to a tire-squealing halt as the drivers see the dragonfly monsters up ahead.

"What did I do?" I say. "Charlie? What the hell did I do?"

"We're outta here," he growls, jamming the gear into drive and swerving the big van back onto the freeway. The sudden maneuver sends me to my butt and Selby to her back on the bed. She lets out a howl and grabs at her belly.

"We still need a hospital!" I shout at Charlie as he shoves the pedal to the floor. In an RV, though, that doesn't amount to much.

"Working on it!" Charlie shouts back. "Just shut up for a sec!"

I get to my feet and then kneel on the couch, splitting the blinds with my fingers to peer out at the wreckage around us. The dragonflies, for lack of a better term, seem indiscriminate in their attacks. Cars explode all around us like giant fireworks, which Charlie narrowly avoids. Any second now, we'll be next. A green flash, and that will be it. Searing heat, agony, then—

Then what?

Nothing?

Just darkness and un-ness? Like a dreamless sleep? Even with the carnage outside and the wholly surreal monsters beating the air like wicked helicopters, still I wonder what we unleashed in that cave. Still I have to ask what power did what it did to my mother and the others, condemning them to a mindless slavery. Is *that* Hell? Is that the price paid by skeptics and nonbelievers in . . . in anything? Is that what waits for us once the dragonfly monsters incinerate the RV?

"Abby, stop it!" Charlie shouts.

I suck in a breath and whirl toward the driver's seat. "Huh?"

"Stop screaming! I can't think, goddammit!"

I close my mouth with a snap, not realizing I'd been wailing since I'd knelt on the couch. I turn back to the window. The dragonfly monsters stay in more or less one place, hovering and swooping. They really can maneuver like hummingbirds, staying in one place or darting in any direction. Even backward. They do not appear to be following us, focusing instead on the cars immediately behind their previous victims.

And somehow, maybe combined with the destruction of the power plant outside Phoenix, I realize what it is they're doing.

I rush to the front of the van. "Charlie, look. They're jamming the road."

Charlie scowls and checks his rearview mirror. "Yeah," he grunts. "Maybe."

"And the power plant. How many nuclear power plants like that are in the United States?"

"Gee, Abby, I don't know off the top of my head."

"Don't you get it? They're *thinking*. Look."

I run back to the bedroom. Selby still lies on her back, pressing her hands to her wound and breathing shallowly. I climb past her and look out the small back window. Black,

cloudy smoke rises in great plumes behind us. Several cars
have raced past the RV by now, and there are no more vehicles
behind us. We're the last. No one else is getting through one
direction or the other. On the other side of us, in the north-
bound lanes, traffic has piled up. Some people try to jump the
median and get stuck, while others head out into the desert,
maybe aiming for the frontage roads.

"They knew what they were doing," I shout to Charlie.
"They're trapping us."

"Uh, excuse me," Selby says to me, her eyes pinched shut.
"But I am in a fair amount of fucking pain here. Can we maybe
do something about that, please?"

"I'm sorry," I say. "Yes. Charlie's getting us to a hospital."

Charlie suddenly cranks the wheel hard to the left, sending
me and Selby tumbling over each other and making her cry
out again.

"Hang on," he says, long after there was time to actually
do so.

"What're you doing?"

"Trying another road."

"Why?"

"Because we're not getting through up there."

I pull myself up and look out the windshield. The road
ahead is a mass of red tail lights and dust. I can't see what
caused the stop, but I don't really want to. I sit back and put a
hand on Selby's shoulder.

"We'll get help," I say, not sure if it's true or not.

Charlie had made his decision at a crossover, and just in time. He sends us bouncing over to the other side of the freeway, and then beyond it to a frontage road. How the big recreational vehicle is able to keep going after everything he's put it through is beyond me.

"Do you have any idea where we're going?" I say.

Charlie picks up his phone. He steers with one hand and keeps glancing into his lap. I get up and join him at the front, taking the phone away.

"I'll do this. You drive. What am I looking for?"

"Maps," Charlie says. His eyes dart nervously from side to side. "Find us another way out of here."

"Out of here to where? Selby needs help."

"We're all gonna need help if we don't find a way to avoid those things out there. So just get us somewhere else."

I slide my finger across the screen, opening up Charlie's maps. "Okay. Got it. But I don't know what we're looking for."

"I—" Charlie says, then stops short. He presses his lips together and shakes his head. "I don't know."

I touch his arm. "Don't lose it. Please, Charlie. We need you. I need you to be here. Okay?"

He takes a couple deep breaths. "Okay."

"Okay," I repeat. I scan the phone screen again. "All right, there's a little highway not far from here. The 79. There're some smaller towns along the way. There's got to be a medical place there. Urgent care or something. Maybe we can get an ambulance for her."

I glance back at Selby. Her body is still, but I can see her stomach rising and falling as she breathes.

"Sounds good," Charlie says. "Get me there."

"No problem." I feel a surge of strength. Amazing what taking action, what having a plan, can do for your spirit. "It's going to be a while. How are we on gas?"

Charlie looks down at his gauge. Back up at the disused road we're traveling. Down again at the gauge.

"Fuck," he says.

Studying Charlie's face over the table as my pizza cooled, I tried to figure the best way to summarize what I thought had happened to our parents. The problem was it all sounded stupid and crazy and frantic, not smart and logical and calm the way Mom would want me to think.

Mom had raised me a skeptic. I found Mrs. Brower's brand of faith to be harmless, maybe even adorable on some level, but not reasonable. Many other people of faith I'd encountered were a far cry from reasonable. The world had shown many of them to be outright violent. So I'd never had any need for ESP, prayer, miracles, or eternal life.

And yet.

After reading through Prinn's book that previous week, trying to decipher his crazier notes, scraping together some kind of theory as to why they'd gone to the cave in the first place and what might have happened to them, I didn't feel there was an accident involved. I hated that I felt that way.

Truthfully, the logical part of me utterly rejected the idea. The not-so-logical side, the side that couldn't reduce every emotion to pure logic or reason—that side *knew* something else had happened.

"Honestly?" I said to Charlie after a long hesitation. "What I think is that I'm losing my own mind. So if I tell you and you laugh, or you act like a jerk, you can take this albeit fantastic freaking pizza and shove it straight up your ass."

"Understood," Charlie said. He wasn't smiling anymore.

I took a deep breath, and focused my gaze over Charlie's shoulder, absently not-reading famous quotes painted on the far wall.

"I think our parents . . . they found something. Or something found them."

Charlie straightened up in his seat.

"I don't know what that is," I rushed on. "But it was something bad."

"What do you *think* it was?" Charlie asked.

"I don't know, Charlie. Seriously. It's not something I can point to or explain, which, by the way, really pisses me off. It's just a feeling, and I don't like that it's just a feeling. I got really used to the idea that there was an accident. A cave-in, probably. But the stuff in your dad's book, it just—it creeps me out. I don't know how else to put it."

Charlie's expression didn't change, not that I could see. After a pause, he nodded slowly. "Okay. That's fine. That's legitimate."

It was like he knew exactly what to say. I let out a breath and felt my shoulders relax.

"So anyway," I said, "I don't know if they're dead or what. Logically, I'm sure they must be. I don't know if anyone can ever find them. But no matter what, my dad hasn't been the same since they disappeared. He's so sad, and even though it's been so long, he still thinks one day she'll come back. I think if we knew . . . if we could say for sure that she was gone, if we knew she was dead, he'd get better. You know?"

"Sure," Charlie said. "Of course."

"So then, regardless of my 'feelings' or using the Force or calling the Ghostbusters, I need to go and see for myself. That's the important thing."

"Totally."

"Okay. That's what I think. So now it's your turn. What did you find out?"

"That you're absolutely right."

Charlie folded his pizza in half and chewed into it like a taco. I didn't mind the pause this time, and took another bite of my own. I could barely believe I'd just said everything I had.

"You know my dad was a skeptic, like your mom," Charlie said at last. "Atheist, logical, scholarly. All that. He got into the show to prove that ghosts and all that stuff didn't exist. It was all things he taught about before the show began."

"Right, yeah?"

"Well, something happened. He changed his mind. Or was in the process of changing it. Before they left to shoot season three—I mean, for the few months leading up to it—something was wrong. He wouldn't talk to me about it, of course. I was, like, thirteen. I don't know if he ever told my mom. I probably would've just let it be, you know? Live my life and whatever. But then you found that copy of his book and . . . did you bring it with you?"

I reached into my bag and pulled it out to show him. Charlie wiped his hands quickly on a napkin before taking it from me. He did not open it, not right away. He merely held it. For a moment, I thought he'd sniff it.

"Do you want to know what's in it?" I said softly, in case he didn't want to be interrupted.

Charlie didn't look at me, but nodded.

"Near as I can tell, your information is right. The stuff in here is about how wrong he was. A point-by-point refutation of his own research."

Charlie nodded again, and set the book down on our table. "That adds up. Or, adds up as much as anything else up to now does. I just found out *he's* the one who insisted they go to that cave for the season-three premiere. No one ever mentioned it to me before. And it was supposed to be a two-parter, did you know that?"

I shook my head, with a flash of anger. Why *didn't* I know that? My anger cooled quickly; it wasn't exactly an earth-shattering tidbit. Still. It bugged me to not know every detail.

"Apparently, Dad was going around telling people it would change everything," Charlie said. "Not just the show.

He meant, like, *everything* everything. Everything the world knew, or thought it knew."

The born-and-raised skeptic in me gave me a slap. "You know how this all sounds, right? How *we* sound right now?"

"Oh, of course I do. It's absurd, at minimum." He rested a hand on top of his father's book. "But now I have to know what he was working on. And why they all disappeared. Sounds like you do too."

"Yeah. Yes."

"Can I ask you something?"

"Okay . . ."

"Is this really the first time you've thought something besides an accident happened?"

Five years apart or not, Charlie Prinn knew me too well. My skepticism faded as soon as he said it. Mom had raised me to ask questions, to think beyond the supernatural and spiritual. I wasn't sure what Dad believed, but I knew he never contradicted her. I'd never needed church, horoscopes, Ouija boards, or anything like that.

Despite all that, yes: From the first moment Dad had told me Mom hadn't checked in, I felt something was wrong beyond a cave-in. Couldn't shake it, even after all these years.

"No," I whispered. "It's not the first time. I felt it from the start. I just didn't want to . . ."

"Admit it?" Charlie asked, matching my tone.

"Yeah." I started trembling, and couldn't stop. I also couldn't stop talking. To confide this in another human being instead of being locked in my brain was like a seductive, palatial bath, cleansing off years of grime and sludge. That it was Charlie, who had been through the same thing, so much the better.

He sat back. "Well, Abigail, we're going to try like hell to find out the truth. Sound good?"

I nodded, fast. It definitely did sound good.

"I found the address of this guy Dr. Riley," Charlie said, with a down-to-business tone. "He was a friend of Dad's and—"

"He guest-hosted once."

"Right. Turns out he lives in Arizona. Not far from the cave, in fact."

My stomach shrank at the word "cave." I tightened my arms around myself.

"I couldn't find a number or e-mail or anything on him, but I did find his house. Out in the freaking boonies. But what I'm thinking is, we drive out there, do a whole scenic-road-trip thing. Talk to Dr. Riley, maybe shoot a good interview with him if he's up for it. Then we go to the cave, poke around, get some good footage . . ."

"Are we really talking about this, Charlie?"

His eyes glittered. "We sure as hell are. I mean, worst-case scenario, we find out absolutely nothing. Well, we know absolutely nothing right now, so no loss there."

I couldn't tell if he was charming me, flirting with me, or if this was just his natural optimism. I also couldn't tell which I wanted it to be.

Charlie continued, "The important thing—the important

things—are, one: What if we were able to find proof of how they really died? Maybe we'd find something everyone else missed. And two . . . I'm willing to bet that you get the dreams too."

All my internal organs froze to ice when he said it. How did he know about the dreams of that place? How *could* he know?

I didn't answer, but clearly, I didn't need to. Charlie said, "That's what I thought. Now, look, I know they might be dead. And probably are. If they are, then okay, I accept that. I've done my five stages of grief. I'm good. But if we could figure out what really happened, it's worth finding out. I'll admit, when you called last week, I was a little skeptical, but after doing my homework, I can't tell you how on board I am."

Yet even as he said it, the spark of a thrill I'd felt when I saw Charlie standing in the hall vanished, extinguished by five years of empty pain. I loved my mom. Not in the past tense, but in the here and now. We'd been happy. Everything had been good, except maybe that Dad wanted another kid and Mom was too busy, or at least that was the reason she always used. I liked being an only child, because it meant I got their combined, full attention. Right up until *TSS* started production, anyway.

Right up until she never returned another text or call. Right up until Dad broke down.

"I mean, *I've* felt it too," Charlie said. "That something else went on, but no one besides the nutjobs online would talk about it. But I did *not* want to sound like a nutjob, so I never brought it up to anyone either."

I twisted my lips around, trying to find words. They didn't come.

"It sounds to me, and correct me if I'm wrong, but in your gut, or heart, or soul, or wherever people feel things, you and I both know they didn't *just* disappear."

A cold breeze dried my mouth, filling me again with autumn chills. Charlie seemed to pick up on it. His voice softened.

"Look, Abby, I know it's been a long time since we've seen each other. But you know this isn't about kidnapping, or our parents running off together, or a cave-in. You know this is about something else. About that *place*. I kept telling myself all these years I was imagining stuff, or was just having trouble getting over losing both of them so close together. But then you called, and . . . I don't know. This seems right."

I tried to get spit back into my mouth and couldn't. I hated Charlie Prinn right then.

Because he was right. I did know. I *had* dreamed.

"And, I mean, it does have a great angle," Charlie added, mostly muttering it.

"A what?"

"The children of the disappeared going out in search of answers. Whatever else it might be, it's good drama. It's a good story."

That he could swing the conversation back around to filmmaking actually relaxed me. It made the whole adventure return to being a lot more innocuous. A road trip, like he said.

"Okay," I said. "Let's do it. What's next?"

"That's it. We'll pick you up tomorrow, unless you need more time. I plan on being back Monday night—does that work?"

"Sure."

"It won't mess you up in school or anything?"

"I take all online classes, so no big deal."

"Okay. Cool. If you have any questions, give me a call."

"Just one. What do you *think* happened?"

Charlie hesitated. "Honestly, I don't have an answer for that. I just know that I'm going to find out."

We'd somehow finished our pizzas without my noticing. Charlie asked if he could hold on to the book, and I said yes, of course. He walked me back to Mrs. Brower's truck.

"So, what're your . . . friends like?" I asked, pulling out my keys.

"Well," Charlie said, leaning against the truck. "Alex is kind of like a puppy. Very excitable. Fortunately, he's paper-trained, so that's good."

I laughed, surprising myself. A cloud of dust may as well have come out of me.

"What about Selby?"

"Yeah, Selby. She's what they call *wicked smaht*. Ivy League material, probably going to win a Nobel Prize before she can drink legally. I think you'll like her."

That was a patent impossibility, but I wasn't about to admit to it.

"Where'd you meet her?"

"Texas State Science Fair last year. I was on a crew shooting a doc about it. She won. For the second time, in fact."

"Wow."

"Yeah. Pretty cool. Hey, you seeing anyone?"

Innocent question, I told myself immediately. *Innocent question—it happens to be the topic of conversation right now, you're the one who started it, do not do not do not read into this.*

"No," I said. "Too busy, mostly. You know."

"Yeah, I hear ya. Well, guess we'll see you in the morning, then?"

"Sounds good."

We hugged again, a little longer that time. Charlie headed back into the hotel, and I took off for home. I again tried, in vain, not to imagine what Selby looked like, how much smarter she was than me, or anything she and Charlie might be doing in their hotel room right that very moment.

After dropping off the truck and keys to Mrs. Brower, I went home and decided to watch season one of *The Spectre Spectrum*. I thought maybe I'd find something on an old ep that I'd missed the previous hundred thousand times.

No such luck.

I once watched a prank video online in which a guy on a cell phone stood at a bus stop and pretended to get world-ending news from a relative. "Dude, Florida just got hit by a tsunami; it's coming this way!" he said to people. "My aunt's going to pick me up over here—come on, we have to go!" And people went. Either they didn't have their own smartphones, like me, or they simply didn't stop to consider whether it was true. They just panicked because of one person's claim.

Somehow I'm thinking about that dumb prank as I scan Charlie's phone for information on what's happening near us. The Internet has exploded with quote-unquote news, but none of it agreed, and all of it was bad. Viral cell phone videos are only making people more confused and scared, which makes them panic, and that makes things worse.

The speed with which people are losing their minds is remarkable. But then I have no room to judge.

"Here," Charlie grunts, and pulls my attention away from his screen.

We catch a break, pulling into an urgent care clinic in the small town of Oro Valley, a few miles northeast of Tucson. Traffic is light. I can see smoke from I-10 billowing in the distance, and guess that everyone has either bailed out of town already, or they're staying home and watching the news.

The urgent care building stands alone, a short building painted adobe red with lava rock decorative gravel lining a concrete sidewalk that leads to the entrance. It looks clean and safe, somehow. Normal. Inviting, even. Maybe that's because inside are professional medical people who can finally help us.

"Get her in," Charlie says as he stops in the parking lot. "I'll go get gas."

"What? No. No, we stay together."

"There's a Circle K right down there. I'll be there and back before you've even finished the paperwork. You're okay."

I don't like it, but can't find a good argument. I help Selby out of the RV and into the clinic. Charlie waits until we get in before rolling out of the lot and toward the gas station. For no good reason, I get a crush of fear in my chest that we'll never see him again. That he'll leave us here, or something will happen the moment we're apart.

Then again, maybe I have a million good reasons.

The urgent care lobby is empty except for a nurse sitting behind a counter. Everything is gleaming white inside except for the lobby furniture, which is the same color red as the lava rock outside. As I help Selby to the check-in, I see a laptop sitting on a desk just below the counter. It's showing live stream helicopter footage of the 10, which looks like a war zone. Flames, black smoke, cars at a standstill, people milling about. Or lying still on the pavement.

"Can I help you?" the nurse asks, barely able to take her eyes off the screen. Her blue-black hair gleams under recessed lighting that gives me the absurd, momentary impression that everything is absolutely okay. This woman clearly dyes her hair; who would do that if the world was really ending?

I know it doesn't make any sense. It's just this fleeting thought. Fleeting hope, maybe.

"She's hurt," I say, holding on to Selby with both hands, her arm slung over my shoulders. "She's been stabbed."

That gets the nurse's attention. She stands up. "Someone stabbed her?"

"No," I say quickly. "She tripped. Fell on something. In our car. RV."

"Fill out her information here," the nurse says briskly, dropping a clipboard onto the counter. "I'll bring her around back."

"I don't know her infor—" I start to say, but the nurse walks away. A moment later, she appears from a door off to our left and takes Selby from me, guiding her into the back of the building. Selby says nothing as they stumble off, her face a grimace of pain.

I pick up the clipboard, but stay to watch the laptop screen.

The laptop is muted, and it feels wrong somehow to lean over and try to bring the sound up, so I just watch.

The blacktop of I-10 is on fire. A crush of vehicles jams the entire roadway for what must be miles. Portions of the road have already literally melted away, creating a roiling tar pit sucking at the burnt-out shells of cars. I do not see any of the hairy dragonfly things.

The nurse reappears behind her counter, drying her hands on a paper towel. "You said you were in an RV when she was hurt?"

"Yes," I say. It sounds confident enough, I think.

"Were you in the wreck?" the nurse asks.

I blink. "What?"

"On Interstate 10. Were you in the big accident?"

Accident? I think. *There was no accident. Not by a long shot.*

"No," I say carefully. "What, um . . . what happened?"

"They don't know. But look at it. Isn't it awful?"

We watch the screen for another minute. Then I start to move to a chair to attempt to fill out the paperwork.

"What did she get stabbed with?" the nurse calls after me.

"Uh . . . knife?"

Nice one, Abigail. The nurse narrows her eyes at me.

"I mean, she was standing up in the RV," I say. "Cutting up vegetables and stuff. We weren't in the wreck, but we saw it, and he—Charlie, the driver—he had to slam on the brakes. She lost her footing and fell against it. You know."

Not terribly convincing, but the nurse seems to accept it.

"How about you?" she says. "You don't look well. Are you all right?"

"Not really." I sit down, and my muscles protest.

I stare at the paper on the clipboard, toying with the pen attached by a string of tiny metal pearls. Name? Well, Selby Lovecraft. Address? Date of birth? Insurance company . . .

I set the clipboard down, lean my head back, and close my eyes. I don't think I fall asleep, but can't say for sure; all I know is that at some point I snap up when someone sits beside me.

Charlie.

"You okay?" he asks.

"Don't know. No. You got gas?"

"All filled up."

A man with short black hair wearing blue medical scrubs comes out from the side door and approaches us. I notice he positions himself between us and the exit. Maybe it's unintentional. Maybe it's not.

"I'm Dr. Kay," he says, not unfriendly but not smiling. "Would you like to tell me what happened to your friend before or after I call the police?"

Charlie and I look at each other. Very smooth. I can't tell if he's thinking the same thing I am: that given what else is happening not far from here, I doubt very much the police will give much of a crap about us.

"It was an accident," I say.

Dr. Kay is silent, keeping his deep brown eyes trained on me.

"She fell against a knife while we were driving," Charlie says. "It's my fault. I shouldn't have slammed on the brakes."

"We were camping," I add, for no particular reason. When did I learn to lie like this? "That's our RV out there. We tried to get to Tucson, but the freeway was all backed up. We came straight here."

The doctor's expression relaxes a little. It's a weak story, but not an impossible one. "How are you related to her?"

"Just friends," Charlie says.

"Mmm." Dr. Kay studies us a moment longer, as if trying to decide his next course of action. Then he sighs. "Well, we do have a bit of a problem. She needs more attention than we are equipped for here."

"How bad is it?" I ask.

"Hard to say. There could be extensive internal damage, or it could have missed everything major. Her belly is not distending and there's no rebound pain. Those are good signs. Right now I'd guess she perhaps hit the liver, which is sort of a best-case scenario. It's always possible, however, that she could be bleeding internally, which is very dangerous. The problem is that I'm the only doctor in town right now, and there are no ambulances to the hospital in Tucson."

"So what do we do?" I ask. "I mean, what's the safest bet?"

"There are two options. She can stay here for observation, which is what I recommend. That way if she gets worse, at least I'd have an opportunity to take action. Or you could try to take back roads to Tucson, which is where the nearest hospital is.

But there's no predicting the condition of the roads and traffic, and no guarantee of reaching the ER in time in the event of a complication. Also, there's likely to be quite a backup in the ER anyway. It is not a good situation, no matter how we look at it."

"So who makes the call?" Charlie says.

"I have treated her as best I can. And I've given her something for the pain. The bleeding has stopped. I would say the decision is up to her parents or legal guardian."

"And if we can't get ahold of them?" Charlie says.

"Then it is up to her. Where are her parents?"

Charlie and I meet each other's eyes. "We don't know for sure," he says. "She moved out a while ago. They don't talk."

Dr. Kay doesn't seem to care much for that answer. "I'll get some more information from her," he says, like we're total idiots. And I suppose we are.

The doctor disappears into the office. Charlie stands and heads for the doors, so I follow. We stand outside together on the sidewalk, feeling the stillness of the town penetrate our bones.

"I don't—" Charlie begins, then snaps his mouth shut.

Not really meaning to, I slide my hand into his. His fingers grip mine tightly, and after everything that's happened, the touch of warm, living skin on mine makes me dizzy for a moment.

"Yeah," I say, and my voice catches. "Me either."

I heard Dad's car pull up a couple hours after my trip to MGM. Hurrying, I ejected the *Spectre Spectrum* disc and shoved the entire box set under my bed just as Dad came inside. He immediately sank into the couch, turned on the TV, and began listlessly watching daytime talk shows. The couch had a divot in it these days, perfectly conformed to his body. I'd only sat in that spot once recently, and immediately gotten back up. It had felt like entering a casket.

He didn't even look up as I stood watching him get settled into his spot. "Dad?"

"Hi, Plum."

"What's going on?" I asked, although I knew.

"I just couldn't do it," he said. "I tried. I went back to the office, and I asked, and I met with my boss, and . . . I don't know what happened. I just couldn't."

"It's okay," I said, lying.

Dad had gone farther and farther between episodes like

this in the last year or so—a huge improvement. But sometimes his depression just got the best of him. He'd always been somewhat predisposed to sadness, I think, from what I could remember as a little kid. Mom's big laugh and love had done a lot to mitigate it. I remember that, even when I was little, it seemed that Dad's smile always came late, like he needed to check everyone around him to make sure it was okay.

Since Dad already felt bad, I had nothing to lose. I sat down beside him.

"Dad," I said, keeping my tone as relaxed as possible. "Can I ask you something sort of hard?"

"If it's about boys, I don't know how much help I can be." He managed a weak smile.

"It's about Mom."

A deep crease appeared between his eyebrows as the smile torqued upside down. "Okay," he said helplessly.

"What if . . . I mean, I don't want to make you mad or sad or anything, but . . . what if we found out for sure that she was gone?"

Dad's voice flattened. "You mean dead."

"Well. Yes."

Dad's head bobbed on his neck—not really a nod, but not really anything else, either. Finally, he said, "Maybe that would be okay. If it was for sure. For definite. What's that word we kept hearing? Closure? I think we'd have closure."

The last of my doubts about going with Charlie disappeared when he said that, but I still didn't want to tell Dad the whole story. Not yet.

I waited until dinner that night to tell my lie. I did not like lying to my dad. It wasn't in my nature or my repertoire. I only knew I could get away with it because if you're not a liar, you can count on being able to tell one really big lie and people will believe you. Also, I didn't think Dad would bother trying to verify my cover story.

"There's an astronomy conference this weekend I'd like to go to," I explained over leftover spaghetti. "I'd get credit for it. It's in Phoenix."

I said it sort of quickly, hoping he wouldn't make the connection. No luck. Dad's shoulders slumped. Phoenix meant Arizona, and Arizona meant Mom.

"So I'd be leaving tomorrow morning. There's a group of other online students who can give me a ride. But I don't have to go if you don't want me to. . . ."

I'd put this idea together—this lie—while watching *TSS*. Now came the part I hadn't scripted. I didn't know how Dad would respond to my being gone.

"The bills," Dad said listlessly.

"They're all paid up, we're fine."

"No, I mean you shouldn't be the one in charge of paying them."

I didn't say anything.

"I have to get better," Dad said, gazing blankly at the kitchen table.

I sat statue still. He hadn't said anything like that before. Ever.

"What can I do?" I said after a long pause.

"Go," Dad said. "Go, and have a good time. I'll make some calls."

"What kind of calls?"

"For help." He shook his head, very slowly. "I can't keep doing this to you. I know what you do. I know how you keep this place up, Plum. It's not fair. To you."

I wanted to reach out, touch his hand, something, but we hadn't made physical contact in years. Not intentionally. I didn't think we knew how.

"It's not fair to you, either," I said.

"Maybe," Dad said. "You should give yourself a raise. In your allowance. Or a bonus. Take whatever you need for this, uh, field trip. If there's any money left. Is there?"

"Some."

"Take it. You've earned it."

"Dad . . ."

He looked up and met my eyes. His eyelids were at half-mast. "Yes, Plum?"

"I don't have to go. I can stay. It's all right."

"No," Dad said. "It'll do you good. It'll do us both good. I'll find a place to go, make an appointment."

"Okay. Sure. Okay."

I realized then that as much as I didn't like lying to Dad, I had no alternative. If I'd told him the truth, about Charlie and all the rest of it, he would not have said everything he just did. If anything, telling the truth would only make things worse, maybe for a long time. Somehow my lie about an astronomy conference had jarred something else loose instead. Something good.

That night, I climbed into my tree house and watched as the constellation Cygnus appeared overhead. It was the first one I could identify without Mom's help when I was little. It was late before I finally came down and tried to get some sleep.

And tried.

And tried.

Charlie either doesn't notice or doesn't care that I'm holding his hand. While it feels great, like my entire heart is located in between our palms, it's not exactly the romantic scenario I envisioned over the years. Mostly, in fact, it's just contact. Human contact.

"I've been thinking about Selby," Charlie says finally.

My heart shrivels a little between our hands. "What about her?"

"About how she did that to herself. In the cave. Something made her do it. Something made her spill her own blood."

"Yeah." While not the most visually terrifying thing we'd seen in the past twenty-four hours, Selby driving a knife into her own gut while desperately trying not to do it . . . that memory wasn't going away any time soon.

"I wonder if it's the same thing that took our parents."

"Sure," I say. "Why not."

"Abby, I'm serious."

"So am I!" I turn to face him, but our hands stay entwined. "Charlie, what are we going to do? I mean, what the hell are we going to do? Alex is dead and we haven't even told anybody yet. There're *monsters*, real giant monsters, out there killing people. And it's our fault. What do we do?"

"Been thinking about that, too," Charlie says. "There's always Dr. Riley. He's the next-best thing to an authority. Maybe he has some ideas, now that all this has gone down."

"I don't know, I just want to go home. I want to see my dad. I want to go to bed."

"I'll take you wherever you want to go, Abby," Charlie says, making sure I'm looking in his eyes. "I'm sorry this all has happened, believe me. I am. I'm already doing math in my head for how much therapy this is gonna cost me, you know? But I don't want to figure out our next move by myself—I *can't* figure it out by myself. We have to find a way to undo this."

"Isn't there something in your dad's book, maybe?"

"We can look. I don't think he knew this was coming, though. I think he just got as far as figuring he could find the pit, that's all. I didn't think we'd go much farther than the first few chambers of the cave, myself."

I hesitate, rocking on my feet. Selby's bloodstains mark my jeans in awful five-fingered streaks.

"The thing with Selby," I say. "Stabbing herself. You're talking about that being some kind of blood thing, aren't you. Like a sacrifice."

"Crossed my mind. Humanity's history is filled with that kind of thing."

"It wanted blood? The ark, or the pit, or whatever the hell it is?"

"Maybe. Does it make any *less* sense than anything else so far?"

"Fair enough."

A choked, exhausted laugh coughs out of me when I say it. Maybe I've already gone crazy, but honestly, it feels like laughing is all there is left to do. Charlie gets caught up in my black comedy, and we both laugh for . . . well, not very long. A couple seconds at most. Still. It's a small blessing.

I sit down on the edge of the walkway, and Charlie joins me. At some point, our hands have become disentangled. He doesn't point out that it even happened, so neither do I.

"Get your phone," I say. "Let's see what's going on out there."

We scan the web for news. It doesn't take long. Our laughter suddenly feels a million years past.

In just a few minutes, we gather all the bad news we can handle. Parts of Phoenix are being evacuated due to the power plant meltdown. Hospitals in Tucson are being attacked. The local news page we're on has a live feed going. Police are surrounding the outside of a hospital building, and I catch a glimpse of a stone sign outside of it that reads MATERNITY.

As the horror of that word sinks in, I see, live on TV with I'm sure millions of others, three police cars get razed by green flame and explode, taking several cops with them.

Charlie's face contracts as we watch the footage. My eyes lose focus as I gaze into middle space and wonder how we could possibly ever make this right.

"Charlie . . . they're just kids. Children and—"

Charlie stands up fast, almost knocking me off my seat. "I'm going to see Riley. I understand if you don't want to come. But he's all we got."

I rise to my feet too, but slower. Every muscle in my body feels twisted an inch to the left. I'm a lot older than sixteen right then.

"Will you come with me?" Charlie says.

"Wh-what about Selby?"

"What about her? She's safest here."

That stuns me. "She's your girlfriend."

"Which means I want her to be safe, and it's safer here."

"No, I can't," I say. "I can't leave her here, Charlie, I can't, I won't do it. She's coming with us. Those *things* are headed this way. You saw them going after hospitals. They'll get here, too."

Charlie wrestles with my logic for a moment, although I'm not sure "logic" is the right word. But I do know I'm not leaving anyone behind. Not anyone *else*, I should say.

"Okay," Charlie says. "Yeah. Let's get her."

We go inside and ask the nurse if we can see Selby. She starts explaining that we can't go in the back, but then Selby and Dr. Kay come out from the side door. Selby moves with stiff, wooden legs and her teeth tightly clenched.

"Let's go," she says.

"How is she?" I ask the doctor.

"I explained her options," Dr. Kay says, clearly not agreeing with the one Selby has chosen. "I strongly recommend getting to a hospital."

"That's the plan," Charlie says. I have the sense to not look surprised at his easy lie.

"Thank you so much," I say, moving to Selby and slipping her arm over my shoulder.

"Watch for swelling in the abdomen," Dr. Kay says. "If you push gently anywhere on her stomach area and it hurts when you let go, that's called rebound pain, and she'll need immediate care. Keep an eye on her vital signs. She's got a few pain pills and antibiotics, but they're not going to last. She needs to get checked out at a hospital as soon as possible. All right?"

"Got it," I say.

We haven't even gotten clear of the door before Dr. Kay has joined the nurse at her desk, watching whatever fresh horror plays on the laptop. Charlie and I get Selby into the RV and settled in the bedroom with much huffing and groaning. Her face seems pale, but her breathing is regular.

"How do you feel?" I ask, pulling a sheet over her.

"Like I fucking got stabbed."

I choose to take her tone as a good sign. I kneel beside the bed.

"I'm not letting anything else happen to you, okay?"

Selby turns her head to look at me, bunching her hair up beneath her on the pillow so it sticks up in the back. I regret saying it, because now that it's too late, it strikes me as condescending. I brace myself for a Selby trademark insult, maybe something to do with me being a Girl Scout.

"I don't want to die," Selby says.

All her characteristic snark is absent. She looks five years younger. Instinctively, I take one of her hands.

"Me either," I say. "So let's not."

The RV engine starts. Charlie pulls out of the parking lot and gets us aimed at the small two-lane highway that will take us toward Dr. Riley's.

I managed to get Dad out the door and off to the library to start looking for jobs again on Friday morning—a major feat. He promised to let me drag him back to the library next Monday and Wednesday for free career workshops and résumé writing classes. Those were some big improvements, and his job hunt that morning helped settle a lot of the lingering doubts I had about the trip. Now I could focus almost exclusively on not being jealous over Selby Lovecraft.

A big brown and tan RV that looked more like a band's tour bus showed up at eight a.m. sharp. Charlie climbed out of the side door as the RV idled, and I met him on the front porch.

"Morning," he said, and smiled. I liked it.

"Howdy. That's quite a ride."

"Adventure in style. Are you ready?"

"Yeah. Let me just grab my bags."

"I'll do it," Charlie said, taking a step closer.

"It's okay." I grabbed my suitcase and backpack from inside the front door. I didn't want him to see inside my house. I locked the door behind me.

Charlie opened the side door to the RV and ushered me in. I climbed two short steps and met the cast of whatever insane reality show this was about to become.

"Hi!" said a guy in the driver's seat. He looked college-aged, with long blond bangs squirting out from under a yellow USC cap. "I'm Alex. You're Abigail Booth?"

"Yeah. Abby. Hi."

"Hi!" he said again.

I thought his smile could power half the Vegas strip. Alex struck me as being an athlete of some kind: broad shoulders and muscled calves, making it easy to picture him playing tennis or swimming laps.

"My mom was a big fan of yours," Alex said. The smile stayed on his face, but dimmed. "Fan of your mom's, I mean. Sorry we're meeting like this."

The person sitting in the shotgun captain's chair snorted. Alex glanced that way, and his smile turned wry.

"This is Selby Lovecraft," he said, gesturing. "Sells, can you say hello?"

"Hello," Selby said without turning the chair. All I could see of her were ankle-high blue Doc Martens and tight black jeans, since her feet were kicked up on the dashboard.

"She's very happy to meet you," Alex said.

Charlie said, "Abby, have a seat. Relax."

I sat down on the couch behind the driver's seat, and Selby whirled in her chair like some cinematic evil mastermind. Her first order of business was to scowl at me, apparently for the great sin of sitting beside Charlie, who'd joined me on the couch. She dressed as if she'd seen what I was wearing that day—jeans, Converse, and a short-sleeved top—and put on the exact same thing except dyed black.

"Okay!" Alex said. "Get the party started! We're moving out, Big C."

"Uh, 'big C' is slang for cancer, you hemorrhoid," Selby said to Alex over her shoulder, her eyes still lasering me in half.

One minute with Selby convinced me to rethink this trip. Charlie shook his head a little, sending me a *Don't mind her* type of look.

"*Gosh*, you're charming," Alex said as he got the big van moving.

I looked through the window and saw Mrs. Brower standing in her front doorway, waving and smiling. I waved back as a million warnings and suggestions for her flew through my head—things she needed to know about Dad, what to look out for, how often she should check in on him.

But I didn't tell Alex to stop. I'd only be gone a couple days. Dad could survive that long, and Mrs. Brower already had a keen idea of how things were going at our house. If anything strange happened, she'd take care of it. A nurse and psychologist—I couldn't ask for much more.

So I just waved again, then turned to assess the RV as Alex revved up the engine.

"This is plush," I said as Alex urged the van toward the freeway.

"I know, right?" Alex said. I hadn't been talking to him, exactly, but I didn't mind that he assumed. He made a nice counter to good old Selby.

When I'd compared the RV to a tour bus, I didn't realize how close I was to the truth. The RV had everything, and everything done *nice*. Thick beige carpet, oak cabinets, double sink with a purified-water spigot, long white leather couch along the driver's side, a table for four behind that, bathroom with a shower *and* tub, and what looked like a queen-size bed in the back. The bedroom even had a ceiling fan. The inside of this thing was more high-end than any given room of my house.

"First time to Arizona?" Alex asked.

"Yeah," I said. "My dad went when . . . you know. But he had to stay awhile, so he had me stay with a neighbor. Mrs. Brower. She's great. She makes us cookies. And dinner."

"Are you sure you're feeling okay?" Charlie asked.

"Sure, yeah, why?"

"You sound nervous."

I closed my mouth. He was right.

"Yeah," I said. "I guess I'm a little scared. Not sure of what."

"Same here," Alex said. "Hey, we can listen to music or something if you want. Or there's some audio books."

"I'm okay," I said. "I mean, unless *you* want to."

Charlie touched my knee. Briefly. Casually. My response inside was anything but. Online classes and Arby's cashiering didn't provide a whole lot of romantic possibilities, or at least not the kind I was interested in. Plus, crushing on Charlie long-distance over five years . . . I guess I was more excited to be spending time with him than I'd realized. Selby notwithstanding.

"Let's get you caught up," Charlie said. He seemed to not realize the effect his quick touch had had on me. "That way we're all on the same page when we get to Dr. Riley's place."

"Sure, yeah," I said quickly. "How long's the drive?"

"Shouldn't be more than eight hours. We'll try to push through to Phoenix before stopping, so that's five. Then it's another couple hours or so to Riley's."

"Are we sleeping in the RV?"

"We could if we had to," Charlie said. "But we've got a hotel near Riley's house."

"When do we go to the cave?"

"First thing tomorrow." Charlie reached over the built-in seats surrounding the table, and picked up a backpack. He pulled his father's book from it and set it on his lap. "So I've been going through this. Where'd you find it?"

Selby lifted her chin, trying to see what we were looking at without actually getting up from her chair. Alex cast a quick glance back at us too.

"In my mom's dresser. I don't know when he gave it to her."

"That was a good book," Selby said. "A little pedestrian sometimes. Solid research, though."

Charlie and I both looked at her. Selby smirked right back, unfazed.

"What is it?" Alex called back. "What's going on, what'd I miss?"

"It's the book my dad wrote before they went missing," Charlie said, dismissing Selby's snark. "Basically it's about how things we consider supernatural are really part of thousands of years of brain evolution. It explains the science behind our belief in mythology and legend. Except something happened."

Selby's eyes narrowed. "Charlie, come on."

"Alex didn't get a chance to hear this," Charlie said—a bit too patiently, I thought. "Dad changed his mind. Or was in the process of changing it."

My eyes darted to the cover, to the big black letters Dr. Prinn had scrawled across the crossed-out title. *Wrong.*

"I talked to some people at the network, and they said Dad found something. Or *thought* he found something."

"Something supernatural, you mean," Alex said.

"Oh *Jesus*, here we go," Selby said with a monumental eye roll. She could have powered the *other* half of Vegas with it.

Personally, my skepticism faded around the edges as Charlie spoke. It was a dizzying tension to live with—what Mom has always taught me versus my deepest fears about what had happened to her. "Work the problem," she'd say when I had a tough word problem in math. "What's the logical thing?" she'd say when I asked her about things like ghosts or the power of prayer. When her mother had a heart attack a few years before the show began, she'd reacted with calm, purposeful steps while Dad and I freaked. I tried hard to be more like her these days.

Charlie turned more pages in the book, examining his father's handwriting as he narrated. "Dad's theory was that religious faiths, from the Greek and Roman pantheons to modern-day cults, were an evolutionary meme, with all the same features you'd find in the evolution of an animal. Mutations, variations, that kind of thing. He wasn't the first person to come up with it, but his approach was based in religious anthropology, all the things he'd been studying his whole career. Basically, it tries to disprove every belief out there."

"Not that that's a challenge," Selby said, swinging her chair left and right.

I thought I saw Charlie tense a bit as he said, "Yeah, well, he was really good at it. Okay?"

Selby sighed theatrically and began smacking a wrapped pack of cigarettes on her hand.

Just how long had this relationship been going on? They were either on the verge of a breakup, or were like some old married couple. I couldn't tell which. I only knew which one I hoped for.

"Do not smoke in here," Alex warned Selby.

"I'm *not*," Selby said. "*God.*" Then she muttered, "Should've had one when we stopped."

"So what's the book got to do with the cave?" I asked. "I mean, Charlie . . . you don't actually think they're alive, do you?"

Charlie's face went in twelve different directions, like I'd asked him if God could make a rock so big he couldn't lift it.

"Probably not," he said.

"*Probably* not?"

"I'll be honest. If I had some kind of tangible proof, I'd obviously be taking it to the cops. But what I've got and what I think we'll find isn't the sort of thing that gets the attention of detectives."

"Oh, *God,*" Selby said, missing her own irony. "They're not alive, just say it. It's certifiably insane. Charlie's dad went crazy, no offense, and it got your families killed, the end."

Neatly ignoring Selby, Charlie said, "When I talked to some of Dad's friends at the university, a couple said that Dad had a . . . an experience, I guess."

"On the road to Damascus," Selby said, rolling her eyes so hard that her entire head rolled with them.

"The what?" I said.

"It's a Biblical reference," Alex said. I *really* preferred his voice to Selby's. "It's where Saul became the apostle Paul in the New Testament. In Acts."

To Selby, I said, "You read the Bible?"

Alex laughed and said, "Right? Surprised she wasn't hit by lightning!"

Selby, though, merely punctuated her response with one

last smack of the cigarettes against her palm and said, "It is wise to know the ways of one's enemies."

Wow. That was brutal. To Charlie, I said, "So he, what, found God or something?"

"Something," Charlie said. "I'm not sure what to make of it all. I'm hoping Dr. Riley can clear some of it up for us."

"What do *you* think happened, Abby?" Alex asked. "To our parents. Just out of curiosity."

Charlie and Selby both turned to watch me. It felt like a trial. I took my time before answering.

"I think our parents are dead. But sometimes, I also . . . I feel like it's not that simple. I don't *believe* there's any more to it than that . . . but I'm *afraid* there is. I don't know what that might be. But it's something bad. I know my mom didn't get to ride off into the sunset, if that means what I think it does."

"A happy ending," Charlie said. "The bad guys lose, the good guys win, and there's always tomorrow."

"Yeah. She didn't get that." I turned to Alex. "What about you? What's your theory?"

Alex drew his shoulders up for a long moment before letting them drop. "I'm not sure either. I know that I'm *looking* for a lot of things, not just my mom. And . . . that I guess I'm hoping to find some of them on this trip."

"You won't find any of them in a mythology book," Selby grumbled, kicking her feet up on the center console. "Whether that's Charlie's dad's, or any other, by which, of course, I mean the Bible, the Torah, the—"

"You know, Sells," Alex interrupted, "you say you're a humanist—"

"Damn right!"

"But you don't treat people like human beings. It weakens your case. Just an FYI."

That settled Selby down for a second, and I liked Alex more and more.

"I tend to agree with you, Abby," he said. "Probably she's gone. But just in case, let's go check this place out. Maybe find out if they really are gone or not. I love her, you know?"

I didn't answer, but I didn't think I needed to. Alex had used the present tense too.

"So then why are you coming along?" I said to Selby. I figured part of the reason had to do with dating Charlie, and that was reason enough, but couldn't resist the question. I hoped it didn't come out sounding like a challenge. But it might have.

Her eyes darted briefly to Charlie before she said, "I was asked."

"Selby's making a name for herself in the online skeptical community," Charlie said. "She's got almost six thousand followers on her blog."

"I've got a book signed by Richard Dawkins," Selby said, raising her eyebrows.

Richard Dawkins was, among other things, one of the world's leading skeptics. I hadn't read him myself, but Mom had been a fan. We still had books of his at the house.

I didn't normally pick fights, of any kind, with any person, but Selby's snotty attitude pushed me over the edge. "Is that supposed to be a credential? Anyone can buy a signed book."

I thought I'd neatly won that one until Selby stabbed back.

"Uh, I'm, like, the Texas State Science Fair first-place winner two years running, I'll be getting my early action results from Caltech in December, which will doubtless be in my favor, my SATs are rivaled only by my prodigious IQ, and I'll probably have my first doctorate before I can buy alcohol. As for Richard, we were having dinner when he signed it, he and me and my older brother, who was working for him at the time. What're your *credentials*, Girl Scout? Merit badge for most Thin Mints sold?"

So that pretty much shut me down.

We use cached maps on Charlie's phone to navigate an out-of-the-way route toward Dr. Riley's house, twisting and squirreling around on back roads as best we can. Again I wonder about the integrity of the RV. We don't see many cars, but at one point, farther out deep in the desert, we spot a short caravan of pickup trucks thumping over dunes and hills, piled high with equipment that looks like camping gear and personal belongings.

"They're bugging out," Charlie says when I point out the trucks to him. "Getting out of Dodge."

"Smart," I say.

Charlie doesn't answer.

About an hour later we pull up to Dr. Riley's house again. Surprisingly, he's sitting on the porch, rocking gently back and forth in the chair Selby was in yesterday.

"Yesterday." That word cannot do justice to how much time has actually passed, how old I actually am now.

Charlie parks the RV and says, "He knew we were coming."

"In like a mystical hell-beast kind of way, or . . . ?"

Charlie climbs out of the driver's-side door while I go back to the bedroom to check on Selby. She's fallen asleep. Her temperature seems okay, as far as I can tell. I do my best to check her pulse, but don't know what would be too fast or too slow. It seems normal to me. I lift her shirt. Dr. Kay has rebandaged the wound, and the gauze is clear and bright; no blood. It doesn't appear to me that her stomach has swelled.

I replace her shirt, thinking I'm an idiot. I'm no nurse, no doctor. How am I supposed to know if she's improving, stable, or dying right in front of me?

I push the thought away and rush to join Charlie outside. As we approach, I see Dr. Riley has set up a metallic TV tray beside him. On it, a bottle of tequila stands guard beside a can of Dr Pepper. Beads of clear condensation well up on the surface of the can, suddenly making me excruciatingly thirsty. His heavy stone ashtray from the house also sits on the tray, while his pipe is clamped between his teeth, smoking lazily from the bowl.

A shotgun lies across his lap.

"Howdy," he says sarcastically. "Wondered if you'd be showing up again."

"What the hell is going on?" Charlie demands, putting on a burst of speed to mount the steps and stand right beside the older man. I grit my teeth and wince, sure the professor won't hesitate to blow Charlie away with the gun. I've never seen a weapon like that in person before. They aren't nearly as sexy in real life as the movies make them out to be. It just looks cold and heavy and serious and determined to destroy anything it wishes.

Dr. Riley arches an eyebrow and gazes up at Charlie. Softly, he says, "Step back."

Charlie hesitates, but must decide he can't take on the shotgun. He takes three steps back, but keeps his body angled a bit, like he's ready to leap at the old teacher if he needs to.

"That's better," Riley says. "Last thing we should all be doing is fighting amongst ourselves, wouldn't you say? Seeing as how there won't be many of us left before long."

"Why didn't you tell us what was down there?" Charlie says. "Why?!"

Dr. Riley looks disgusted. "Oh, you think I knew? You think I had inside knowledge of what the leviathan was? The nephilim, the behemoth, the seraphs? Where were you when he laid the earth's foundation?"

"What?" I can't help but say. I haven't climbed the porch, choosing to stay on the hard-packed brown earth.

"Bible stuff," Charlie says, not taking his eyes off Riley. "He's just quoting Bible stuff. So, what? You're . . . you're this religious fanatic now? You believe in God?"

"Son, it doesn't matter what I believe. I thought you all would've figured that by now. Even your sassy little scientist . . ." He trails off. "You're two people short."

"*Yeah*," Charlie snaps. "You could say that. Keep talking."

Riley considers this for a second before speaking again.

"Belief doesn't mean anything, Charlie. You wanted proof, you got it. This isn't about faith. This isn't about religion, or about God. This is about reality. And our reality has come crashing right down."

"How do we stop it?" I ask. "Please."

His red-rimmed eyes unsettle me, which, after everything we've seen, is really saying something.

"Stop it?" he asks. "Now where is *that* written?"

"People are getting killed. Kids . . . *babies* . . ."

Something in his face slackens. "The slaughter of the innocents."

"That's from the Gospels," Charlie says. "You just said—"

"No, the Bible never uses that phrase," Riley says. Ever the teacher. "You want to know what I knew? Nothing. I knew nothing, not for sure. I *feared* there was something down there, yes. Or, *believed*, if you like. I sometimes believed that something was down there that should've damn well stayed down there. Something that we had no business messing around with. Whoever put them there had a reason. Well, take a look around. Now we know why."

"Why didn't you stop us?" Charlie says.

"What conversation were *you* having? I tried to stop you. You wanted to know what happened to your family, so you went. I couldn't wrestle you all to the ground." He shakes his head and works his mouth as if he's going to spit. Instead, he says, "Now here's a fun thought for you: Maybe none of us had a choice."

I don't like the sound of that.

"But it's been done before," Charlie says. "They *were* put there. So there must be a way to do it again."

"Sure," Riley says. "Why don't you find yourselves a good righteous man and his three sons to build you a zoo attraction for them, hmm? Maybe that'll work."

"There's got to be a way!" Charlie shouts.

Dr. Riley calmly swigs from his tequila bottle, and smacks his lips afterward with a sigh.

"If I thought that," he says, "I wouldn't be out here with a gun I've never fired once in my entire life."

"Can they be killed?" I ask.

"Sure, why not. Give it a go. But from what I've seen on the news so far, things aren't going real well for the human race. Oh, we'll raise the stakes as time goes on. More guns, bigger guns, then the rockets and missiles and bombs. Maybe we even bust into our chemical and biological weapons when we get desperate enough. But kill them? The gods had a tough time, I don't see where we stand much chance."

"So that's it," Charlie says. "That's all you've got. You and my dad knew more about this than anyone, right? Don't you have more notes, an idea, some theory? Anything?"

Dr. Riley taps out his pipe.

"Children," he says, and somehow, it actually sounds paternal rather than patronizing, "you might want to start adjusting your-selves to the idea that the rest of your lives will be spent in Hell."

Funny. I'd been thinking the same thing.

"Sorry," I said to Selby, feeling stupid for having doubted her prodigious IQ. Then I couldn't help adding, "But could you at least just chill out for a second so I can talk to you like a normal person? We've got a whole weekend to go, here."

Selby held her glare a moment longer, then said, as if doing me a favor: "Sure."

"Thank you."

I took a deep breath and shut my eyes, rubbing my hands hard against my forehead, thinking this might be an awfully long forty-eight hours or so if I couldn't make peace with Selby.

"Okay," I said when I felt like I could speak again. "So, if I hear you correctly, you're going along specifically because you *don't* believe anything supernatural happened to our parents."

"Correct," Selby said. Her tone was neutral. "There's an explanation for everything. There's always a scientific explanation. Always."

"We need a reporter," Charlie said. "Keep our *Spectre*

Spectrum skepticism going. We need someone who *will* fight us, or me, on anything we find. Keep us honest-like."

"And add drama," Alex said dryly.

"Voilà," Selby said, striking a glam pose in her captain's chair.

"Why don't you believe something supernatural could have happened at the cave?" I asked her. "I'm not saying it *did*, I'm just curious."

"There's no proof. I mean, it's really just common sense. Like on *Ghost Hunters* and *The Spectre Spectrum*, people would say, 'An apparition of a woman in an old-fashioned dress will appear!' Okay, so . . . does this ghost exert free will? Did she *choose* to appear right then? If so, was her goal to frighten the observer? And if so, why? There's no logic at work. If ghosts were real, we'd have proof. Not evidence, proof. Everyone would see one. Why would a spirit make a chandelier swing, or a chair rock? What is the ghost trying to do, exactly? What's its point?"

"They may be psychic energy," Alex said. "Impressions left in rooms, the residual of heightened emotion, things like that. It's a theory."

"Okay," Selby said, like she was accepting a dare. "Let's just pretend that's possible. Let's assume traumatic events can somehow imprint themselves on a building or an object. Maybe trauma releases some kind of eternal photon that sticks to the atoms in a wall or a chair or something. Let's call them ghostons."

I actually caught myself grinning at that. *Damn.*

"And those ghostons stick around for ages and ages until suddenly one day they light up out of nowhere," Selby continued. "And someone happens to see it and says, 'Oh, wow! A ghost!' All right. Cool. But come *on*! A full-torso vaporous apparition like in *Ghostbusters*, for God's sake? No. We'd have it recorded by now, unless you count the dumb shit on You-Tube, which is hardly the zenith of hard science. People want to believe in something, I get that. God, their Buddha, nature, whatever. But existential dread isn't evidence of an afterlife."

I realized then that she'd dropped the snotty tone from her voice. She sounded like a professor, and not at all eighteen.

"Existential dread?" I asked, slowly, not wanting to stumble on my pronunciation in front of Selby. "You mean—"

"We're all afraid to die. So we pretend there's something else out there for us to make ourselves feel better. Only, there's not. We're all alone."

Well, that pretty much sucked the sunshine out of the day.

Feeling an absurd need to say something to Selby, I came up with this: "I wasn't a Girl Scout."

I may as well have said, *I'm rubber, you're glue.* Everyone froze. Then . . . they laughed. Even Selby.

And I joined them. Not a lot. But some.

"Just out of curiosity, what if you're wrong?" I said.

"I'm never wrong. But just for shits and giggles, about what, exactly?"

"About . . . afterward. What if we're not alone? What if

there's a heaven or a hell or something else entirely? What would change for you?"

Not bitchily, she asked me, "What do *you* think happens after we kick the bucket?"

"Nothing," I said automatically. My default skepticism came back, and I welcomed it. It warmed me as surely as a favorite faded hoodie. But I couldn't help adding, "Or, *probably* nothing. If I found out for sure there was an afterward, then that would be kind of great. I guess I'd see my mom again someday."

Selby took that in for a moment before leaning forward toward me. As she spoke, her tone still wasn't bitchy or condescending, but she definitely sounded like a teacher.

"Abby, there's a scientific, logical reason for everything. Even things we don't understand yet. I want to see my dad, too. But based on existing laws, it's not going to be on some cloud playing a harp, or making inarticulate noises and rattling chains in some attic. Know what I mean?"

"Your dad?"

"He died when I was ten. Random brain thing."

"I'm sorry, I didn't know."

"S'okay," Selby said with a shrug. "But thanks."

The rest of the drive was not exactly a party, but it was cordial. I didn't mind. It still beat being at home in the dark. At Selby's insistence—she was having what she called a "nic fit," and the term suited her demeanor—we stopped for food at a little fifties-themed diner outside Phoenix.

Charlie, Alex, and I talked while Selby chain-smoked out-side. I tried hard not to show my surprise when Alex men-tioned that, until recently, he'd been attending a seminary in order to become a youth pastor.

"Oh!" I said. "So, you're like a . . . Christian, then? Or . . . ?"

"I'm not going to throw any Bibles at you," Alex said, grin-ning. "You don't have to cross your arms quite so hard."

He was right. I'd practically shrunk two sizes, sinking into myself and away from him. I hurried to drop my arms and sit up. Alex and Charlie both smiled through all my nervous acrobatics.

"So, who did it to you?" he asked. "Was it a specific pastor, or one particular church, or . . . ?"

"Huh?"

"Usually a response like yours comes from someone who got beat up by a religion. Physically, sexually, emotionally, spiritually. What's your story?"

"Oh. Nothing. I mean, nothing like that ever happened. My mom was just really, you know . . . reasonable."

"Ah, so I'm *un*reasonable."

"No! I just mean—"

Alex poked my arm. "Only teasing. I understand, trust me. The ones who show up wearing crosses generally intend to crucify someone."

"Does Selby know that you . . . ?"

Alex and Charlie both started laughing. "Are you *kidding* me?" Alex said. "I've been living with that little troll for two days already. The last thing I need is for her to go off about me and make-believe Jesus."

All of us laughed at that. Frankly, I'd take whatever brand of faith Alex had over Selby's caustic attitude anytime.

"So why'd you stop going?" I asked. "If you don't mind."

The mirth left Alex's face. "I started asking certain questions, and those questions were not met with the *lovingness* I had expected. Eventually, it was decided that maybe it would be best if I took a break."

"'It was decided'? Meaning—"

"Meaning I was *gently*, with the guidance of the *Holy Spirit*, of course, asked to 'hate the sin and love the sinner,' and would I please fuck off and never come back."

The booth seemed to cool by twenty degrees.

"Maybe not in those exact words," Alex said wryly. "But where I come from, the meaning comes through loud and clear. But don't worry. They're *praying* for me."

An echo of Mrs. Brower's frequent promise to do the same bounced back at me. I wondered if she was the type of person who could hurt someone like Alex. I didn't think so, but you could never tell with religious people.

"You ever read it?" Alex asked. "The Bible, I mean? It's okay if you didn't. I'm still not going to walk you through the Four Spiritual Laws or anything."

"What are those? I'm probably breaking them."

"Trust me, it's better if you don't know. But have you? Ever read it?"

"No."

"Well, lemme tell ya, there's a lot of weird stuff in there. I know that. I'm not stupid. Believe me, nothing messes with your faith more than going to Bible college. But then there's a few things that strike me as pretty clear, you know? Like, I dunno . . . 'Love people.' 'Don't judge.' Those seem like easy ones to remember. Maybe not to *do*, but to *try* to do. I mean, I even feel bad for calling Selby a troll."

"Oh, don't feel bad about that," I said. "It's not a sin if it's true."

Alex looked me square in the eye, and for a second, I thought my joke had totally misfired. But then he laughed hard, and we were okay.

"I'm sorry about whatever happened," I said.

"Thanks," Alex said. "It's been a long couple months, and I haven't really had anyone I could trust to say any of that to. Just Chuck here, I guess, since he took me in."

"He's been staying with Stephen and me for a few months," Charlie said.

"Right, but only, and I mean *only*, until I figure out what the fuck to do with the rest of my life," Alex said. "As soon as I know that little tidbit, I am *gone*."

That was good for a smile.

"What about you?" Alex asked. "You're, what, a junior?"

"Essentially. Yeah."

"What're your plans?"

Not intending to, I let out a sigh. "I'm not sure. I'd like to go to college and maybe study astronomy, I guess, but my dad . . . I just mean, I might need to stay close to home, is all."

I must have zoned out then, because Alex touched my arm and said my name. I shook myself and blinked. "Hmm?"

"We lost you for a sec. You all right?"

"It's just this trip. The more I think about it, the more I want to really find something concrete. One time, my dad told me, 'Give a man enough hope and he'll hang himself.' I know hope is supposed to be a good thing, but in his case, it's killing him slowly. Like cancer. I don't know that giving him any more hope would be a good thing."

Alex sipped his Coke. "Well, with cancer, sometimes you have to be aggressive. It can save your life that way. Can I make an observation based on my years of accumulated wisdom?"

"Sure, why not."

"Whatever we find or don't find, move out of your house," Alex said. "Because if you don't, you'll resent your dad. Or worse."

What I did not say was: *You mean resent him more than I already do.*

Because I did. I knew it. I hid it, I didn't dwell on it, but I knew. And after so many years, I could feel that resentment hardening, petrifying, calcifying into something much darker than resentment, maybe something I couldn't undo later.

"I don't want to hate him," I said.

"Of course not," Alex said. "But you've got a life too, you know? You get to live it. You deserve to live it. Just sayin'."

I didn't find it easy to think about much else during the rest of the afternoon. Selby came back inside as our food arrived, grabbing and reading a yellowing newspaper from a stack near the door. I earned a burst of fire from her eyes when she saw she couldn't sit beside Charlie, but he didn't try to change the seating arrangement.

Other than that, lunch was kind of fun, in an odd sense. Selby read yesterday's news and started a crossword, while I methodically ate. One of the best meals I'd had recently, and most important, not roast beef or curly fries.

After, we got right back on the road. We followed Interstate 10, which eventually ran parallel to railroad tracks. Enormous orange, blue, or black shipping containers trudged alongside of us. Near Tucson, we exited the I-10 freeway to a frontage road, then followed that to a dirt path carved only by previous tires. Back at the frontage road, there'd been a post with four mailboxes tacked to it, but other than that, no sign of life. The dirt road took us up and over a rise, and once down it, the frontage road was out of sight. We hadn't been able to see the freeway for ten minutes or more by then.

Riley stands up, resting the shotgun over his shoulder. The gun doesn't suit him. He doesn't handle it with practice or ease. He takes one more drink from the tequila, then pops open the Dr Pepper can for a long slurp. He lets the can dangle in his fingers by his thigh.

"I got a Jeep in the garage," he says. "It's a four–wheel-drive. There's a bit of food and water in the house. The satellite for the TV's still working, though I doubt for much longer. Got a portable CB radio for emergencies. King bed, pretty comfy. You can stay here, or load up and head out. That big bus won't get you too far, I don't think. Do whatever you think is best. There's a Bible on the bookshelf. And a Koran, and a Bhagavad Gita, a Book of Mormon, a few others like that. On the shelf below that is everything your father ever sent me. It's not much. Ramblings, mostly. Maybe there's something in there that'll help you, but I doubt it. My advice is to just hunker down and enjoy whatever time you got left. I wish you both well."

Riley comes toward the steps. I step aside to make room. He doesn't even look at me.

"Where are you going?" Charlie asks, crossing to the railing.

Dr. Riley hesitates, then turns around to look at us both.

"God bless," he says. It's the closest I've seen him come to a smile.

With that, he starts walking into the desert. Charlie and I watch him go until he turns a corner around one of the small hills that shield his house.

"I don't get it," I say. "What's he—"

Then the shot.

We both jump and automatically clutch at each other. The reverberation echoes for years, a deep, thundering *boom* that rattles my organs.

We stand there silently until the last of the echoes dies away.

"Well," Charlie whispers. "That's not a good sign."

Thirty-six hours ago, the idea of someone committing suicide with a shotgun just a few hundred yards away from me would've given me a seizure. Now it just seems anticlimactic and sad.

And, as Charlie said, it definitely doesn't bode well for us. Dr. Riley either knew a lot more than he told us, and it wasn't good . . . or he simply meant what he did say, and we were all doomed.

Once I've got my bearings again, I check on Selby—the sound did not disturb her at all—then join Charlie inside the house. CNN blares from Riley's big flat-screen on the chimney wall, facing his couch. It takes all of about thirty seconds to see why he lost hope.

It appears the world is coming to an end.

Charlie and I sit down on the brown leather couch and watch what the newscasters keep calling "disturbing footage." They're right about that. What I had assumed, or hoped, was local to this area has spread. Other power plants are being assaulted by otherworldly beasts. The Hoover Dam, which I'll have to cross to get back home, is under attack. I learned about Hoover in grade school, and didn't think the dam itself could really be damaged . . . but the electrical and mechanical parts sure could, and the potential damage from *that* I couldn't even fathom. It seems the entire Western Seaboard is under siege, and footage is piling up on newsroom floors of strange and enormous creatures being behind it all.

"We've got bases," Charlie says nervously, sitting on the edge of the couch cushion. "Bases here in Arizona, in California, Nevada. The army will wipe them out."

"Unless they've already been taken out. If those things know what they're doing, maybe they targeted military sites first."

Charlie frowns, and remains silent.

"How'd they get so far, so fast?" I say. "I mean, Hoover Dam . . . That's not far from where I live, that's hundreds of miles from here."

Charlie only shakes his head, keeping quiet. We watch for a few more minutes, each video more dire than the last: people panicking, people shooting at the creatures with little or no effect, police and fire departments stretched well past their limits, hospitals overcrowding and then being attacked when at capacity. It does look like the end of the world out there.

I wonder if Dad is watching it all. I wonder what watching might be doing to him.

"Charlie?"

"Huh."

"I want to go home."

He pulls his gaze off the TV. "Right now?"

"Right now."

Charlie clenches and unclenches his jaw for a minute before saying, "I don't think that's the best idea."

"I didn't ask."

"You're serious? With all that shit flying around and burning things to ashes, you want to try a drive to Nevada? I don't think we'll even get past the dam, Abby. I'm not sure we can make it a mile away from this *house*."

"There're ways around the dam."

"*Long* ways."

"But my dad." I leave it at that, letting him fill in the blanks.

Charlie puts one hand over mine. "Hey. I got family too. I'm scared. I'm worried. But the fact that we got this far . . . man, my survival instinct is pretty fucking honed right now."

I don't answer.

"Why don't you give him another call," Charlie says. "Just to check in, make sure he's okay."

I hold up my phone. Charlie looks at it. "What . . . ?"

"No service."

He reaches for his cell.

"Yours won't either," I say. "No one's will. They've already taken them out."

"How do you—"

"I just know. Look at what's going on out there. They're smart. They know what they're doing. These phones are done."

Charlie, staring at the screen of his phone, swallows. "The army will—"

"We don't know that. Riley might've been right. These things aren't scared of us. They probably have no reason to be. Charlie, this might be it."

"Abby—"

"I know what happened to my mom now. And it sucks, and . . . it's *okay*. I can deal with it. But I need to deal with it *with* my dad. Whatever happens. I can't let him go through this alone again."

Charlie tilts his head. "Again?"

I face the TV, numb already to the latest images of twisted creatures tearing our world apart. Amazing how quickly the numbness came.

"Three years ago. With a razor. I found him in the bathroom. It was close. *He* came close. If I hadn't found him when I did, he would've . . . anyway. I can't help but wonder what he's seeing right now. What he's feeling. If Dr. Riley couldn't handle it . . ."

I stop there. I don't need to say anything else.

Charlie stands and walks into the kitchen area. I sit, still and small, watching the news unfold. Every minute brings a new horror to the screen. Schools knocked to the ground by brute force of the rhino-rex creatures. Power poles burnt to cinders by the dragonfly beasts, and blacktop highways turned to sludge by fiery breath.

There were *so many*. So many out there.

"He was right about the food," Charlie calls from the kitchen. "We're all stocked up here. Abby, no kidding, the three of us could live for a month here, easy. Hunker down and wait it out, see what happens. Driving around the desert to get to your dad . . . I get it, I do, but I still think it's the wrong call."

"What about Selby? She still needs more help than we can give her."

"How'd she look when you checked?"

"I'm not a doctor. She's breathing, and there's no blood on the bandage. That's all I know. Staying here—"

The TV goes dark.

I sit up straight. Charlie, realizing the sudden silence, comes back into the living area. "What . . . ?"

"It's not the TV," I say. "Look, it still has power." It slowly dawns on me what the blank screen indicates. "It's the station that's dark."

I try other channels, and get things like History Channel, A&E . . . all sorts of entertainment channels. Nothing network. Nothing with information.

Charlie laces his fingers behind his neck and groans.

"Told you they were thinking."

"Or being controlled," Charlie says.

"Whichever."

Charlie spots Riley's tall wooden bookcase. He rushes over and sits cross-legged in front of it.

"He said Dad's stuff was here," Charlie mutters, pulling out a three-ring binder. "Maybe we can figure something out."

"Charlie—"

"Just wait!" he shouts at me, and his face is wild. It's as if the TV going blank was his last straw.

I shrink back. Charlie sees me do it, and forces a deep breath.

"Just wait," he says again, holding up a hand. "Till . . . till tomorrow. Give me that long. Maybe the stations will come back, or maybe we get someone on the CB radio, or . . . I don't know, but please, Abby, come on, just give me till tomorrow morning. Okay?"

I stand and bury my fingers under my armpits. I feel absurdly cold.

"Okay. Tomorrow."

He starts to say something else, but I turn and walk toward the lone hallway before he can speak. I use the bathroom, then find Riley's bedroom. It's been perfectly and simply made up, as if he was expecting guests. It'll do.

But first, I go back out to the RV and climb inside. Selby hasn't moved even a little, to the point that my heart stops for a moment, thinking she's died. Then I see the white sheet over her rise and fall, and I sigh with relief. I stand in the doorway to the bedroom, watching her breathe, struggling with an overwhelming sense of sorority. I've only known her a couple days, and they haven't exactly been a good couple days, but I meant what I said to Charlie at the urgent care clinic. I will not let anything else happen to her, no matter what.

The question is, now what? She's as comfortable here in the RV as anyplace else. I don't think waking her up to move her inside is necessarily a good idea. The RV might not be the safest place if something comes after us, but then the house isn't either, based on what we've seen on TV. If something attacks us here, I don't think there will be much we can do about it.

Better to let her rest, I decide. The RV sits within a few yards of the porch, not that far. Charlie and I can take turns checking on her.

For all the good it will do if her condition worsens.

I push the thought away and go back into the house. Charlie still sits on the floor in front of the bookcase, with a different binder in his lap now. He doesn't even look up as I walk past.

"Keep an eye on Sells," I say. "She seems okay, but I'm leaving her in the RV. I don't want to wake her up or move her."

Charlie nods absently.

I stop walking. "Charlie."

He finally looks up, face wrinkled in irritation.

"I'm not letting anything else happen to her. Okay?"

His face relaxes. "Okay. Get some rest."

"That's my plan."

I go to Riley's bedroom, where I take my shoes off and crawl under the comforter. I don't know when I fall asleep, but it's long before dark.

"Sure this is right?" I asked Charlie.

"Pretty sure," he said, consulting his iPhone. A second later, he frowned, shoved it in his back pocket, and began opening cabinets. "Signal's already shot. Is there a map around?"

"Charlie, there is nothing out here," I said, watching the Sonoran Desert tumble by outside the window. Severe saguaro and prickly paddle-shaped cacti dominated the gravel floor. Mountains loomed in the distance, purple and blue, their peaks reminding me of shark teeth. Shorter, rounded hills surrounded us, punctuating the otherwise flat desert.

Perhaps not the best possible introduction to driving into the middle of nowhere to meet a stranger.

"There it is," Alex said a minute later as we drove around a hill.

A simple wood-framed house sat in the middle of a sort of valley. I found myself surprised to see there were no horses anywhere, just mesquite trees, more saguaro, and a huge satellite dish planted into the ground.

"This place *has* an address?" I said.

"There were the mailboxes," Charlie said. "We're not that far off the main highway. It just feels like it."

"If you say so. Where are the other houses?"

"Beats me. They could be anywhere in these hills, I guess. I doubt they're very close together." Then he added, as if just reaching this realization: "You don't move out here to be near people."

The professor's house didn't seem much bigger than mine, and mine wasn't very big. It looked sort of diminutive, sitting there alone in the middle of all that nothing. Just a dark green splotch against a backdrop of browns and tans. The house sat in the middle of a sort of valley, with hills surrounding most of it, starting at maybe two hundred yards away. No fence marked off the property, and I wondered how much of it Dr. Riley owned. As far as the eye could see? Farther?

Alex stopped the RV in front of the porch, which ran the width of the house, Southern-style. A picture window took up much of the wall, with the front door implanted a few feet to the right of the window. Thick drapes were drawn across the window, blocking any attempt at looking inside.

Selby's first order of business upon exiting the RV was to light a cigarette. Alex, after grabbing the video equipment bag, fell in beside Charlie, who climbed carefully up a short flight of wooden steps to the porch. The lumber warped mildly, as if warning that one more year out here was apt to result in all planks springing free of their nails. All of us seemed to be scanning the area as if expecting snipers to open fire, except for Selby, who paced back and forth in front of the RV with her smoke.

Charlie knocked on the door. We waited. He knocked again.

The curtains in the window fluttered.

"Dr. Riley?" Charlie called.

The front door opened, revealing an older man with a few weeks' worth of gray beard growth, deep crow's feet around his eyes, and dry, parched skin.

"Christ," the old man said, like he'd stepped in dog shit. "What do *you* want?"

Charlie reared back at the snarl in the old man's voice. "You know who I—"

"Of course I know who you are, Charlie," the old man growled. "You look exactly like your father. What do you want?"

Charlie took a second to compose himself, then said, "Your name showed up in some of my dad's notes. We were hoping you could help us. We're here about the disappearance."

The old man snorted. "They're still calling it that?"

Even Selby, farthest away from him, looked unsettled at the tone in his voice.

"And we're off to a good start," Alex muttered beside me.

Riley's eyes darted to him, assessed briefly, and zipped

back to Charlie. "I have nothing to say, to you or anyone else. So have a nice day."

He began shutting the door. Strangely, I felt a surge of disappointment. Up until this brisk dismissal, my subconscious must have been really expecting something from the professor. It's weird how your real desires sneak up like that, like when a friend gets you some gift you had no idea you even wanted.

I also figured we'd finished this leg of the journey. But Charlie didn't sway as easily as I did.

"Okay," he said, projecting his voice through the rapidly closing gap between door and jamb. "We have the RV out here, so we'll just camp out till you change your mind."

The door stopped, then swung back open. Riley stuck his face past the threshold, closer to Charlie, and snapped, "What was that?"

"Yeah, this big camper here," Charlie said. "There's room for all of us. We'll be happy to wait."

Riley squared himself up and took a step outside. Charlie—and the rest of us—matched it backward.

"Listen up, smart-ass," Riley said. "I have nothing to say. Get your big rig out of here, or I'll call the cops to come out and give you a hand."

Alex turned and took a step toward the yard, making a grab for Selby's shirt on the way to drag her along. Charlie, on the other hand, fired right back.

"Go ahead," Charlie challenged the older man. "We'll keep

coming back. I'll park it past your property line if I have to, but we're not going anywhere."

Riley put his hands on his hips. The gesture made me suddenly think he would look different—and, somehow, more normal—in a casual suit. Something for an office. His red flannel shirt and dusty jeans struck me as idiosyncratic, or even a put-on of sorts. Like he was trying to fill a part he was never meant to play.

"Maybe you don't understand," the professor said slowly, "the concept of a man living by himself out in the middle of a goddamn desert."

"Maybe *you* don't understand how far some kids are willing to go to find their parents."

A studying look crossed Riley's face as he tried to suss out what cards Charlie might truly be ready to play. I wondered the same thing myself. Alex stopped with one foot on the steps, and relinquished his hold on Selby, who, by that point, appeared delighted to stomp out a cigarette butt in what passed for Riley's front yard.

"They're gone, Charlie," Riley said, suddenly opting for a paternal tone. "You have to know that. They're gone."

"If that's the case, maybe you can make me understand the concept of a friend of my dad's living by himself out in the middle of a goddamn desert, so close to where it happened."

Wow. I think the scientific term for that was "zing." Riley looked like he'd been shocked with a Taser as he absorbed Charlie's words.

Dr. Riley shifted back to his grizzled old miner persona, or whatever role he felt compelled to play. "You scrawny little son of a bitch," he said, and pointed a thick finger in Charlie's face. "And I mean every word of that."

"No argument from me, sir," Charlie said, straight-faced. "But I really do need to talk to you about my dad. Please. We won't keep you long."

Dr. Riley eyeballed each one of us, maybe to see if we were dangerous muggers or something. "All right. All right, fine. But I warned you. I warned you."

He stepped into the house, calling over his shoulder, "I don't have anything to drink except tap water and tequila, and I don't recommend either one."

Charlie hurried to follow with the rest of us trailing behind him. Selby came last, stomping her second cigarette out in the dirt yard, half-smoked.

Dr. Riley's house had an open floor plan, with the kitchen, dining area, and living room all part of one big space. He'd decorated it in what I took to be Aging Bachelor Chic, with mismatched but functional furniture, a bookcase that took up the entire wall, and an impressive flat-screen hanging against the opposite wall on the redbrick wall of a chimney. A single hallway led, I presumed, to the bedrooms and bathroom.

Dr. Riley sat at the kitchen table, which looked like it had been nice once, and proceeded to pack a pipe full of tobacco from a pouch.

"Welcome to the embittered professor archetype's house," he grumbled. "Couldn't be more trite if you tried."

"Uh, so, I can smoke in here?" Selby asked.

"Cigarettes? Christ, no. You got a pipe, be my guest." The professor got his pipe going, and the room slowly filled with the scent of cherry.

"So?" Riley said, squinting through his own smoke. "What do you want?"

He focused on Charlie. Selby, pissy about the cigarettes, flung herself into an old wooden rocking chair in the living area. Alex set the camera bag on the floor, and he and I sat tentatively on the edge of a cracked brown leather couch. Charlie stayed on his feet.

"We're making a pilot, sort of," Charlie said. "A video. About the disappearance. Would you mind if I taped you answering a few questions about it?"

"Guess I don't have to tell you who you remind me of right now." Riley sighed. "Go ahead. I don't care."

Charlie nodded to Alex, who nodded back and spent about five minutes setting up a camera on a tripod, and something Charlie called a key light. Alex obviously knew what he was doing, working with the smooth efficiency of familiarity. Riley sat watching the setup and eyeing Charlie.

After Alex finished setting up the camera, Charlie pulled a kitchen chair beside the tripod and sat down. Alex said, "Rolling."

"You worked with my dad," Charlie began.

"We've established that," Riley said.

From where I sat on the couch, I saw resolve harden Charlie's expression.

"And you just so happened to retire a few miles from where he disappeared," Charlie said. "Can you tell us about that?"

Riley snorted. Smoke streamed from his mouth, dragon-like. "I see. You think I did them all in. Is that it?"

"No, sir. But I think you know more than anyone else might be willing to believe. I think you've kept things about their disappearance to yourself. I want to know what those things are. We just might believe them."

Charlie used the word like bait, hanging it out there for the professor to latch on to or not.

Dr. Riley's eyes narrowed. He examined all of us from his chair, each in turn, like the bad cop in an action movie. I didn't like what I saw in his expression—bitterness, suspicion. Fear.

"I had a friend once," Riley said. "Nuclear engineer. Worked on building bombs. When he retired, he moved to New York City so he could be as close to a primary nuclear target as possible. So he wouldn't suffer if the Russian missiles hit. People think they can survive if they buy enough canned beets and ammunition. But sometimes it's better to die in the first wave."

No one said anything. I, for one, had no idea what he was talking about, and it didn't seem anyone else did either.

"I'm sorry," Alex said, actually raising his hand like we were in a classroom. "There's a bomb that's going to go off here?"

Dr. Riley smirked a bit. I suddenly had an image of having him as a teacher in college, and how much that would suck.

"Oh, I doubt it," he said. "But if John Prinn was right . . ."

He paused. Charlie leaned forward. Maybe we all did. Riley shook his head.

"All right," he said. "You really want the whole story? Fine. Buckle up, kids."

A red digital clock on Riley's bedside table reads 6:04 a.m. when I open my eyes. I slept for more than twelve hours. I see light coming from the living area, but hear nothing. The house is perfectly still. Calm.

I slide out of bed, moaning. My muscles are knotted tight, like they can never be undone. I move out of the room, down the hall, and into the living area. Charlie is asleep on the couch. The TV is on, but the screen remains black. Books, notebooks, and papers lay strewn across the floor and on the coffee table. Two cans of soda and an empty frozen dinner tray stand guard over it all. For no good reason, I realize Riley had told us he had only tap water and tequila to drink. I couldn't help wondering: *So what else did he lie about?*

Since there's no telling how long he's actually been asleep, I choose not to disturb Charlie. I go out to the RV, picking carefully through the dirt and rocks. Selby has moved around some during the night, but is still out cold. I check her bandage—no blood. I opt not to lift the gauze and see underneath. I put a bottle of water on the drop-down table beside the bed within easy reach for when she wakes up, then go back to the house. I figure I'll make some breakfast, maybe shower, then come back and wake her up if she's still sleeping.

I search the rest of the small house to see what we have to work with. Riley's food supply veers more toward frozen and canned food than fresh, plus generous supplies of Dr Pepper and the same brand of tequila he'd been drinking. A door off the kitchen leads to a tiny garage. A blue four-door Jeep Wrangler sits there. Already inside are two full ten-gallon gas cans and several jugs of water.

Going back out to the RV, I pull all our stuff out from the storage compartments, then go back inside the house to use the bathroom and shower, trying to scrub everything that has happened to us off me. I try not to think about Alex's bags, about the fact that he will never open them up and sort through T-shirts and underwear and shorts and jeans and socks that will never be used again—

I turn the hot water on stronger, until it's so hot I have to turn it back down before it scalds me. I barely care. The piercing, blessed heat brings me the closest I've ever come to believing in God.

I climb out of the stall reluctantly. I could stay in there another year or two, but now I'm starved. I go out into the kitchen for a glass of cold water, only to find Charlie sitting at Riley's table, staring blankly at the top of it.

He looks up when I come around the corner. I imagine my face turns a little red since I'm wearing only a towel, but Charlie doesn't ogle me or anything like that. I should've just dried off and gotten dressed. Guess I wasn't thinking clearly. Maybe never would again.

"You're up," Charlie says listlessly.

"Yeah."

"How was the shower?"

"Good."

"Leave me any hot water?"

"I think so. Quite possibly not, I'll be honest."

He nods, then waves weakly at the kitchen. "Making coffee. Hope you like it caffeinated."

"Yeah."

"Good. I should check on Selby."

"I just did. Before I showered. She's asleep. Figured I'd wake her up after breakfast."

"Okay."

Charlie stands, and somehow, he seems to have shrunk overnight. He'd been so tall standing on my driveway two days ago. Now he looks old. Decrepit.

"I'm gonna go clean up," Charlie says. "You should eat."

I nod and sidestep out of his way, brushing my still-wet hair behind my ears as he passes. Charlie pauses in the hallway and looks back at me.

"You look good."

I have no response and Charlie doesn't wait for one; he

stated it as a matter of fact, a point of interest, not with a leer. I'm not sure whether to be disappointed or not.

I get dressed, grateful for the clean clothes, then make myself breakfast. My belief in a higher power surges again as I eat microwave sausage, a sweet roll from the oven, and hot coffee. For a few minutes, I'm just on a retreat, a little trip, a cabin somewhere to relax.

Charlie also takes his time in the shower. I rest his bags outside the bathroom door, knocking and telling him I've done so. By the time he reappears, I'm flipping through the channels on TV. More of them have gone off the air now. The few channels that remain on the air consist of home shopping or, perhaps ironically, religious programming.

"That shower . . . That was a beautiful thing," he says, pouring himself coffee.

"I know." I gesture to the notes spread over the floor. I haven't looked at any. "Find anything?"

"Ideas. Leads, maybe. At best. But mostly no. Not really."

"I had a thought about the professor."

"What's that?"

"It's just that . . . we didn't see him die."

Charlie pauses with a mug halfway to his mouth. "Why would he . . . I mean, we heard him. I don't think there's much room for error."

"But we didn't *see* him."

He gives me a worried look. "You don't want to go out there."

"I don't want to, but I think we should. The sun's up. I just want to make sure before we leave."

"You still want to try to get to Vegas."

"Yes. I *am* going. It's just a question of whether you're coming with me or not. I'll take the RV or the Jeep. Either one, doesn't matter. And I'm taking Selby with me."

"I thought you hated her."

"I never said that."

"You didn't have to."

"Yeah, well, that was two days ago, wasn't it. Things are slightly different now."

Charlie resumes his sip, frowning as he does it. I wait.

"If we avoid the dam," he says finally, "that's got to be, like, four hundred miles. That's a lot of time out in the open without any real protection."

"I don't know that there is any protection short of a tank."

Charlie shrugs, conceding.

"You can stay if you want," I tell him. "Either way, there're two vehicles and . . ."

As I speak, Charlie puts down his mug and walks over to me. I stand up as he does it. Then his arms are around me, pulling me close, tight, surrounding me. I hug him back and shut up, my cheek pressed against his collar. He's trembling, and I realize he isn't hugging me for me; he needs me to be holding him.

So I do.

After a few minutes—what feels like hours—Charlie lifts

his hands to either side of my head. He pulls away just enough so that we are touching foreheads, our mouths only an inch or two apart. Still he shudders. I raise my own hands to hold his wrists.

"I—" Charlie whispers.

I slide my hands under his forearms and touch his chin, then pull him close.

We kiss hard, though not passionately . . . desperate, perhaps. At first our mouths are closed, but soon we open them, and tear fiercely into each other's lips. Our hands find each other, and link together, pressing tightly, squeezing hard. We gasp and twist our heads around each other like snakes, eyes shut tight, using nothing but lips and teeth and tongues to find each other. I lose all sense of time.

We end up in the same position as before, with our foreheads touching, Charlie tilting his head down and me tilting up. Our eyes stay closed. Or at least, mine do.

"I . . ." Charlie breathes, and catches his breath. "I . . . want . . ."

I grabbed double fistfuls of his shirt to keep my hands in place, so they don't travel anywhere else the way they want to. I know what he wants. *We.* I know what *we* want.

He tries to say it again: "I want . . . to . . ."

I move my head away from his, and he nearly topples forward. I hug him.

"Get me home," I say. "Get me home first."

We don't move for a bit. Then slowly, we untangle and each

take one step back. Charlie sniffs and runs both hands down his face, giving his head a shake like a wet dog.

"Okay." He clears his throat, trying to make it appear nothing just happened. "So we try to get you to your dad. Okay. Okay."

"Thank you."

He's about to say something else when his attention shifts to the plateglass window behind me. Looking over my shoulder, Charlie manages to say one word:

"What—"

The room explodes. The window blows inward. Shards and needles of glass slam into my neck and back. The noise muffles my hearing and ties my lungs into a knot. I fall to the floor, hands over my head, even as a little survivor's voice inside me whispers that I know this sound, have heard it recently, that the next few seconds are very likely going to be my last because it was, without a doubt, the blast of a shotgun.

"Any of you kids read the Bible?" Riley said, like he knew the answer already.

"Cover to cover," Selby said, bouncing a foot over one knee.

If she meant to impress him, it didn't work. "Good for you," he said with a derisive tone that put Selby's icy glare to shame. "Tell me about the flood."

"Should I use the original Hebrew?"

"Pop quiz, smart-ass. Question one. There once was a man with a wife and three sons who survived a global flood. Name all five."

"Noah, and I don't know the rest, because I could not care any less," Selby said.

"Noah, Shem, Ham, and Japheth," Alex said. "I don't think his wife is ever named."

"Not bad. But wrong."

Alex's eyes bugged. Riley plowed ahead.

"Question two. Once upon a time, God told the men to go into a ship. They took all sorts of animals with them. The floodwaters rose, covering the mountains. Later, to check whether the waters had dried up, they sent out a dove, and it came back to the ship. Where can I find that story?"

"Genesis six, seven, and eight," Alex said, a little forcefully.

"Wrong again."

I thought Alex might tackle him.

"Question one refers to a man named Tumbainot, his wife Naipande, and three sons, Oshomo, Bartimaro, and Barmao. That's the Masai flood account. The second question refers to the flood story from Tanzania. Neither of which have anything to do with the Biblical flood. Last count, there are at least five hundred similar flood accounts from all over the world."

"Okay, didn't know *that*," Alex admitted quietly.

I felt myself nod in agreement.

"Know what that means?" Riley asked. "It means something happened. The details vary, sometimes a little, sometimes a lot. But something big happened several thousand years ago, and almost every culture we know of recorded it."

"What's that have to do with my dad?" Charlie asked, polite but firm.

Riley squinted at Charlie. "Myths aren't about fact, they're about truth. You hear the difference? It's not important that God saved a righteous man and his family along with two of every animal by sealing them into a boat. It's important that our world underwent a profound change at the behest of God."

"You're saying 'God' like he exists," Selby said. "I thought you were a scientist."

"Oh, I apologize. I meant *gods*."

We all looked at one another. Dr. Riley appeared pleased—in a cranky way—that he'd made an impact.

"Islam states there is but one god," he said. "Not many other religions make this claim. Very few, in fact."

"Christianity, Judaism—" Alex started.

"Say to have no *other* gods before him," Dr. Riley said. "You want to show me where it says there's only one? The Old Testament, or the Tanakh, the Torah? They'll tell you you're not supposed to have any other gods before Yahweh. You'd be hard-pressed to find anything in there about him being the *only* god. Have any of you ever *really* examined the weird stuff in the Old Testament alone? Giants, fallen angels, demons, leviathans, nephilim, the behemoth, ghosts. There are people out there who think the Bible proves the existence of the Loch Ness Monster, for crying out loud."

"Uh, is that what you think?" Selby asked. "Because if it is . . ."

Riley fixed her with a glare that even Selby couldn't beat. She sucked her lips between her teeth and shrank back into the chair.

"Four thousand years ago," Riley said, "in the place we now call Iraq, you have lots of cultures running around, and they all worshipped a lot of gods. The sun, moon, fire, water, animals, you name it. But along comes this fella who says no, no, there's one god above all the others."

"Abraham," Alex said.

"Father Abraham, correct. So that's about two thousand BCE. Well, guess what's already happened here in the good old US of A? There's a group of people called the Patayan, who lived not far from here. A little farther west, maybe. They'd been around since ten thousand BCE. That's eight *thousand* years before Father Abraham in Iraq. Now, all the Patayan's neighbors worship the sun, the moon, fire, buffalo . . . all the usual suspects. But not the Patayan. Know what they say? There's only one god. How about that? Guess what else—they got a flood story too. Just like four hundred ninety-nine other prehistoric cultures all over the globe."

This wasn't a story I'd heard before. I could tell Alex was thinking the same thing. Selby . . . well, Selby tried to look as unimpressed as ever, but she was paying attention too.

"But the Patayan flood is a little different," Riley said. "See, their god isn't out to get rid of naughty little humans. He said some of the *animals* were too wild for Earth. They had big teeth, and big claws, and were dangerous to man. And there were too many of them. So he decides to kill them off with a flood. But before he can wipe all of them out, his people actually beg him to stop, because he might kill off all the good animals too. So he relents. And we never hear anything more about the animals with the big teeth and big claws. Where'd they go? We haven't seen any in a while. What happened to them? It's like he's put them away somewhere for the safety of his human followers. Maybe he put them into an ark for safe-keeping. And maybe they're still there."

"I thought the ark was a boat," Charlie said.

"That's one possible definition," Riley said. "The Old Testament uses the word '*tebah*.' The only other time the word '*tebah*' is used in the Old Testament is in reference to the basket Moses was put into. In both cases, the word could refer to anything meant to protect people. Maybe by the time the flood story got to the Middle East two thousand years ago, things had been switched around. In the Noah story, human beings are put into a *tebah* to protect them from what was happening outside of it. In the Patayan story, maybe the humans are protected by what's put into the ark. Into the *tebah*."

Tebah. One of the words I'd seen scrawled in John Prinn's book. That at least confirmed Riley really knew about Mr. Prinn's research.

Selby, unsurprisingly, made a quick recovery from her bashing. "Sorry, I nodded off there for a minute while you were speaking nonsense. You're saying, what . . . Noah built a boat that rescued American Indian monsters from drowning? That's your theory?"

"Did I go too fast?" Riley mocked. "You're free to leave any old time. Bye."

"Please," Charlie said. "Keep going."

Riley chewed his pipe for a moment as if deciding whether or not to pay attention to Charlie. Then he spoke.

"Your dad did a better job of tying up all the threads, but this is how it finally breaks down: You look at all those ancient myths, from all over the world. You start seeing their commonalities. How far back they really must go. You start studying the places where beliefs intersect instead of diverge. Pretty soon you got a whole heaven full of gods and a whole Earth full of monsters."

"Uh, that's a *swell* story, I'm sure it'll make a great Brad Pitt movie someday, but I thought you were a scientist," Selby said. I could practically feel waves of nicotine depletion rolling off her. "You don't seriously believe all that crap, right? Did I miss the part where Santa Claus fought off the Martians? Or when Harry cast a spell on the vampires?"

Riley smiled, but it was anything but friendly.

"Science, eh? I see you're quasi-intelligent. I respect that. But you lack imagination. And imagination is what puts men on the moon. Without that, facts and figures are just that, nothing more. You're not grasping a holistic view of creation, the universe, and our place in it."

"I'll grasp it fine if you want to try using, I dunno, *science.*"

"Oh, you want to talk testable and repeatable science?"

"Yes!"

"Okay. Let's do that for a bit."

Dr. Riley stood up and went into the kitchen. He crashed around in the large drawers for a few moments before pulling

out a glass casserole dish that had seen better days and a few
Brillo pads. He came back to the table and stood beside it,
holding the casserole up for us to see. Alex adjusted the camera to follow.

"Look at this dish. Nice and clean, thank you very much.
Do my own dishes by hand, always have. How many dimensions does it have?"

"Uh, three," Selby said.

"Correct. Now look at its shadow on the table. How many
dimensions does that shadow have?"

"Two?" I asked.

"Correct again. But what if the dish, the physical object in
its three dimensions, was only the *shadow* of something else?"

"That's not possible," Alex said, but I could see him wres-
tling with the idea.

It made no sense to me, either. I looked at Selby, figuring
she'd be gearing up for another retort. Instead, she now sat in
concentration as if scrutinizing each of Dr. Riley's words. I
guess he was finally speaking her language.

"Actually, it is possible," Selby said. "In theory."

"Go ahead," Riley said, arching a bemused eyebrow.
"Explain it to them."

She glowered back, but did face us. "So there are lots of
theories in physics, okay? String theory, M-theory, the holographic principle . . . all kinds of stuff. We live in four dimensions, right? Three plus time. Well, the holographic principle
suggests that our dimensions are only a shadow of a fifth

dimension that we can't perceive with our senses, or our technology. Not yet, anyway. It's only ever been suggested on paper."

"Well done," Riley said, giving her a nod, which only elicited another glare from Selby. "Now. What kind of beings might be capable of residing in that fifth dimension of reality?"

"What, *God*?" Selby said, not trying to conceal a sneer.

"No," Riley barked back. "Give the gods a few more dimensions than that. I'm talking about flesh-and-blood animals that maybe used to exist *here* until they were sent *there*."

"Monsters from the fifth dimension!" Alex said in a movie voice-over.

"Laugh it up," Riley said, and nobody did. "You all asked the questions. I'm giving you possible answers. Use your imagination and consider what a giant Biblical carnivore who's been locked away for milennia in a fifth dimension of reality might look like. What it might be capable of. I'm talking about creatures with, let's say . . . big teeth. And big claws. And they're dangerous to humanity. And maybe there were too many of them. And they were supposed to get killed off. In a flood. Am I ringing any bells, children?"

Echoes of his Patayan flood myth circled the room like hawks before landing on my scalp with curved nails.

"So," Riley said with a dramatic shrug. "Maybe some of those creatures were put into an ark, a *tebah*, in order to preserve ancient humanity, and maybe that ark has nothing to do with our four dimensions."

He tossed the dish to the table, where it clattered loudly and made me tense up. Riley crashed back to his kitchen chair and relit the pipe. His hands trembled as he did it.

Selby stood. "Okay, this is ridiculous. You are obviously, like, insane or senile or whatever, but this is bullshit. There was this brief, *brief* moment where I was tracking with you, but then you went off the goddamn rails again. I'm going to have a smoke."

"It's a big world, and an even bigger universe," Riley said as Selby reached the front door. "And there's probably something even bigger than the universe. I don't know, and I don't want to know. But John Prinn might've figured it out. And it might've gotten him killed."

"Well!" Selby said. "That brings us to the end of Crazy Time here at Uncle Nutzy's Funhouse. I'm going to go spread carcinoma in my lungs to sooner rid myself of this type of execrable scholarship. Peace out, folks."

She marched out the door, but didn't close it behind her; she left it swinging open on its hinges. It gave me the impression she didn't want to be left out of anything else that might be said as she smoked on the porch.

Riley turned his gaze to us, as if assessing. Maybe trying to decide if we were worthy of what other information he had. But *was* this information? Or just mad ramblings? Selby had a point: maybe he suffered from senility. He didn't look or sound like someone having cognitive trouble. So that left insanity. Much more likely, but somehow, it didn't seem right.

"Dr. Riley?" I said.

He met my eyes. His seemed tired now.

"I'm sorry, but wouldn't we already know about all this if it were true? Giant animals, all that sort of thing. Wouldn't that be clear in the fossil record or something?"

"You're not grasping *scale*. Do you know how many new species of animal are discovered every year? Have you ever been through the Sonoran desert here? Or the *Sahara*? Brazilian rain forests, arctic tundra? The square mileage of earth that's never been excavated . . . There could be entire civilizations right under us and we might never know it. There are *known* archeological sites in the Holy Land, sites with enormous archaeological value, and they haven't been excavated because of politics and religion. Those are sites we *know* about, and that don't date that far back, comparatively. What else is out there we don't know about?"

"There would still be proof," Charlie said.

The words went up like a target, and Riley shot right at them.

"Glaciers grind stones and metal into powder. Even Styrofoam won't last a thousand years. You're still dismissing *scale*. On the scale of the three or four billion years this planet's been around, humans aren't much. Our best concrete will turn to dust after six hundred years. Steel rusts and disintegrates. Solar radiation destroys plastic very quickly in geological terms. Even Kevlar crumbles because of ultraviolet radiation if it's not treated with certain paints. The older a thing is, the harder it is to date, and the harder it is to find. And if you're talking fossils, those are extremely rare things. Just the right set of environmental factors has to be at play for us to get fossils. Now you throw one or a couple hundred transdimensional deities into the mix, and it's no wonder there's no proof. Evidence, on the other hand, is exactly what your dad was collecting. I think he found it."

Riley hoisted himself up and shuffled into the kitchen. He poured himself a shot of, I assume, tequila, downed it, shook himself, then leaned against the countertop. I wondered if he was neither senile nor insane, and was instead just plain drunk.

"You're here about that cave," he said. "Well, caves have a very long history with us. As far back as our brand of mankind goes, caves have been places of magic. Maybe there's a reason for that."

"You believe in magic?" Alex said. His voice was gentle but sincere.

"Of course not. What I mean by 'magic' is a science utterly above and beyond anything our young little brains can fathom without resorting to lunacy to protect ourselves. Flying in the sky was once magical. Ships to other worlds were once magical. Right now, proving something as simple as string theory would be magical for all of a day or two, before it became common sense. *This* science, *this* magic Prinn talked to me about . . . it goes well beyond that."

We remained silent for a moment, until Selby stomped back inside, trailing the scent of smoke behind her, went straight to Dr. Riley, and jabbed her finger at him.

"You know what I think? I think you're like a freaking Scooby-Doo villain. And this is all bullshit, and stupid, and dumb. I cannot believe I wasted all this time to have an insane old man try to fill us all full of such shit. A doctor, no less. What a waste."

"Young lady," Dr. Riley said, unimpressed, "there will always be frontiers. You're on one right now. It's always frightening when the old order crumbles. So I don't blame you for being so disagreeable. Having said that, I truly do not care what you think."

He looked past her at the rest of us. "The official explanation was a cave-in, kids. Let it go at that."

"Gladly," Selby said, and crashed out of the house. She didn't stop at the porch this time, veering instead straight for the RV.

"Okay." Charlie sighed. "Cut."

Alex hit the record button on the camera.

"Thank you, Dr. Riley," Charlie said, and got up from his seat.

"Go home, son," Riley said, with that oddly paternal note in his voice again. It made me wonder how Dad was doing. "Go home, and make a movie about bad guys and good guys. Let this thing go."

Charlie peered closely at the old professor. "Why? How come?"

"Because no matter what, nothing good comes out of this for you. Nothing."

"Maybe we find out what really happened."

"Maybe. Or maybe you just get hurt. For months, I listened to your dad go off on all this stuff." He gestured around the room. "This is where it got me."

"He's why you left teaching?" I asked.

Riley snorted like I was the dimmest bulb in this box he'd had to deal with. "I was a tenured professor at a prestigious university with a boatload of annual endowment money. After John Prinn dragged me into his research, I ended up a broke-ass alcoholic living in the desert waiting for Armageddon. If I thought Prinn was alive, I'd be first in line to punch his face off."

He eyed each one of us. The look on his face froze me.

"Children, listen to me. You want to know if I believe in the supernatural. No, I do not. As your little scientist there has said, I'm a scientist too. And what I'm telling you is that humanity's imaginary supernatural stories, our monsters and ghosts and demons . . . they are a pleasant walk in the park compared to what science is going to prove about this universe someday. Someday soon." He looked specifically at Charlie. "Your dad was close to accomplishing just that. To opening a door that will change everything we know and accept about our teeny-tiny so-called reality. And children? My plan is to be long dead before that happens."

I noticed Charlie wiping a hand on his jeans, as if in preparation to shake the professor's hand, but he didn't do it.

"You could blow it up," he said instead. "Dynamite the entrance so the cave couldn't be accessed."

Riley literally laughed.

"Dynamite?" He kept laughing. At the tail end, he repeated it. "Dynamite. Huh. You didn't hear one goddamn word I said. Just like your dad. Get on out of here."

Charlie gave him a nod, then nodded at me too, and together we walked out of the house.

The blast from the shotgun reverberates through my body. I roll over onto my back, unable to grasp the meaning of this fresh new hell.

It's Dr. Riley. He has the shotgun leveled at the place where the window had been a moment before. How Charlie and I avoided the pellets, I don't know. Then again, maybe we haven't. Maybe the pain just hasn't reached me yet, and maybe Charlie is behind me, dead, and I'm already bleeding out . . .

The top half of the professor's head is missing.

He turns to look down at me. I can see he must have placed the shotgun a few inches above his eyes and pulled the trigger. A crater of bone shows the pulped remains of his brain open to the air. But his eyes . . . his eyes swim with malicious green-black liquid smoke, mesmerizing me away from the horror of his ghastly appearance.

I try to get to my feet, but succeed only in digging glass into my palms. I cry out and worm my way up by bracing my back against the couch. Dr. Riley—if he can rightly be called that anymore—follows me with those green-black eyes. They're like the fluid insides of a glow stick mixed into motor oil. Not a bit of whites, cornea, or iris is visible.

The Riley-thing takes a step, clumsily lifting a foot over the short wall that remains of the windowsill. He scans the room mutely as I finally get to my feet and shuffle back against one wall, holding out bleeding hands to ward him off.

But he doesn't want me. He walks—toddles, really, like a little kid—over to the kitchen. That's when I spot Charlie. He's hunkered down, shaking glass from his hair as the professor stomps past him. Charlie sees him, looks for me, and rushes to my side.

"Okay?" he says, or seems to say, because I still can't hear much of anything.

Instead of answering, I just watch in awe as the zombie creature goes into the kitchen and opens a drawer. Good God, is he making something to *eat*?

No. He needs something. He pulls out a small white-and-red box and dumps the contents onto the counter. They bounce and clatter, several red cylinders spilling onto the floor.

Shells. For the gun.

Riley still holds the shotgun in one hand, where it dangles from his fingers. With the other hand he tries to pick up any one of a number of the shells.

Charlie looks wildly around the room, then lunges at one of the chairs at the kitchen table. He picks it up in both hands and swings it hard over the old man's back. Riley lurches forward over the counter, dropping the cartridge he'd managed to get hold of.

The chair hasn't broken, and Charlie uses it to prod the zombie away from the box. Riley stumbles backward, dropping the gun. Charlie grabs it and swipes a handful of shells off the counter and toward me, like his hands are too numb and clumsy to fit the shells into the shotgun. He trips over his own feet and heads back toward me.

Charlie falls at my feet and manages to get the shotgun cracked open. Two green shells pop out. I smell something smoky. Charlie grabs two of the shells he'd knocked this way and stuffs them into the chamber. Dimly, I hope he knows what he's doing.

Riley gets back to his feet. Instead of rushing for us, he turns toward a butcher's block and pulls a cleaver out of it. He starts tottering in our direction.

He doesn't make it far. Charlie, from a crouched position, fires the shotgun.

The old man's chest bursts apart and scatters pulp throughout the kitchen. It sends him reeling back several feet into the garage door. There he stands for a moment before falling against the tile.

And something else comes out of him.

A viscous, nearly liquid smoke pours from his mouth. It moves first languidly, then quickly, jerking back and forth like a silken scarf or an anxious school of fish. It's not the only time

I've seen this happen, I realize suddenly, but it's the first time it's been in full daylight.

The first time was in the cave, before the pit opened.

The black cloud swims before us for a moment, then slips out through the hole where the window had been. Charlie and I both instinctively follow, stopping at the window, watching the black thing hesitate outside the RV.

"No!" I scream. "Stay away from her!"

The black cloud whirs and dances, cobra-like, before bolting up into the air and out of sight.

The side door to the RV opens up. Selby stands in the doorway, bracing herself against the frame.

"Uh, what the hell was all that noise?" she says, pressing her right hand against her wound.

I race outside and look into the sky, trying to track the black cloud. It's already disappeared.

"Are you okay?" I call to her.

"Still stabbed," Selby says. "Otherwise, yes. Hungry. Isn't this that professor's house? What are we doing here?"

I back up to the RV door before turning and offering a hand. "Come on. We'll get you some food. You can get cleaned up inside."

Selby takes my hand and lets me help her to the ground. We step slowly toward the porch.

"Where's the prof?" she asks, wincing. "And what the hell happened to the window?"

I glance at Charlie. He meets my eyes, then looks at the gun in his hands as if surprised to see it there. He tosses it onto the couch with a look of fierce disgust.

"This way," he says to us, and joins me and Selby at the steps up to the porch. We go inside, and I realize Charlie is keeping Selby positioned in a way to prevent her from seeing the professor's body in the kitchen.

We escort her to the bedroom, where she gives her arms an obligatory shake to get us to let go of her. "I brought in your clothes," I say, trying to control the shaking in my voice from leftover adrenaline. "If you want to shower or something."

"Yeah, okay." Selby reaches for the hem of her shirt, but sucks in a breath. "Ow. Can you . . . ?"

"Oh. Sure."

"I'll go, um . . . clean everything up," Charlie says to me.

I nod quickly. He leaves, shutting the bedroom door on his way. To Selby, I say, "Why don't you sit down. I need to clean up my hands."

"You're bleeding," she says, gingerly taking the edge of Riley's bed.

"Yeah. I . . . yeah."

I go into the bathroom and run water over my palms, biting my lips together. The damage isn't awful, but the glass hurts something fierce. I find a first-aid kit in Riley's cabinets, and bandage my hands as best I can before returning to Selby. She's still sitting on the bed, motionless, her shoulders slumped.

"I can't even take off my shoes," she says.

I kneel in front of her. "It's okay. I got it. It's your

core—everything moves from there. It makes sense that you can't do much."

I begin unlacing her blue, now-dusty boots and slide them off her feet. Next, I peel off her socks, which are cold and damp with old sweat. If I hadn't had to take Dad's shoes off so many times while he was passed out on the couch, maybe it would have grossed me out. Plus, after today, is there anything that could gross me out?

"Here, stand up," I say, pulling her to her feet.

"I can do my own goddamn zipper," Selby grouses.

She braces herself on my shoulder while she gets undressed.

"So how long have you guys been going out?" This question pops out of me like a bubble. I couldn't have stopped it even if I'd wanted to.

Selby rolls her eyes a bit. "Few weeks."

Fortunately, I manage to bite back my first response, which would have gone something like, *That's it? Are you freaking kidding me?*

"That's not very long," I say.

"I just moved out of my mom's place. Long overdue, really. We don't, uh . . . get what you'd call *along*. So I split. Took a bus to Los Angeles to stay with Charlie for a while. We'd been talking on the phone and online. You know, usual stuff. Then you called."

Those last words come out even, but I can tell it's hard for her to make them sound like it.

"Don't you want to go back? I mean, to see if your mom is okay?"

"No."

"It was that bad?"

"It was that bad."

"But—"

"Abby."

I shut up.

"Let me deal with my own shit," Selby says, but somewhat kindly. "Okay?"

"Okay."

I help her crawl out of her shirt as she gasps and swears through the whole thing. "That'll do," she says, and limps over to the bathroom. As if an afterthought, she adds, "Thanks."

"No problem."

I let myself out, closing the door behind me. Charlie's in the kitchen, staring at what's left of Dr. Riley.

"Yeah, so, we're getting out of here," Charlie says.

"Right," I say. "Told you."

He holds my hand.

"So I guess that's what they call reality TV," I said to Alex as we walked to the RV.

"At its finest," Alex agreed, grinning.

"Certified can of nuts," Selby announced as we got into the RV. "That's all he was. People like that are in desperate need of a Darwin Award."

"You know what you sound like right now, Sells?" Alex said, climbing into the driver's seat. "An extremist. You sound like a person who would happily behead someone who did not share your beliefs, or who doesn't come around to accepting the way *you* say things are. Just sayin'."

It's outdated, I know, but the first word that came to mind after Alex said that was *Snap!*

We all got inside and Charlie shut the door. Alex started the RV.

"Know something, Alex?" Selby said. She snatched up yesterday's newspaper she got from the café and sat on the couch. "You

might think I'm this ice-princess atheist bitch. And you'd be right.
But you know what else? I loved my dad. A lot. He was a good
guy. And made living with Mom easier to deal with. So I miss
the righteous holy hell out of him, but I'm not about to go pin-
ning any hopes to some lame-ass professor living in the middle of
nowhere who's so drunk and senile he thinks there's an afterlife."

"Technically, he didn't say that," Charlie said.

"He implied it with his crazy talk, come on."

"That's fair," Alex said, steering the RV back to what passed
for a road. "But just because you don't know something yet,
that doesn't mean it's impossible, does it?"

"Uh, in this case? Yeah, it does." Selby folded the paper
to the obituaries page and flung it onto the console between
the two front seats. "Look at these people. They died, but the
world moved on. I moved on. All of us did. That's all I need
to know."

"But that's not proof of anything," Alex said. "I thought you
were scientific."

"And pragmatic." She slapped a hand on top of the obits.
"These people, they didn't matter."

Alex said, "Yes, they did! They mattered to the people who
are still here."

"Yeah, but in a hundred years, *they* won't matter either.
Even if you had a kid right now, just popped one out, in a
hundred years, it won't matter, he'll be dead too. The Earth will
still be torn apart by humanity, but you'll be long gone, and so
will your kids. Maybe even grandkids. It doesn't matter."

I shook my head and stared out at the desert whipping by outside the passenger window. "You're a great big ray of sunshine, anyone ever tell you that?"

"Yeah." Selby sat back on the couch again. "My dad. How's that working out for me?"

I'd had it with her. On a number of levels, one of which was—maybe she had a point. In any case, I just wanted her to stop.

"Wow," I said, spinning the captain chair toward her. "That was like a . . . like a little zing there, wasn't it?"

Well, that clearly wasn't the reaction she was looking for. She kept her bitch face on, but I saw something deeper in her eyes twitch. Plus, I saw Alex stifling a sigh and Charlie rubbing his eyes. Geez. They didn't need me contributing to the mobile bitch factory.

"I'm sorry," I said right away. "That wasn't cool."

I thought I saw Selby's shoulders spasm upward, like she didn't want to shrug a *No big* back at me but couldn't help it. I took that as a good sign.

"I'm just saying," Selby said. "We play with death, and I'm sick of it. We fetishize it, glorify it. Movies, books, video games. We treat it like this great drama. Like when it's our turn, there will be this great orchestral swell and there will be a fade to black, and the credits will roll, and it will all be nice and dramatic and touching. Maybe a slow pan across the faces of people who loved you. Maybe even some slo-mo, *ooo*! But we'll see that actor again. We can reset the video game or reread the story, and nobody ever dies. Except that's not how it really goes, now, is it."

Nobody had anything to add. I thought of my dad, and wondered if maybe Selby had a pretty damn valid argument.

"You were paying attention to some of the stuff Riley said," I pointed out. "How come?"

"Because he wasn't totally stupid. His bit with the glass dish was mildly entertaining."

"Okay, I did not understand that even a little bit," Alex admitted, slapping a hand against the steering wheel. "How can a three-dimensional object be a shadow?"

"Things get weird when you start adding dimensions," Selby said. "Here, hold on."

She went to the fridge and helped herself to a Diet Coke. Coming back up front, she said to me, "Trade me places?"

It might sound funny, but it was the most polite, civilized tone she'd had so far. I gave up my shotgun seat in a hurry, anxious to keep her going down this unbitchy road.

Selby sank into the chair, which now faced toward the driver's side of the van on a swivel, so the three of us could see her.

"Okay," she said. "Imagine a perfectly flat world. Everything is in two dimensions. We can move side to side, up and down, around and around. But there is no *out* or *back*. We lack that third dimension. Okay?"

Alex and I both nodded. I actually found myself enjoying this side of Selby. She was enjoying *herself*.

"Now one day, we find a circle. We can move all around it

and measure it, say this is a circle. Then we find a rectangle. We can move all around it, measure it, just like we did the circle. We know this is a rectangle. No problem, right?"

"Sure," I said.

"Great. Now here's the twist. Can a circle ever be a rectangle?"

"Um . . ."

"Not a trick question, Abby. Can it?"

"No."

"Right. A circle can never be a rectangle, and a rectangle can never be a circle. So far, so good. But what if we take this soda can—"

She set it on top of the console.

"And we draw an outline of it on top of our flat world. The outline is a circle. A two-dimensional circle. But if we tip it on its side . . ."

She chugged the last of the soda and set the can down lengthwise.

"And we draw an outline of it, what do we get?"

"A rectangle," Alex said, starting to smile.

"Aha, and presto," Selby said. "A circle can be a rectangle if you add another dimension."

"That's kind of cool," Alex said. "How'd you come up with that?"

"I didn't. A guy named Edwin Abbott did, a long time ago. It was a story called *Flatland*. It was actually a social satire, but there's this physics aspect too, whether he meant it to be or not."

I spoke slowly, trying to sound the idea out. "So the point is that once you add another dimension . . ."

"Things that shouldn't be possible suddenly become possible," Selby said. "Hey, there's hope for you yet."

She said it in a way that made me feel good about myself instead of wanting to smack her silly.

"So now, tie that back to everything Riley said," Alex pressed. "I still don't get it."

Selby's eye roll returned full force. "Sounded to me like he was trying to argue that somewhere out in the middle of the desert is a fifth or sixth or bazillionth dimension. I find that mildly difficult to believe. I'll admit that crazy shit happens at the subatomic level, but none of it extends to matter bigger than those particles."

"But is it *possible*," Alex said.

"Given the current laws of physics, no, it isn't. We've never observed phenomena like the kind Riley tried to pawn off."

"The current laws, you said," Alex replied. "Which can change, right? I mean, the more you learn."

"Sure, yeah. I mean, that's what M-theory is. Trying to draw connections and overlaps between ideas to explain the stuff we don't know. Like, there's quantum physics, which is how things work on a very small level, and there's gravitational physics, which is how things work on a huge level, like the universe. We know both of them work, but we don't know why. They should cancel each other out, but they don't. Some of the top minds the world has ever known look at some of the mathematics, and the best answer they've got is *Uhhhhh . . .*"

"Hmm," Alex said. "Sounds like physicists have to take a lot on faith."

Selby's eyes wrinkled to slits. "No, it's actually nothing like that."

"Take the next left," Charlie said.

I'd nearly forgotten he was there. He seemed lost in his own little world. I couldn't tell if it was because of the stuff Selby said, or what Riley said, or if maybe he'd just had it with the whole goddamn lot of us.

Selby calls for me after she's done with her shower. She's taken the bandage off, and I help her rebind it with stuff from the first-aid kit after she's gotten mostly dressed. The wound is ugly, a yellow-blue bruise surrounding the dimpled skin around her stitches.

"Does it hurt?" I ask, putting the last piece of tape into place.

"No, it fucking tickles. Of course it hurts."

"Is your stomach . . . Can you tell if there's any swelling?"

"Maybe a bit, I don't know. That's probably normal, huh?"

"Probably," I say, not believing it.

"I want to go home."

"We're working on that," I say, and squeeze her hand. I hand her a clean T-shirt from her bag. "There's breakfast in the kitchen."

Charlie and I had wrestled Riley's body out back, and done a good job of cleaning up the blood and . . . stuff. There's no real evidence of what had happened by the time Selby comes gingerly sliding into the kitchen.

"So where is the old prof?" she asks, lowering herself gently into a kitchen chair. "And what happened to the window?"

"We don't know," Charlie says. He sets a plate of food in front of her, and for a moment, it feels like we're all playing house. Here's Daddy, home on a Saturday, making breakfast for his little girl. The image made me sick somehow.

While Selby eats, Charlie and I stuff the Jeep full, with only barely enough room for us in the front seats and Selby behind the driver's seat. We give the TV one last chance, but now *all* the stations are dark. Not what we'd hoped for. Then we sit down with our maps and try to find the best way to get me home.

"What about you?" I ask Charlie once we've got a plan to get to Vegas.

"What about me, what?"

"Don't you want to get home?"

Charlie runs his hands backward through his hair. "Yeah. But Stephen's probably already hunkered down in the woods somewhere. That's his style. Once he sees how things are going, he'll bug out, see what happens. In any case, I'm not leaving you guys."

We leave everything the way it is. I can't help thinking that now two people are dead because of us. Two directly. How many more have died since the ark broke open? Maybe Charlie was right—staying at Riley's house would be safer— but maybe, too, this is a risk I have to take. What right do I have to live, after everything I'd been a part of the past couple days? The least I can do is go out into the ravaged world and take my chances like everyone else.

I don't say any of that to Charlie. What I said about my dad and wanting to be with him, that was all still one hundred percent truth. The rest of it I'd keep to myself.

Charlie drives the Wrangler carefully. Both of us try to keep an eye out in every possible direction, waiting for mutated dragonflies or clouds of black possession or goddamn Godzilla, for all we know. But the immediate world around us is quiet until we reach the freeway.

That's when things get tougher.

Everyone with access to a vehicle seems to be out on that road and along the sides of it. There's a fleet's worth of SUVs and trucks taking off through the desert, roughly following the direction of the I-10, but staying well clear of it. Fancy sports cars give it a shot too, but end up stuck or worse. There are no commercial planes in the sky, but several times we see serious-looking military helicopters cutting through the air overhead. Not long after that, we also see jets screaming past, low in the sky.

Charlie guides the Jeep beside a fairly steady flow of other cars like ours. Strangely, to me at least, they seemed welcoming, as if the drivers are saying, *Hey, here's a guy who knows what kinda car to drive during an apocalypse! C'mon in, son!*

"Why don't you try the CB, see if we can raise somebody," Charlie says.

"Like who?"

"Like anybody. I'd ask these guys, but I don't think anyone's in the mood to stop and talk."

I turn on the CB radio, utterly unsure how to use the thing. I try holding down the button on the side of the microphone.

"Hello? Is anybody there? Hello?"

"Ten-four," a male voice says.

I look at Charlie. He gestures for me to talk. I hold the mic up again.

"Um, hi. Hello? My name's Abby, who is this?"

"Name's Orson. Abby, how you doin' out there?"

"Not great. Where are you?"

"I'm passing Marana right now. Things're jammed up all to hell, though. Where you headed?"

"We're north of Tucson . . . um, I think south of you. But we're trying to get to Las Vegas. Do you know what's going on that way?"

"Boy, Abby, I tell ya, this country shit the bed somethin' fierce," Orson says. "Guv'mint projects, secret stuff t' use against the Middle East, who knows. But they jacked us up real good."

This was not the type of hard-hitting reporting I needed.

"Sir, can you tell me about the 95? Is that still clear? Do you know?"

"Got a buddy headed that direction right now," Orson says. "I could check in and give you a call back."

"Would you? I'd appreciate it."

"This your first time on a radio, Abby?"

"Um . . . yes, sir."

Orson chuckles. "No 'sirs,' thank you. I was just curious. You in a four-wheeler?"

"Yes."

"Good. You go ahead 'n follow ten up. Most of the worst of it's gettin' focused on the cities now. Best make good time while you can. Hey, Abby."

"Yes?"

"You know if we lose Hoover, Vegas is gonna get itself emptied real quick. No power in Sin City, see what I'm sayin'? Things're liable to get ugly. Might want to find another place to hole up."

"My dad's there."

"Well, that's bein' a good girl and I appreciate that, but just be careful. I'll get back to you. Don't change the channel or turn off the radio, copy?"

"Um . . . copy."

"Atta girl. Ten-four."

I almost say it back, but feel a little silly, then feel even sillier that something so stupid would make me feel silly in the first place.

"He's got a point," Charlie says. "About Vegas. It's not like that's a big self-sustaining agricultural community. If they lose power, that's it."

"I don't think it's a question of 'if.'"

"I need to ask you something." Charlie grips the top of the

steering wheel with both hands, staring straight ahead. A tan Chevy pickup drives in front of us, its bed piled high with camping gear.

"Okay."

"What would you be willing to do to make it stop?"

"All *this*?" I say. "Are you crazy? Anything!"

"Anything."

"Yes! Charlie, what is it, did you find something at Riley's?"

"How far could you really go, Abby?"

My excitement pivots to suspicion. "What do you mean, how far?"

"I mean *how far*, Abby?"

"Charlie—"

"Could you kill?"

I stare at his profile. His jaw is set.

"Who?"

"So you could," he says right away.

"No, I—"

"You didn't say no," Charlie insists. "You went immediately to 'who.' To a subjective judgment call. You're implying that some person's death would be okay but another's might not be."

"All I said was *who*, Charlie. What did you find, goddammit? And why didn't you say something earlier?"

"I'm not saying I found anything. But the word 'sacrifice' did keep showing up. Which makes sense, since nearly every world religion ever known is based on sacrifice in one way or another. Sacrificing the self to service, or sacrificing a person to a god, whatever. It's a common theme."

"So you think—"

"I *don't* think," Charlie says. "I said I don't *know*. I'm just trying to sort through what I read last night, and that's a word that kept cropping up, that's all. It worries me."

I shift in my seat to look out the side window. "I'm not getting into a morality debate. If you don't have anything helpful to say, then don't bring it up."

I feel him eyeing me, but ignore it. We drive for a long time in silence, right up until Orson crackles to life on the CB.

"Abby, you there? Come back."

"Here I am. Yes. I'm here."

"All right, here's what I got," Orson says. "95 is not free and clear, but it's currently doing better than anything else that way. That could all change by the time you get there. You got a map?"

"We have a paper map and a GPS."

"Don't know how much longer that'll be any good. Use your paper map. Take all the back roads you can. The major arteries are clogging up. People are running like hell. It's a great big mess out there."

"Yeah. We've seen it."

"All right, then. You stay in touch you need anything else, hear?"

"Yes, sir. I mean, yes."

"Good. And, hey, Abby?"

"Yes?"

"You into prayin' much?"

I don't know how long I hesitate, only that I do. "Not much, no."

"Well, you might wanna reconsider, the way things're going," Orson says. "Not to throw no Bibles at you or nothin'. You take care now. Orson out."

I cradle the mic. The CB stays dead. We stay quiet. When the Wrangler finally coughs itself out of gas, Charlie dumps the two cans of extra into it and we're off again.

Selby, as far as I can tell, sleeps through all of this until Charlie starts the Jeep up again. When she speaks, I jump.

"There're no planes," she says.

I whip around. "Hey. You all right?"

"Stop asking me that. There're no planes."

I don't roll down the window, but scan the sky as best I can. "No, you're right. A couple army helicopters went by an hour ago or so, but—"

"And jets," Charlie grumbled. "We've seen three so far."

"How much are you guys not telling me?"

Her question surprises me. Charlie, too, I think.

"I'm not an idiot, remember? You're hiding shit. What is it? Just tell me."

Charlie grits his teeth. "Riley's dead. He shot himself in the head. But then he came back. Or something got in him and made him come back."

"I see."

"It's bad," I tell her. "The things out there, they're just . . . they're tearing everything apart."

"I see."

"Any theories?" I ask, only partly kidding.

Selby lets her head shake slowly back and forth. "Not at this juncture. I think I'll be taking another pill now."

"Is there anything else I can do?"

"No. I choose to medicate." Selby pulls the bottle from her jeans carefully, so as not to move her belly any more than necessary. She swallows one of the pills and wipes her mouth. I struggle to see if she's more pale than usual, but can't tell.

Another jet streaks past, gone by the time we hear it.

"How am I going to explain this?" I say, half to Selby and half to myself, watching the jet disappear. "My dad will never—"

"You don't know how to explain because you *can't* explain it." Selby's eyes have closed again. "We don't have language for it. I'm not stupid. Maybe you missed that memo."

"No. I didn't miss it."

"There's no language for it because the language doesn't exist on this level," Selby goes on, speaking in one long breath. "When we talk about subatomic or cosmic levels, which *is* what we're talking about, then language gets superfluous. Things are either too small or too big to even talk about. You can only use math."

"Okay," I say cautiously, giving Charlie a worried glance.

He returns it. I don't know where this sudden lecture is coming from, and it sinks hard into my stomach. If Selby's blathering, talking nonsense, that's definitely a bad sign. But who can tell if she is? Her science is way beyond my English.

Selby coughs out a weak chuckle. "Jesus, Abby. I'm trying to help you here. I'm not crazy."

It sounds like she's read my mind. I don't answer.

"The problem is that there are places in the universe where even math doesn't work anymore. Can you imagine that? Now, that sounds like hell to me. No logic, no systems. Nothing you can count on. That's hell."

"What kind of places?" Charlie says.

"Black holes. Singularities. Places like that. Did you know that, Charlie? Did you know that there are things we don't even have a theoretical basis to observe? It's that weird out there. When we talk about things so big or so small that talking means nothing, well, then what's there to talk about?"

Out ahead of us, a jet screams past. I watch it fly over thick plumes of smoke, which seem to rise from every direction. I wonder where it's going, what good it can do.

"I don't understand," I say.

Selby takes a slow breath before answering. "Physics is eternal."

Then her eyes flutter to a close, and she takes another breath and falls asleep.

"Did you get any of that?" I say to Charlie.

"No. But now I'm glad she's still with us. When she's feeling better, maybe she'll come up with a way out of this."

"Besides killing someone."

"Yeah. Besides that."

We drive on.

The cave mouth yawned in a vertical slit right in one side of the base of a mountain, only wide enough for one of us at a time. For some reason it reminded me of ice, like a giant cube of it had cracked under pressure. As I followed behind Charlie—unsure how I got elected to go second, or why it would even matter—I also became aware of a strange aspect to the cave: There was no smell.

We'd spent the night in a cheap motel not far from Tucson, three rooms total. I made sure Alex got the middle room, because on the chance the walls were thin—and they almost certainly were—I didn't want to risk hearing anything Charlie and Selby might be doing overnight.

The trip to the cave went uneventfully, though it took us a solid hour on the freeway, and another hour bumping through the desert in a vehicle never designed to go off-road. But following Charlie's notes and map, at last we'd pulled up beside the entrance. When we did, I got struck with a peculiar déjà vu, even though I'd never been there before.

Having not spent an extraordinary amount of time in any caves, anywhere, ever, I don't know what I'd been expecting. An odor of bat crap, if nothing else. Maybe something musty or moldy or damp. But the cave had no discernible scent at all. I could detect the faint odor of Selby's cigarettes on her clothes, and the pleasant scent of desert plants, but that was it.

Charlie removed a few nylon bags from the RV, and slung the largest over his shoulders. He lifted one of the others, a plain black Jansport.

"This one's food and water," he said, handing it to Selby. She took it without complaint. Alex and I took the others.

"What's all in here?" I asked.

"Camera, infrared, EMF detector, triangulation mics, stuff like that," Charlie said.

"You know this gear is all pseudo," Selby said as she shrugged into her backpack.

"Yeah, I know. That's why you're not carrying it."

"We're a pretty gosh-darn bright group of kids," Alex said, grinning. "Looking to capture good footage of real ghosts. I think we're gonna be famous!"

Charlie pulled out flashlights and handed them to us— two heavy-duty police-style ones, a couple cheap plastic types stamped with EVEREADY on the side, and two headlamps on elastic headbands. Alex pulled on one, Charlie the other. Selby and I took flashlights.

Following Charlie, we went in.

Our flashlights pierced the gloom like needles through black leather. For one fraction of a second, I had the absurd impulse to douse everyone's lights and just be plunged into this darkness, an emptiness I had never experienced before in my life. There's not a lot of literal darkness in Henderson, Nevada, so close to Vegas. Metaphorical darkness, maybe, but not the real thing.

And back home, we had *noise*. Maybe not New York City noise, at least as I imagined it, but residual noise—or maybe it's just imaginary sounds wafting over the suburbs from the casinos. In any case, this cave was silent. I had nothing to compare it to. Quiet so deep I almost lost my balance.

We pushed about ten yards through the narrow crevice opening and into a massive first chamber. A couple school buses stacked bumper to bumper vertically could fit inside. I expected stalactites and stalagmites, but again my expectations came to nothing: the ceiling appeared quite smooth, dimpled only by occasional holes and bumps of rock. The floor felt slippery from hard stone coated in fine gravel and dirt.

"This isn't so bad," Alex said. "You want me to shoot any of this?"

"Not yet," Charlie said. "Let's just stroll along and we'll shoot if we find something."

"Something like this, you mean?" I said.

They came over to where I stood beside one wall. On it, several glyphs had been etched into the stone. Barely visible.

Charlie ran his fingers over one of them. "That's . . ."

"Yeah," I said.

Selby shot us both suspicious looks. "What? What are you two talking about?"

Charlie dug in his bag and produced Dr. Prinn's book. He flipped through it for a moment before stopping on a page and pointing at a symbol sketched in ink.

"That's it," Charlie said. "They match. Holy shit."

"*X* marks the spot?" I said.

"Looks like it," Charlie said. He raised an index finger, lifting it toward the painting, but did not touch it. "These markings may be thirty thousand years old or more," he said with wonder in his voice.

"Your dad had been here before?" Alex asked, squinting from the page to the cave wall.

"I don't think so, at least not to my knowledge," Charlie said. "I think these are symbols he found during his research."

"There're more of them in the book," I said. "All over the place. I wonder if . . ."

Charlie glanced at me. Even in the darkness I could see the agreement in his eyes.

"Only one way to find out," he said.

"What?" Selby demanded. "What is it?"

Charlie led the way again, deeper into the labyrinth, while Selby scrambled to keep up. "Goddammit, what are you two talking about?"

"There will be more symbols," I said. "I mean, there *might* be more symbols, the deeper we go. They'll point us to . . . to something."

"That's insane," Selby said.

"Yeah, probably," I said, because I didn't want to get into it with her. She wasn't going to change my mind, and I wasn't going to change hers.

At first the cave offered only one long, tunneled route, so we followed it. The floor continued to slope downward, and I tried not to dwell on the mountain overhead. As we went deeper, the mountain went higher; who knew how deep this could go?

The tunnel finally emptied into another cavern, about the size of the first. Several branches snaked out from the cavern, as if a colossal squid had once stretched out its tentacles and bored through the solid rock. I counted ten options of where to go next, and those were just the ones we could walk through easily; besides them were six more crevices we'd have to crawl through. I suddenly thought about the entrance again, how narrow it had been . . . and compared it to how big and broad this passage had been so far, as if we were in the broad end of a funnel, with the entrance a tight spout.

"There's more markings," Alex said.

I hadn't seen them at first, but as we stopped and looked around, I saw another symbol carved into the rock beside one of the branch tunnels. I flashed my light around and checked out a couple of the other caves. They, too, had symbols beside them: a figure or design had been etched beside each opening, like prehistoric address numbers. Even at a distance, I thought I could recognize animals like wolves painted in dim reds and yellows and faded blacks, while others seemed to look like repeating patterns of diamonds chipped into the rock itself.

"Which one?" Alex asked as we flashed our beams at the passages.

"There," Charlie said, pointing.

"Whoa, whoa, whoa, wait a second," Selby said, taking a step back from Charlie.

He held up the book. "Here it is. It matches up, see? The other ones on the walls aren't in the book."

"So he *had* been here," Selby said.

"Maybe," Charlie said, and his tone reminded me of my own; now that we were here, he didn't want to get into a shouting match with Selby. "It doesn't matter. What matters is we have a map."

Charlie's eyes gleamed. What had begun as a quirky little road trip now took on a whole new meaning—I could see that in his expression.

"Isn't it weird that no one else has been here?" Alex said. "I mean, a place this big, shouldn't a lot of cavers come hiking around?"

"We don't know that they didn't," Charlie said, putting the book away. "All we know is that it's massive. Maybe there're bodies down here no one even knows about, or maybe there are cavers who come all the time but don't tell anyone else. Who knows."

We all glanced around uneasily at the idea of explorers' bodies being somewhere nearby. Then Charlie kept moving, and we followed him.

"Okay, listen, not to be the voice of reason or anything, but maybe we should head back," Selby said.

"Feel free," Charlie said.

Uh-oh. He may as well have smacked her upside the head. She half whined, half shouted his name. Charlie spun.

"Look!" he said. "You knew what we were coming here for. You knew the point. Now, I'll admit, I didn't think we'd find much, but I figured it was worth the trip. But this stuff on the walls and in Dad's book, that's not a coincidence, all right? He knew something. I'm going to find out what it was."

"Well, whatever he 'knew,' it got him killed," Selby snapped back, but like she wasn't sure she should.

Charlie's expression hardened until it matched the rock walls.

Alex jumped in. "How long would we be in here? And can we find our way back out?"

"I have chalk," Charlie said, staring at Selby. "We can mark as we go."

"We'll probably be in here for a while," I said. "A few hours, at least."

"So why not take the book to the cops and show them this little so-called map you're making up as we go," Selby said. "We don't have to—"

I unleashed.

"My mom's been gone for five years," I said with a voice that sounded like my vocal cords had been scraped with sandpaper. "But my dad's been *dead* for that long. Dead to me, dead to himself. You at least know what happened to your dad. At home, I have to ask every day, is he going to get out of bed? Shower? Eat? *Speak?* I don't know. I don't know because *we* don't know what happened to Mom. This is the only chance I can see to get an answer, so I'm going in that cave. I'm following these symbols, because if at the end of it is a big sign saying HA-HA, JUST KIDDING, NOTHING NEW HERE! then you know what? Then I can go home tell that to my dad, and we can fucking move on."

I had to stop. My lungs ached. No one spoke. I dragged an arm under my nose and forced in a deep breath.

"So if you need to wait in the van, go for it. I don't blame you. I'm sorry if this isn't the peachy keen time you were hoping for, but I'm going."

Selby stared at the stone wall, like she couldn't bear to look at me, or Charlie, for that matter. Alex stood patiently waiting. I had the sense he was coming with us, that he wanted answers too.

At last, Selby nodded, gripping her big black flashlight with both hands like something out of *Star Wars*. "Okay. Fine, you win. I'll go. I must be out of my mind."

"I think maybe we all are," Alex offered. I expected his sarcastic grin, but he wasn't joking.

Charlie assessed us each, as if to make sure there would be no more delays. "All right. Let's move out."

We walked deeper into the cave.

We drive in silence, bumping over gravel until we hit an empty road. Charlie steers us onto it. The sun begins to set, and we haven't encountered any more creatures. Cars, too, have become rare, and then are gone altogether until we are the only ones on this road headed north.

"Looks like we might make it," Charlie says.

His voice startles me. I'd been partly dozing while trying not to. Now that the sun is disappearing, the wisdom of being out in the dark in a world full of unknown monsters doesn't sound so smart.

"To Henderson, I mean," Charlie says. "Lotta traffic going away from there. See those campfires?"

He points, and I see a few pinpricks of light out in the desert mountains surrounding us.

"My guess is they were told to evacuate," Charlie says. "Maybe the emergency broadcast system was working, and they were able to bug out. Doesn't look like anyone's headed our way at the moment."

"Okay," I say, and open a fresh bottle of water.

"Problem is, we're almost out of gas. We might be rolling to a stop in front of your house."

"Okay."

"You could get clean clothes, anyway."

"Anyway . . . ? You mean if my dad's not there."

"Abby—"

"He will be. Trust me."

Charlie seems about ready to reply, but then snaps his mouth shut and slows down. As we slow, it becomes clear why no one else is headed out of town or following us in.

There had been a roadblock here earlier. Military. We pass two of those big drab brown Hummer jeeps. One is on its side, showing us its belly. The other is bashed into rubble where it stands. Just beyond the glare of our headlights—it's now fully dark—I see prostrate bodies in digital camouflage clothing.

Charlie hits the brakes. I catch myself on the dash, and Selby wakens with a sharp cry. Before I can say anything, Charlie, with a look of terrified determination, leaps out of the car, runs to a soldier lying half on the blacktop, and picks up his gun. Charlie rushes back to the Wrangler, shoving the rifle or machine gun or whatever it is into the back, and stomps on the gas before he's even gotten his door closed.

"The hell?" Selby groans.

"Sorry," Charlie mumbles.

"What's *that* for?" I say, pointing to the gun.

"For whatever did that to them."

"Right, but if those guys had guns and it didn't help—"

"Just let me have a fucking gun, Abby."

I shut up. I also consider asking him if he has even one clue how to shoot it, and I stay shut up instead.

"Where are we?" Selby asks, wincing.

"Almost home," I say automatically.

I hear her fish for her pills and take one. I ask how she feels, and she grumbles, "Fine." We leave it at that, but I suddenly get anxious to look under her bandage and verify her claim. She slept most of the day on those pills. I suppose that's okay, but something about it doesn't sit right with me.

We drive on through a darkness rivaling that of the cave. It feels as though the moon has taken off too, like she'd seen what's happening down here and said, *Thanks but no thanks, I'm outta here.*

As we go, there seems to be a haze on the horizon, one that I should be able to identify but can't, not right away. When we crest a hill, Charlie again slows the car, just to take in the magnitude of it.

Las Vegas has been devoured in flame.

It is destruction of Biblical proportions. I wonder if this is what happened to Sodom and Gomorrah, and have to resist taking Orson's suggestion to pray about it. Except for the lack of a crater, the Strip looks as if it's been struck by an asteroid. Anything and anyone within miles of the Strip has surely been blown away or burnt up.

"Abby . . . ," Charlie says.

"No. Henderson's that way. Keep going."

"But—"

"Look, it's mainly the Strip. The suburbs aren't on fire, see? Keep driving."

Charlie inhales deeply, then slowly accelerates again. He doesn't mention what I've already noticed: while Henderson doesn't seem to be on fire, there are no lights on anywhere either. Not that I can see from up here.

Fortunately, I'm right about the suburbs. We manage to get into my hometown and to my neighborhood without huge difficulties, though there are burnt-out cars we need to maneuver around along the way. We're lucky that there's more gas in the tank than Charlie had feared, though the needle hovers on E. We don't encounter a single living soul.

But we do pass bodies on the road. Neither of us looks closely at them. I don't want to know how they died.

We pull up to my house, to the same old dirt yard with its yellow weeds, and that's when adrenaline dumps into me again. With the electricity gone, my house has only starlight above to see by, and even that is obscured by dust and smoke. My house looks like a crypt.

Charlie shuts the car off but leaves the lights on, pointed toward the house. He pulls out the army rifle.

With one hand on the door already, I ask, "What are you doing?"

"We don't know what's in there."

"*We* don't care. Put that thing away."

"No."

"Fine, then stay here with Selby."

"I'm not letting you—"

"Shut up," I say, and climb out of the Jeep, marching toward the front door.

Which, before I can reach it, opens by itself.

Despite my bravado in front of Charlie, I freeze in place, sucking in air, thinking it might be my last breath.

"Abby?"

Dad steps onto the porch. He wears jeans and a long-sleeved turtleneck against the chill. I run full speed up to him and surround him with my arms.

"Come in," he says after a second. "It's not safe out—who is that?"

"Dad, it's Charlie."

"Charlie Prinn?"

"Get Selby," I say to Charlie. "We should get inside."

Charlie helps Selby climb out of the car. She isn't moving any faster than she did this morning.

"I'm so glad you're okay," I tell Dad as Charlie and Selby come toward the front door.

"Of course I am," Dad says. "Come on. Come in."

Still clinging to him, we sidestep with each other into the

house. I don't let go until we reach the kitchen. I look back as the door closes, and watch Charlie setting Selby down gently on the couch, where she lets out a pained sigh. Charlie joins me and Dad in the kitchen tentatively, clearly not sure what kind of reception to expect from Dad.

He still carries the rifle.

"Did the rescue teams make it this far?" Alex asked as we continued down through the cave.

"I don't know," Charlie said. "There were, what, ten options back there? No telling how far they snake out, or come together and double back. This isn't someplace you want to get lost."

"Brilliant," Selby muttered. Her old snarkiness actually made me feel a bit better about being however deep into this cave we were.

We moved carefully down the passage, shining our lights in all directions but paying close attention to our feet.

"What kind of cave is this?" Alex asked. "I mean, do you know what formed it? Water, I assume?"

Charlie shrugged. "Don't know. That's probably a reasonable guess."

"So smooth," Alex muttered, tracing his fingers along the wall for a moment. "And dry. I don't even hear any water dripping. Isn't that kind of weird?"

"Whatever caused it must've just dried up over a long period," Charlie said, but I could hear the uncertainty in his voice. It occurred to me then that the others sensed it too: that this cave was wrong somehow.

"What time is it?" Selby asked suddenly.

I checked my phone. No service, of course, but the clock worked fine. "Almost eleven."

"We've been in here an hour," Alex said. "How close are we?"

"To what?" I said.

We aimed our lights toward Charlie's back. He seemed to sense the attention and answered, "I don't know. I don't have a destination in mind. We'll know it when we see it."

Twenty minutes later, we stopped to take a break, eat warm Lunchables, have some water, and listen. We didn't talk much. What would we have said? *Seen that new horror movie?* Feeling slightly better but not exactly refreshed, we pushed on.

We reached another chamber with spider-leg tunnels branching off from it. These, too, had distinct cave art beside them. Charlie consulted the book, chose a tunnel, and on we went. After that, we encountered branching tunnels more often. We'd find a side tunnel with no markings, and go past it, then a three-way split with drawings or carvings. They were becoming more and more frequent, and it became clear how search parties couldn't have checked out every passage.

We kept trudging through, deeper into the labyrinth and

farther under the ground. We saw dozens of branch tunnels leading in all directions, all of them large enough to at least crawl through. At one point, I got the unsettling impression we were in a giant ant farm. Charlie kept referring to the book and matching up symbols and drawings on the walls with things his father had written down.

"Stop!" Charlie said.

We did.

"Hold on a sec. It looks like there's a drop-off up here."

He let his bag slide to the ground, then got to his hands and knees and inched forward with his flashlight.

"Well, that was close," I muttered.

"Alex," he said with a sort of enforced calmness to his voice. "Hand me your bag."

"What—"

"Just do it."

Alex frowned and unshouldered his large, square bag. He eased his way to Charlie and set it beside him. Charlie rummaged through the bag and pulled out an EMF reader. He turned it on, and we all watched the needle instantly jet to the far right. A red indicator button lit up like an evil eye.

"We've got something," Charlie said. "There's a big electromagnetic field."

"That's not possible," Selby whispered. "Not down here."

I didn't have to ask what they meant, because Mom had explained EMF meters to me a long time ago. Ghost hunters used the meters to locate and measure energy fields, but they were designed to be used to find problems in power lines. Ghost hunters claimed spirits generated their own energy fields, which the meters could detect.

And Selby was right: this far into an underground cavern, there should not have been anything for an EMF meter to pick up. Not that strongly.

Charlie gently set the EMF down and picked up a small camera. He opened the viewfinder and pointed it down the dark, sloping tunnel. The rest of us strained to see what he was looking at on the screen, but none of us wanted to move from our sure footing.

"Something's moving down there," Charlie whispered. "But it's . . . it's cold. The thermal is just barely picking them up. . . ."

"They?" I said, and my voice sounded as taut as a spiderweb.

Charlie put the camera into the bag and crept farther along the floor on his stomach. The drop was so steep, we couldn't see his head as he shined his heavy flashlight down the tunnel.

Charlie's voice sounded as if it came from the bottom of a pit of quicksand.

"It's them!"

Selby, Alex, and I traded looks, then shuffled over to Charlie. He lay grasping the edge of a steep drop into darkness, shining his flashlight down. We gathered around him, pointing our lights.

The first flash of red nearly made me scream, except at the

same moment, I recognized it. A shirt I'd seen before. On at least one episode of *The Spectre Spectrum*.

My mother's shirt.

We'd found our parents.

Alive.

My house is dark but for a single lit candle on the kitchen table. I could have cried; the smell of the house, the feel of it . . . Being home takes on an entirely new meaning, no matter what's happening outside.

Dad pours a mug of coffee. "Does your friend . . . ?" he asks, gesturing to the living room with the mug.

"Selby?" I call. "There's coffee."

"No."

Dad hands the mug over to me. "It's not too hot. The power went out a few hours ago, and I had this pot going. Better than nothing, I guess."

Dad hands another full cup to Charlie. Dad's eyes seem recessed into his head, concealed by shadows thrown by the candlelight as he stares at Charlie. Charlie obviously feels the scrutiny. He takes the cup and stands against one counter, resting the rifle on top of it. It looks like a demon in its own right.

Dad sits down at the table and I join him, taking a sip of the coffee. Unbelievably curative, like the sun was yesterday.

"Have you seen what's happening out there?" Dad asks.

"Yes. We've seen . . . a lot. You're sure you're okay?"

"I'm fine."

His head turns toward Charlie. "So, Charlie. How have you been?"

All of us, I'm sure, hear how much he does not care what the answer is. Charlie sets his cup down with a sigh and says, "Mr. Booth—"

"We found Mom," I say.

Dad turns slowly around to me. "What?"

"Daddy, listen to me." I take one of his hands in both of mine. His fingers are chilly, as if he made the coffee specifically to keep them warm. The lines of strain and age on his face deepen in the flickering candlelight, which smells of pine.

"We found Mom," I say again. "We found all of them."

"Not all," Charlie says.

"What?"

Charlie's eyebrows shoot upward. "You didn't . . . ? Abby, they weren't all there. There was one missing."

I scan that awful memory and come up blank. "Who?"

Charlie gapes, then snorts, then shakes his head. "Gotta use the bathroom," he says, and walks out of the kitchen.

Dad's hand is limp in mine. "What are you two talking about?"

"Dad, listen. I lied to you about going to a conference. And

I'm really sorry, but that's not what matters right now. Charlie and I and two other people went to the cave. One of them was Marcia Trinity's son."

I pause, trying to edit myself on the fly while still dedicating resources to figuring out what just went wrong with Charlie.

"They were dead," I say. "We found their . . . you know. Remains."

At least I haven't lied yet. Not directly. To specify what happened doesn't seem useful.

But Dad has other ideas. He pulls his hand away from me and scoots back in his chair, dumbfounded.

"You found the ark?"

I would've choked on my drink if it'd been in my mouth. Instead I just choke on air.

"Wh-*what*?"

"You did," he says softly. "John wasn't going crazy. You two, you really found it, didn't you?"

I lurch to my feet and stumble back away from Dad. "What are you talking about? How did you know about that?"

"Dad must've told him," Charlie says from behind me, startling me.

"John told your mother," Dad says. "She told me. Then he told us both, next time we were all together. We laughed about it. He sounded like a crazy man. I'd never seen him act like that before."

Charlie takes a chair opposite Dad at the table. "What exactly did he tell you, Mr. Booth?"

"I don't recall exactly. Quantum physics, alternate realities, the creation of the universe . . . no. *Multi*verse. That's what he called it. My apologies, Charlie, but honestly he came close to raving. Annie almost canceled the shoot." His head dips. "I wanted her to. I should have made her."

"Daddy, please, stop. You can't go there right now. Please."

Dad picks up his head. Good. He's still with us. He gazes across the table at Charlie, though in the shadows, I still can't see his eyes clearly. Sort of disconcerting, like those poker players who wear sunglasses and don't move their faces, so you can't tell where they are looking.

"John was right, wasn't he?" Dad says. "And you found it."

"Yeah," Charlie says, barely above a whisper.

"That's why all this is happening, isn't it?"

Dad's insight cuts me like a razor, like the spectres had done back in the cave. I think I managed to fend off one certain emotion with large amounts of terror, adrenaline, and panic. Now that I'm home, now that I know Dad is safe, that certain emotion finally lands, and lands hard: guilt. A tangible thing, the weight of two bodies, the onus of countless souls pressing down on my ribs, caving me in.

"It wasn't intentional," Charlie says.

Dad holds up a weak hand. "Doesn't matter. It's here now. So what are you going to do about it?"

"Charlie wants to kill someone," I say spontaneously, I guess to try and alleviate the crushing weight inside me, push some blame somewhere else. It doesn't help.

Charlie glares at me. "I didn't say that. All I said was that the word 'sacrifice' kept coming up in Dad's notes, *and* that it didn't mean anything."

"How is your old dad these days?" my father asks with uncharacteristic sarcasm.

I gasp as I realize what upset Charlie earlier.

"He wasn't there," I say in disbelief, not that it was true, but that I had somehow blocked that truth from my mind this entire time.

"No," Charlie says. "He wasn't."

"Where is he, then?"

Charlie shrugs, just a bit. "No clue. Been trying to figure that out since it happened."

"*No* sign? No trace of him down there, anywhere?"

"Not that I saw. I mean, we could have missed something, who knows? But I didn't see him."

"You say there are notes?" Dad asks. "Something that might help?"

"Notes, yes," Charlie says. "Whether they'll help or not, I don't know. Nothing has so far, but like you said, it sounds like raving, most of it."

"Dad?" I say. "Are you sure you're okay? I don't mean to . . . it's just, you sound . . ."

"Lucid?" Dad asks, and, surprisingly, adds a smirk.

"Honestly, yeah."

"I'm okay, Abby. Better than okay, maybe. I know things have been hard here, and I'm not saying they won't be again,

but it's funny how the end of the world clarifies a man's prior-
ities."

I sit back down in my chair. He leans forward and touches
my cheek with one finger.

"Hey," he says. "You saved my life. I know that. And after
what I've seen today, I'm in no hurry to die."

"I'm sorry," Charlie says, lifting his palm off the table.
"What exactly do you mean 'what you've seen today'?"

"I mean that you'd have to be a fool not to see that those
things out there aren't from this world," Dad says. "Which at
least opens up the possibility that there's something else, too.
Something good. There has to be, to counteract it."

"God?" I say.

"I hope so, at least," Dad says. "I hope so."

No one adds anything else for a minute. Then two. And
well into a third.

"So what now?" I ask. "We find a church? Try praying?"

"Stay here?" Charlie counters. "Unpack the Jeep and stay put?"

"Or go fix it," Dad says.

"Fix what?"

"Fix what's wrong out there. In the world."

"How would we do that?" Charlie says.

"Oh, I'm not sure it's even possible," Dad says. "But if you
find your father, that would probably be a good start. Any
ideas?"

"No. No, not at all. It's been five years. He could be anywhere. Alive or dead."

"I'm sure he's alive," Dad says. "We'll just have to figure out what he might have been thinking, retrace his steps. He's out there."

I almost smile. I haven't heard Dad sounding so optimistic since . . . well, I guess that went without saying.

I reach for his hand, noting again how cold it has gotten. Then I notice a small spot of something dark on the tabletop.

"Daddy, are you bleeding?" I pull back his sleeve.

Yes. He'd been bleeding. Past tense.

In fact, everything about my father is past tense.

Without stopping to think, we all slid down the embankment toward the movement we'd seen. Honestly, at that moment, I think we were acting independently of one another, not caring if anyone else was coming along or not. The floor sloped down at nearly forty-five degrees, so we slid on our butts all the way down, knocking gravel loose as we went. Some distant part of my brain pointed out we'd have to find a way to climb back up this slippery slope, but mostly I didn't care. I didn't think the others did either.

Our families were down there. In the dark. Alive. Moving around.

It did not occur to me—not for one instant, not for one heartbeat—that there had to be something very, very wrong with this situation.

Five years, and they were . . . what? Living down here in a commune? Taking eight-hour treks to the surface for food and water? Had they all collectively agreed to hide from us, from the world, for all this time? In the *dark*?

It was so wrong, so contrary to common sense, yet not one of us said it—none of us even hesitated to slide toward them. I guess when you miss someone, you just lunge for a thread of hope, no matter how thin.

Nor did we say anything *else*. We didn't shout their names, try to get their attention, ask if they needed help first. We just slid down toward them. Unstoppable.

We reached the bottom of the slope after maybe ten seconds, and stood up side by side, shining our flashlights around. Alex's beam found someone first.

"Mom?" Alex whispered. My heart would've broken for the awe and pain in his voice if, a moment later, the beam of my light hadn't caught my own mother too.

They were working.

All of them. Their clothes hung ragged and faded off them, as if they'd never changed since that last day.

I didn't care. My mother was alive, on her knees, digging in the dirt with both hands, hair hanging in her face. She shoved small piles of dirt into some kind of pit nearby, where I heard the pebbles and dirt tumbling down . . . but not landing.

"Mom," I said and took a step.

This cavern stretched out at least two football fields long, half that in width. Piles of dirt and rock lined the outside edges where the floor met the wall. The floor beneath shone brown and tan, shot through with tendrils of black. And so very, very flat. Almost like glass. Not accidental, not natural.

But those were details I took in only peripherally. All that mattered at that moment was Mom. And I was going to go to her.

Except someone grabbed my arm. Charlie.

"Wait," he said. *"Look."*

I started to shake my arm free, but my gaze fell on Alex's mother. She crouched nearest, bathed in the soft glow of our four flashlights, not quite lit up. Like the others, she dug in the dirt, slow scoops, which she'd pile up beside her, off the smooth rock floor. She still wore a blue scarf that had frayed like a rope noose around her neck. At first I just wondered crazily what they were looking for. Then I wondered how they'd survived for so long in this cave. Then I wondered what happened to their hands.

Because their hands—

My breath caught somewhere in the middle of my lungs and sat there, heavy and dead. I heard Alex gasp and Selby give a little whine. Someone said, *"No."*

Bones. Just bones for hands. The skin and sinew and muscle had been worn away and all rotted off long ago. Even their skeletal fingers, which through some malevolence were still able to bend and flex, were starting to wear down, the tips rounded from five years of digging.

"Oh, God," Selby chanted. "Oh God, God, God—"

I couldn't stop myself. I tried but couldn't. It wasn't the last thing I'd regret doing, but it ranked up there.

"Mom!" I screamed.

They stopped moving.

All at once, like a switch had been flipped.

Then, as one, they turned to face us. Slowly, as if mesmerized, their movements strangely in sync.

When I saw my mother's face, my hands came up and covered my mouth. From the corner of my eye, I saw Selby shut her eyes and spin away, while Alex clutched his stomach and gurgled. Charlie froze solid, eyes wide. It became clear why the thermal camera had not detected any heat.

Like dried corn husks, the flesh of their faces had desiccated and drawn tight over their skulls. Their eyes had long since dried up and fallen out. Or maybe disintegrated. Their mouths were hollow holes the size of fists, their teeth like long yellow pieces of corn. They looked like unbandaged mummies.

"We . . . gotta go," Charlie stuttered.

"It's them," I said involuntarily. "We can't, it's them."

"Not anymore," Charlie whispered.

Then they came for us.

The way the candle lit the room, I didn't see it before. Or maybe I just didn't want to. Maybe I disassociated the swirling black and green in his eyes, dismissed it as a trick of the candlelight. Maybe I didn't see it at all. I don't know.

My father's forearm is slit from wrist to elbow. It isn't a gory wound, just a thick line of black, caked with scabbing blood. But he isn't bleeding currently. And I know, either by deduction or just instinct, it's because he has precious little blood left in him.

Charlie gives a guttural curse and flings himself backward just as Dad, or what is *passing* for Dad, flips the table up toward him with a roar. The tabletop catches Charlie clean in the chest, sending him pinwheeling back into a counter.

I squeal and fall backward myself, scrambling to get away, but my legs fill with molten lead and pin me to the tile. I vaguely hear Selby shouting in the living room.

Followed us, I thought distantly. *The animator followed us*

from Riley's, and Daddy was already dead, has been for a while,
or maybe it's another thing something we haven't seen yet and
Daddy was gone before we even talked on the phone—oh God,
Daddy, I am so sorry.

My father—the thing pretending to be him—snarls and
leaps on top of me, clasping my throat in both frigid hands.

"Where is he?" the thing roars, and its voice comes from a
pit of torment, some spirit tortured for millennia.

I claw at the hands, try to pry them away, and can't. It
allows me only the barest of breaths. My father's face contorts
into a mask of hate that forces spit from its mouth in rivulets
and its lips to almost split apart.

"No—" I manage to squeak, and that's all.

"Where is he?"

Tears, or possibly blood, trickle from the corners of my
eyes as I keep clawing and kicking at the demon above me. I
can't do anything. I make no impact, leave no mark.

The thing lifts my head off the tile and holds it close to
its mouth. Fetid air cascades into my nostrils and coats my
tongue with the black pepper–and-cinnamon taste I remember from the cave.

"We know who you are."

A bare moment later, it's flung off me and I can breathe
again. I also realize I'm suddenly deaf. Only after that do I feel
the *thud* of the rifle going off.

Charlie takes a step over me and fires the rifle again.
Unable to help myself, I turn my head to watch my father's

body jump with a spasm. Charlie fires again, and again, and again. Daddy's body jerks and jumps like he's having a seizure. The next shot is dry, but Charlie pulls the trigger anyway. After a few moments in which Daddy's body does not move, I climb unsteadily to my feet and back into a wall. My hearing slowly fades to normal, and I hear Charlie swearing gruffly and still pulling the rifle's trigger. He sounds as demonic as the thing in my father had.

I stay put. Eventually, with one last incoherent scream, Charlie throws the rifle at my father's lifeless form, and stands, heaving hard, shoulders drawn back as if awaiting another attack.

The attack doesn't come . . . but we both watch a black cloud issue from Dad's mouth, just as it had from Dr. Riley. I shrink back and cover my mouth, as if to prevent it from getting into me. From the corner of my eye, I see Selby standing up with her hands over her ears, eyes fixed on the cloud hovering above Dad.

The smoky black-and-green cloud whirls and twists, jerks and dances, then slides from the kitchen and disappears under the bottom of the kitchen door, out into the night.

So, I think. *We can't kill them. We can't kill any of them.*

I don't move. I barely breathe, partly for fear of Charlie insanely attacking me, and partly because my windpipe feels crushed.

Charlie suddenly loses strength, and collapses to his knees.

"We—don't—know—" He coughs. Finally, he shifts around

to look at me. "We don't know who to trust," he says, wiping his mouth. "The guy on the radio might have been with them. Maybe they cleared the road for us. Maybe that wasn't luck. Maybe they wanted us here. We can't trust anybody."

I lick my lips. Taste bitterness. Spit on the floor. Then turn and walk carefully into my room and fall onto my bed.

A few minutes later, just before passing out, I feel someone get in beside me, behind my curled body, and assume it's Charlie. Except at that point, I don't care. If it's a zombie or a monster or a ghost and this is the end, that will be just fine.

"Stop it!" Selby screamed.

She wasn't even looking at the things our parents had become; she still sat hunched over, gripping her hair, her eyes squeezed tight. Some atom of my brain not devoted to the horror of what we were witnessing said, *She believes now. Now she's a believer. And it's her worst nightmare.*

Somehow, her scream triggered Alex. Not to run, not to scream himself, but to do what I intended a second ago.

He went to his mother.

Alex rushed toward her, weeping openly. Like he couldn't see or had already dismissed the decayed state of his mom's body—*body*, because whatever they were, they were not alive. Alex smacked into her just as his mother got to her feet, and wrapped his mom in a bear hug.

I heard a sound like pencils snapping, dozens of them, all in sequence. It was the dry xylophone cracking of Mrs. Trinity's rib cage and spine. Some sort of purple-green fume erupted from her leathery mouth and coated Alex's face as if forced from long-dead lungs. Her body bent backward and dangled from Alex's arms like a rag.

And yet, even with her back broken, Alex's mother still reached for him.

The bones in her hands still clenched and flexed as if surrounded by invisible muscle. For a second, I allowed myself the luxury, the total beauty of the idea that this was all on television, that we were being pranked unlike any prank before. Must-see TV. Any minute, giant floodlights would pop on and everyone would come out laughing. . . .

Mrs. Trinity's fleshless fingers sank into Alex's throat.

Alex stood still, petrified by the sheer terror of having crushed his mother's bones. Motionless, his eyes giant in disbelief, Alex did nothing while his mother drove her skeleton hands into either side of his windpipe. Alex gasped and choked and at last released the mummified body, grabbing instead at the fingers digging into his skin. Blood poured instantly from the wounds, and Alex dropped to his knees, taking the horrific body of his mother with him.

By that point, Selby had knelt on the ground, her back curled, arms over her head for protection. I wanted to join her, but could not make myself move.

Charlie at last reacted. He raced forward and attacked one of the things, perhaps once a cameraman, shouting and kicking out with one foot. The shot connected with the man's withered face, which disintegrated into dust, leaving a gaping, awful hole. The result caused Charlie to bellow in disgust and step back as the cameraman lumbered awkwardly to his feet and stepped toward Charlie, arms upraised, skeletal fingers seeking—still moving, still animated by whatever stygian force was working in this sunless place.

Charlie stumbled backward, right fist raised to punch the cameraman tottering after him, but he didn't swing. What would his target be? The cameraman's skull remained more or less intact, but his face was gone, a gaping, lurid hole, yet still he shambled toward Charlie with arms outstretched. Whatever evil thing animated their corpses—because that was all they could possibly be—hadn't protected anything but their hands. Alex's mother lay in a dusty heap on top of her son, but those bones still dug and worked at Alex's throat; the cameraman hadn't had eyes two minutes ago, and now he had no face, yet still he could pursue Charlie.

The only possibility, I realized with a sort of religious awe and hopelessness, was that we had entered Hell.

"I'm sorry I'm sorry I'm sorry!" Selby screeched into the dirt.

Charlie was right. We had to go. Should never have come. Alex was dead. Alex . . . yes, Alex now lay still, as his mother's claws kept digging deeper and deeper into his neck. From four people who started the adventure now down to three, and things were only getting worse.

I tried to tell Charlie we had to leave. To run. To get out, and get out now. But then I felt a pinprick of ice against the back of my neck that forced me to turn.

I'd actually forgotten about her. About the rest of them. Up and on their feet and headed toward us. I must have backed up at an angle while watching Alex. The pinprick became spider legs, dancing little dots of icy chill on my skin as I turned.

It was her.

Mom.

Her skeleton hands grazed my neck, my face inches away from her taut, dry, brown skin. Her eyes and mouth were as black as char. Through her stretched and tightened lips, I heard two syllables whisper:

Aaaaaah-eeeeee.

My name.

I screamed from the bottom of my soul and pushed my mother with both hands. She fell backward a step. I kept screaming, and vaguely thought I heard Selby echoing it.

My mother regained her balance and stepped toward me again.

Then her head exploded into brown powder and stray bits of hair.

Charlie stood behind her recovering from his swing of the heavy black police-style flashlight. My mother collapsed with the sound of kindling dropped before a fireplace. Charlie stood above her and pounded down with the flashlight as if it were a sledgehammer, crying out with each blow.

I watched him, screaming over and over, as he pummeled my mother into dust and bone.

I heard my own scream begin to die, winding down like a

siren. Maddened, Charlie raced around the cavern, attacking the other mummies, swinging wildly.

At some point, I know I sat on the ground. Watching, mouth open, and perhaps drooling senselessly. I don't know how long his rampage lasted, only that eventually, the entire crew and our missing family members lay in puddles of crushed bone and hair, no longer animated, and the cavern became silent.

No, not silent. Not entirely.

I wake up under my comforter, my shoes off. I have a brief and glorious moment of joy that I've just woken up from the worst dream in recorded history . . . but the penetrating silence outside is enough to convince me I'm wrong.

I know I should be hungry, and my stomach even makes warning noises to that effect, but I can't eat. Can't move. Here, I am warm. Here, I am home. Or at least what was home. The word "orphan" pops into my head, and once there, I can't get rid of it.

With no electricity, my clock shows only a blank, uncaring rectangular face. I watch it for a while, thinking maybe it will somehow blink twelve at me again, ready to be reset. It doesn't. All that matters now is drawing another breath. One after the other.

When I can't take the silence anymore, I swing my feet out from under the comforter and aim myself at the kitchen. I stop at the end of the hall and see Charlie is sitting on the couch, staring at nothing. I don't see Selby. And my father is no longer lying dead or worse on the kitchen floor.

Charlie turns to look at me. He's aged a decade.

"Hey," he says. He's in the same clothes as yesterday. Whenever "yesterday" was.

I take a step closer. "Hey."

"I put him in his room," Charlie says. "Cleaned everything up. It's safe to go in. There's some food in the fridge and cabinets and whatever. I guess you'd know that."

"Where's Selby?"

"Out back."

"Is she okay?"

"You mean the wound? No idea. Outside of that . . . well, I still have no idea."

I will myself to get as far as the threshold of the kitchen doorway. Charlie is right; all evidence of last night's fight is gone, including Dad.

"Abby?" Charlie says from the couch.

"Yeah."

"Have we gone absolutely fucking insane?"

"That would be great. But I don't think so. How long have you been up?"

"No idea."

"What's it like out there?"

"Smoky. And it stinks. Like . . . like—"

"I don't want to know," I say. "Have you eaten?"

"Tried. Not much. What the hell are we going to do?"

"Let me eat. And we'll talk."

Charlie doesn't nod or say yes. He just turns his head away and stares at our blank TV. I make myself a peanut butter sandwich, thinking maybe this will be our new diet staple. I eat it at the table with a warm bottle of water. I smell antiseptic as I eat. Charlie did a good job cleaning. Probably better than I ever did, or Dad ever did. But Dad will never clean again. I won't either.

These thoughts make me sick. The peanut butter sticks in my throat and it takes the entire bottle of water to wash it down. I stop eating then.

I go back into the living room. Charlie doesn't seem to have moved.

"There might be hot water still," I say. "If you want to shower. And Dad's clothes might fit you. If you want. Or I could try washing your clothes in the sink."

Charlie gets to his feet and walks past me into the hall. "Thank you," he says, and that's all. He goes into the guest bath—basically my bathroom—and the water turns on.

I peek out the front window blinds. Our street looks cold and deserted. Amazing how quickly a normal street in a normal town can turn gray and lifeless in just a couple days. Mrs. Brower's truck is in her driveway, and I debate going next door to check on her. I know I will at some point, just to see if she's alive, but not yet. Maybe later, with Charlie, if he's up for it. Not now. Too dangerous. Charlie was right: We couldn't trust anybody. Having an actual former nurse take a look at Selby's injury would definitely make me feel better, though.

Reminded of Selby, I go out to the backyard, and find her sitting with her back against my tree-house tree, knees drawn up to her chest. I imagine her smoking a cigarette, and it actually takes a moment to realize she isn't. I walk over and sit down beside her.

"I wanted to climb up," she says, her head tilted back to look at the stars. We can't see many; the layer of smoke is too thick on the one hand, but the lack of electricity has darkened the world so more stars can shine. "I think I would've popped a stitch."

"I'm glad you didn't try."

"Why do you care?"

"I don't know how to put in stitches, for starters."

"No," Selby says, and drops her chin. "I mean, about me. At all. Ever since the goddamn cave, you've been all worried about me. How come?"

"Because we're in this together. I think we're family now, whether we like it or not."

"Fair enough."

It's not exactly a *Hug me* kind of moment, but it's about as warm a reception as I've gotten from her since this whole thing began. I watch her out of the corner of my eye, not wanting her to catch me doing it, as she gazes at the sky, eyes wide, eyebrows furrowed.

"Can I ask you something?" I say after a minute.

"Sure."

"What did you mean when you said 'physics is eternal'? Do you even remember that?"

"I remember. It means the universe came with certain rules. We might not know what they all are, but they're there. The world can be known and understood. Everything can be quantified, eventually. There're still some big questions. But we'll get there."

"What if what's happening right now is the answer?"

"Then we're fucked."

I almost laugh.

"Alex told me you were an astronomer or something," she says. "You should know this stuff about time and space."

"I can name stars and tell you where to find Venus in the morning. I know where Mars is this time of year. That's about it. It's a hobby. I was going to study it after next year because I didn't know what else to do. I probably would've changed it at some point once it got too smart for me."

"You're smart."

"Yeah?"

"Well, you know, not as smart as me, but . . ."

"High praise." I bump my shoulder into hers.

Selby faintly smirks. "It should be."

We both let a long silence grow. When Selby speaks next, it's as if it is the only thing she *can* say, the only thing that will make sense.

"I'm sorry. About your dad."

"Thank you."

Another pause stretches out.

Quietly, Selby says, "*I* don't know how to find Mars."

Somehow, that's what gets to me. Hurriedly, I point up and start explaining how to find the red planet, because if I don't, I'll start crying and never stop.

I don't know how long we sat in the dirt as Selby, no longer screaming but still chanting, "I'm sorry, I'm sorry," over and over, rocked herself back and forth on the ground. Somehow, I found the strength to crawl over to her and pick her up into a kneeling position. She could not, or would not, meet my eyes.

"Selby," I croaked, my voice as raw as sand.

She began shaking her head, eyes wild. "Sorry, didn't know, sorry, didn't know—"

And so for the first time in my life, I hit a human being. I slapped Selby once across the face, probably not hard because my muscles were next to useless, but enough that she shook herself and stared into my eyes.

"We're okay," I said. Probably the biggest lie I'd ever told up to that point.

Selby swallowed. Then nodded.

"You with me?"

She nodded again, or perhaps shuddered so hard it merely made her head bob.

I started to climb to my feet, but Selby grabbed me back. "Don't leave."

"I have to check on Charlie," I said. "Then we're getting out of here. Okay?"

"Where's Alex?"

I licked my lips, tasted something like black pepper and cinnamon. Tried not to think what it might actually be.

"He'll meet up with us later," I said, my voice shaking.

To my shock—relatively speaking, of course—Selby accepted that response. She crept backward to the base of the earthen ramp we'd slid down, holding her knees tightly to her chest.

I stepped slowly and carefully over to Charlie. He'd ended up more or less in the middle of the flat cavern floor, heaving heavily. I dropped down beside him, careful not to let my flashlight crash.

"Are you okay?"

He nodded. Then shook his head. Then cried.

I didn't move. I put a numb hand on his shoulder and just left it there. I don't know for how long, but eventually, Charlie's sobs slowed, then stopped. He raised his head, staring into me with bloodshot eyes.

"What the fuck," he stated.

"I don't know."

"How could they be alive?"

"They weren't. Pretty sure about that."

"What *is* this place?"

"I don't know. But we need to go."

"What about . . . ," Charlie began, but shut up and looked to his right. Toward Alex. His flashlight, still on, lit up his sneakers and calves, but the rest faded into darkness. A small favor.

"Can you carry him?" I said.

"I don't think so. I can try, but . . . I really don't think so."

I nodded, more anxious to leave than anything else. Maybe that made me a bad person. So what? How bad could Hell be after this?

"Okay," I said. "We know how we got down here. With the book. We can give someone directions. Rescue workers. Or whatever."

"Yeah," Charlie mumbled. "Rescue."

"Come on," I said, putting a hand under his arm.

I lifted, but Charlie mostly stood on his own, which was good. We started to trek back toward where I'd left Selby, but her piercing scream froze us.

"Help!"

Charlie and I ran.

Selby walked in horrific spasms toward the equipment bags. She looked like a marionette resisting its strings, joints haphazardly jutting and jerking forward.

"I can't stop, I don't want to move, help me!" she shrieked.

"What . . . ," I said, and couldn't say any more.

Selby reached one of the bags and bent over at the waist as

if flung into that position by an unseen entity. Still, she cried out to us, "This isn't me! Please, help! I can't stop it, it's not me, help me!"

Unsure what else to do, Charlie and I ran to her and each grabbed an arm. That lasted all of a half second—she flung us off as if we were motes of dust.

She—or whatever had ahold of her—unzipped the bag and tossed out an assortment of film and ghost-hunting gear before finding what it wanted: a lock-blade knife.

"Selby, stop!" Charlie shouted.

"I can't!" she shouted back. "Please, make it quit, it hurts, it's inside, I think, *oh God*!"

Charlie tried to tackle her as she spun around with the knife, but Selby backhanded him away effortlessly. Still crying, she slid one foot after another until she reached the center of the smooth floor.

We followed her, yelling now too, not knowing what else to do. Moving in distinct tweaks, her hands unfolded the knife and raised it high.

"Help me!" she screamed one last time before the knife came down. It stabbed deep into her abdomen, and she tore it back out.

"*What the fuck?!*" Charlie screeched. His eyes showed that he was a man who'd lost all sense of control, and he knew it.

Blood dripped from the blade onto the floor. In an instant, Selby groaned and keeled over, dropping the knife. Whatever had gotten inside her seemed to have left.

Charlie and I rushed to her side and got her turned onto her back while blood coursed down her hips and splashed onto the ground. Charlie chanted cuss words. Maybe I did too.

As Charlie and I both pressed hands against the wound, making Selby cry out, I turned away, not wanting to see the hole in her flesh. Instead I got a good look at the blood-soaked ground and noticed just how smooth the floor really was where the crew and our parents had been digging.

I pulled my hands away from Selby and shined my light on the ground. Stared at the strangely colored stone. Stone that, now that I studied it, appeared to have cracked in almost perfect horizontal lines. Stone that, if washed and polished up a bit, wouldn't quite look like stone anymore . . .

Something like an electrical sensation rippled through my body right then. All the elements of this crazed trip came together in one flash of insight, awe, and disbelief. I'd seen that kind of stone before. In Arizona, as a matter of fact. On a family trip before *The Spectre Spectrum* ever started, at a national park.

"Charlie," I whispered.

"What, what, what, Jesus, *what*?"

"The floor. It's not rock."

"Selby's bleeding, Abby, help me!"

But I couldn't. Not quite yet. They both had their hands on the incision and the blood already had started to slow.

It took several tries to get out my next words. "It's petrified wood."

Charlie slowly swung his head around to face me. I followed suit to meet his gaze in the reflected light bouncing back at us from the floor.

"Abby, are . . . you saying—"

"I think it's the ark."

Selby says she wants to be outside for a while longer, so I go back in alone. When I get to the living room, I hear Charlie still in the shower. Because he'd be unable to hear me, I make a rational, cognitive choice to stop fighting the thing I've resisted for so long. I walk down the hall and into my bedroom, wrap myself in the top blanket, and weep into my pillows.

It physically hurts. Part screaming, part silence from a grief that goes too deep for sound. My entire torso feels compressed from the weight of it all, from the loss and the death. Everything is gone. This is what Dad felt, every day of his life since Mom disappeared. And now both of them are gone for good.

I don't know how long I lie there, but when I peel myself up, I see Selby standing in the doorway, leaning against the frame. She still has a hand pressed against her side.

"You know," she says, in such a way I can't tell how long she'd been waiting there. I also realize the shower has stopped running.

"Once upon a time, it was a heresy to say the Earth moved around the sun," Selby says. "But now we know it's true. When we know true things, we can ask more questions. Find more answers. A lot of things used to look supernatural, like comets. But science proved they weren't. Maybe that's all this is. Something we can question and find answers to."

I sniff and stand up from the bed, wrapping my arms around myself. "Physics is eternal?"

"Something like that. And, you know, there've got to be all kinds of people all over the world working on this. We're not alone. We can't be. We'll figure something out."

"How can you really believe that? After everything?"

"Because we both know what hopeless looks like. Now, I'm a *lot* of things, but I'm not going *there*."

Selby pushes herself away from the doorframe, wincing. "I'm going to get something to eat."

She moves away from my door, and Charlie takes her place, toweling off his hair.

"You okay?"

"No," I say. "But, you know. Sure."

He nods his understanding. "How do you figure the animator found your dad?"

"One of them went through me, in the cave. I felt it go through. Maybe it knows everything about me." I grunted a sick laugh. "How's that for a happy thought?"

"Yeah," Charlie agrees. "That's, um . . . that's troubling on a number of levels."

We go into the kitchen, where Selby is making herself a sandwich. I make her sit down and take over. I need something to do. We don't talk until the three of us are seated around the table. My stomach gives a tentative lurch, reacting, I suppose, to being where the thing inside Dad had revealed itself. But the lurch doesn't last.

Maybe I'm adjusting. That happened much quicker than I would have thought.

"I was thinking," I say to Charlie. "And if I'm totally crazy, just say so, but . . . I've been thinking about your dad."

". . . Okay?"

"It's just that he's unaccounted for. But he's the most likely person on Earth to have any ideas of what we can do to reverse all this. Or end it, anyway. That animator thing inside my dad, that's who it wanted."

"Animator?" Selby says. "Oh. So that's what we're calling them?"

"Till they tell us something different." I look at Charlie. "Is there anyplace your dad might be? Someplace he might have gone into hiding? I mean, it's a long shot, but—"

"Cedar City."

"Utah?"

"Yeah. Mom used to make him take us to a Shakespeare festival up there. And we'd go camping, hiking, that kind of thing. Population density is pretty low. Lots of places to hide out, or blend in." He tries a weak smile. "I've been thinking too."

"What do you figure are our chances of finding him?"

"Realistically? Slim to none. It's a stupid and suicidal idea." Charlie pulls the towel off his head. "But honestly? I think we should try. I mean, what's the worst that could happen, right?"

"We could stay here instead."

"Yeah, but you don't want to. It's in your face. You want to get out of here."

"Pretty much."

"Is this because of what happened to your dad?"

"No."

"Then why?"

I force myself to take another bite before answering. Not having an appetite is a luxury for a world surrounded by grocery stores and Arby's. I have a feeling from now on, eating whenever possible will be the best choice.

"It looks to me like the animators can only inhabit the dead. And Dad died because he gave up. He might still be here if not for that." I glance at Selby. "We know what hopeless looks like. I'm not ready to go there either."

She nods, just once. It's enough.

"That's pretty harsh," Charlie says.

"It's a pretty harsh world," Selby says. "Not sure if you noticed."

"Sure did," Charlie says, but with a crooked grin. "Okay. So we go. Thing is, I don't know about gas. Pumps run with electricity. I'm not sure I want to hoof it the whole way."

"We'll use physics," I say, still looking at Selby. "That solves everything, right?"

Selby Lovecraft, two-time Texas State Science Fair champ, her mouth full of peanut butter sandwich, smiles.

Charlie folds the towel neatly and sets it on the remaining chair. "How much of what your . . . of what the animator said do you think was true? About my dad, and the—what do you call it—multiverse, all that?"

"I think most of it was true. The devil doesn't need to tell lots of big lies. One small one is probably enough. We'll just have to figure out which one that is."

"You believe in the devil now?" Charlie asks.

I eyed him cautiously.

"Don't you?"

Selby coughed. Charlie shook his head as if to be rid of me and my theory. That dismissive gesture broke my trance and I raced for the gear bags. Gambling and coming up lucky, I found a small first-aid kit in the bag. Trying hard to keep my flashlight steady under my arm, I brought it back to Selby and pulled out what I hoped would be a large enough pad of gauze and some tape, then ran back to Selby.

"Stay still," I ordered.

Selby did, her face twisted in pain. I made Charlie hold both flashlights, worrying vaguely how much battery life we had left.

"Just use one. Save the batteries. Selby, I'm going to lift up your shirt."

Selby *laughed*. "Wow, this really hurts."

I ignored her. My heart raced, and my tongue swelled from lack of water. I mopped up the worst of the blood and pressed the pad against the wound. Then I taped it in place as best I could. The blood didn't bother me—I can't imagine what *would* have bothered me by that point—but I was no trauma surgeon.

"I don't think the conditions are right for petrification," Charlie said suddenly, watching me work. "So this can't be the . . . No, it can't."

"Maybe they aren't now. But they might have been. A long time ago. When the land was wet. Or submerged."

I stood up and automatically wiped her blood off my hands on my jeans. Denim, of course, disinfects everything.

"We have at least a six-hour hike out of here, and that's moving at top speed," I said to Charlie. "Can you carry her? She's a lot smaller than . . . Can you?"

Charlie swallowed, still staring at her. Then he nodded.

"Good," I said. I took my flashlight back. "I'll carry the bag with the food and first aid. We're out of here."

"Sure, now's a good time," Selby groaned.

I turned and looked down. Fresh blood stained the gauze on her wound and trickled down her side, dotting the wood stone beneath her.

Selby pressed a hand to the wound. "Better hurry."

I gave Charlie a shove, and he went to work. He slid his flashlight into his back pocket, and bent down, picking Selby up under her knees and armpits. He grunted a bit, but when he stood, he stood straight.

"How do we get up the hill?" he said as we quick-stepped back the way we'd come.

"I don't *know*, just try." I didn't like that he was asking me for direction. I didn't want to be the boss anymore.

We reached the bottom of the steep incline. I shined my light up it.

"It's kind of bumpy," I said. "We should be able to find handholds. How about . . . Do you have rope or anything?"

"Uh—no—wait . . . light cables."

"We'll have to drag her up," I said, dumping out the contents of the backpacks until I found the cords. "And don't forget the goddamn book. We still have to use it to get us out of—"

A noise cut me off. A dim and faraway sound that I might have felt more than heard at first. I tilted my head.

"Do you hear that?"

Charlie frowned and nodded. My heart began to race all over again.

"What is it?"

"Don't know," Charlie said. "Sounds like a . . . helicopter or something."

I understood his comparison, but disagreed—not a helicopter: more like a hummingbird. They make a deep thrumming sound in flight as their little wings beat so fast they are a blur. There's sort of a bass component to it that always made me think of big black bumblebees. A resonant, vibrational sound.

That's what it sounded like. But bigger.

Much, much bigger.

Charlie turned to face the planks. I turned to follow his gaze, shining my light on the floor.

"It's coming from down there," Charlie said, his voice low and parched.

"Let's go," I whispered.

I forced myself to turn back to the lighting cord, moving as deliberately as I could make myself. After everything we'd witnessed over the past few hours, I was surprised my body had any adrenaline left. But it did. It most certainly did.

I knelt down and picked up a cord. I motioned for Charlie to set Selby down; she'd passed out cold, which I took as both a blessing and a very bad sign. I tied the end of the cable under her back and beneath her arms, then pointed mutely to the hill as if Charlie weren't sure where to go.

He grabbed two handfuls of the cord and sat back against the incline, searching for footholds. He found a couple, and pulled back hard on the cords. Selby slid upward about an inch.

This was never going to work. I looked up into the darkness at the top of the incline. How high up was it? How far had we slid down?

More to the point, could I live with myself for leaving Selby behind? Because as that bass thrumming sound got louder, starting to rattle the pebbles on the cave floor, leaving her was exactly what I felt like doing.

I didn't have time to make that call.

We finish eating.

"So we'll go through the house, pack up anything use-ful," I say. "Then I want to go next door and check on my neighbor."

Charlie stops in place. "What do you mean, check on him?"

"Her. Mrs. Brower. She's a friend. And really old. I need to see if she's okay."

"Why'd you wait till now to bring that up?" Selby says.

"Because I realize it might be dangerous, for one. And for two, I don't know about you guys, but I've been feeling just a bit distracted."

Charlie shakes his head. "Abby, listen, I appreciate what you want to do—"

"Good, because I want you with me."

"—but we won't know if she's really who she says she is."

I don't answer.

"I mean, even if there are no visible marks, if she had a

heart attack or something, and if you're right about those animators . . . she might be one of them."

"I know. But she isn't."

"You can't know that."

"No, but I can believe. I have to. I think I'll be able to tell now. My dad wasn't acting like himself. Riley . . . well, you saw Riley."

Charlie nods, but doesn't look convinced.

"I have to at least check in on her. I'm *going* to check in on her."

"But you understand the risk."

"Yes. Do you understand the risk of *not* checking?"

"Um . . . no, not really."

Selby raises her hand a little. "Me neither, not getting it, sorry."

"Guys, if I don't at least try . . . if I don't *attempt* what would be, in any other circumstance, the right thing to do, then . . . then, Jesus, this world isn't worth saving."

They both stare at me for a long moment.

"Look, I don't want to die. Okay? I want to survive. Badly. But at the same time—survive as *who*? You know?"

"Damn," Selby says. "Here I thought you were just a Girl Scout all this time. Instead you're all philosophical and shit."

"All right," Charlie says. "But at the first sign of—"

"The very instant. Yes. Agreed."

Dad never had a gun in the house, and now that the army guy's gun is empty, we're without a major weapon. I put a butcher knife in my waistband, and Charlie grabs a three-pronged, curved garden tool from the garage, from back in the day, when Mom and Dad would compost our food scraps.

"Selby?" I say.

"Oh, I'm not staying here by myself. But I'll be staying a bit behind you."

"That's fine. Mrs. Brower was a nurse. If she's safe, we'll have her take a look at the bandage."

"Yeah, or maybe she'll take a bite out of me."

"We won't let that happen."

The three of us walk to Mrs. Brower's house. Like every other up and down the street, it's dark. But since the truck is there, I have to believe she's home.

I try the door without knocking. It's locked, and I take that as a good sign. I bang on the door. "Mrs. Brower? It's Abby. Are you all right? I'm here with friends. Mrs. Brower?"

The dead bolt slides, and Mrs. Brower opens the door. In what would otherwise be quite amusing circumstances, I see she's holding both a flashlight and a butcher knife of her own.

After peeking through the gap and counting us, she unlocks the security door. "Abby! Thank goodness you're all right! Come inside, quickly."

We go in. Charlie immediately, like some kind of commando, breaks right and scans her living room. Selby, true to her word, stays behind me; in fact, I feel her grasping lightly to the bottom of my shirt, like a kid sister.

Mrs. Brower puts the knife down on a side table and fusses

over me. I let her, waiting for some clue she's not herself. I don't see or feel anything different about her.

"I'm okay," I tell her. "This is Selby. She's hurt. It's a knife wound. She's got stitches, but I was hoping—"

That's as far as I get. Mrs. Brower takes Selby's hand and leads her gingerly to the kitchen and gets her to sit down on top of the table. "Show me where."

Selby shows Mrs. Brower the bandage while I hold the flashlight beam on it. Mrs. Brower studies the wound underneath the bandage.

"I've seen worse," she says. "The stitches are holding, but there's no way to know how much damage there is in there. There's some abdominal bruising—that could be internal bleeding, or it could be something else."

Mrs. Brower bustles out, then comes back in with a first-aid kit. It's bigger than the one we have. She starts cleaning and redressing the site. "She needs a hospital. Unfortunately, there is a shortage of those anywhere near here."

"What have you seen?" Charlie asks. He has not set down his rake.

"Whatever insanity has been unleashed out there, they're not just stupid animals. They targeted infrastructure. Power, first responders, hospitals. And schools. Children. I don't . . ."

She pauses, covering her mouth. I put a hand on her shoulder.

"We know. What's your plan?"

Mrs. Brower wipes her eyes. "Stay here. Pray. Hope for someone to get us out of this mess."

The three of us trade glances.

"Will you come with us?" I ask. "Charlie's dad . . . well, we don't know, but we think he might be able to help. We're going to try to find him. We could use a nurse."

Mrs. Brower shakes her head before I've even finished. She double-checks her work on Selby, then tugs her shirt back into place. "Do you have antibiotics? Painkillers?"

"The urgent care guy gave me some pills, yeah," Selby says.

"Good. Take them as directed. It's the best you can do. That, and pray."

Selby bites her lips shut and nods.

"Mrs. Brower?" I say as Selby slides carefully off the table. "What do you think? Come with us?"

"This girl is not leaving this house," Mrs. Brower says.

"Oh yes, this girl is," Selby says.

Mrs. Brower frowns. "I suppose I can't stop you."

"No, but thanks for trying." Selby moves over to stand nearer to Charlie.

"So come with us," I say again to Mrs. Brower.

"Love, I can't. I can barely walk. I'd slow you down. And for what it's worth, you're making a mistake. You should stay here too. We could combine our food, our forces. Barricade ourselves inside."

"I'd like to, but we can't. It's a long story, but you have to believe me when I say we have to do this."

She pats my hand. "I understand, dear. Here."

Mrs. Brower goes to the counter and comes back, handing

me the keys to her truck. "You may as well take this. I won't be needing it."

"You might need to get out of here," Charlie says.

"Oh, son. I'm too old to run away from anything. If the things loose out there want me, they can come get me."

Mrs. Brower then scours her house for things of use. No guns, but then I don't know what good guns would be anyway. She insists on our taking her larger first-aid kit, as well as extra batteries, candles, and canned food. I try to protest, but as always, Mrs. Brower is the stronger of us.

We all thank her profusely as she marches us out the door.

"You can always come back," she says as Charlie hoists bags into the bed of her truck.

"I know. I will. I'll come back regardless, I promise."

The expression on her face shows she doesn't think much of that promise. "God's peace go with you, Abigail."

"Thank you. You too."

Mrs. Brower shuts the door. I hear the bolts get thrown.

"So," Charlie says. "Take the Jeep, too? Split up? Or no?"

"I don't like that idea. There's more room in the truck for gear, but the Jeep's got the four-wheel drive."

Charlie looks over at Riley's Jeep in my driveway. It hits me for the first time it's right where Mom's old Jeep used to be parked.

"Honestly," Charlie says, "I'd prefer the Jeep for that reason, except that I wouldn't know four-wheel drive from training wheels. Maybe the truck is better. Plus, is there gas in the truck?"

"Probably full. All right, then. I'll drive."

"Are you sure?"

"I've been driving this thing for a year. Yes. Let's move the other stuff over and get out of here."

We make Selby climb into the cab and wait as Charlie and I transfer the items from Riley's Jeep into the truck. Since I was the last one to drive the truck, the tank is filled up. That'll get us about three hundred freeway miles—provided there's a freeway to follow.

Charlie takes over navigation, folding and refolding a map until it shows him what he wants. Just as we reach the end of my street, he asks, "You're sure you're okay with your dad being . . . I mean, just being in the house?"

"I don't think he'd want to be buried. Too claustrophobic. And I can't imagine . . . you know. Burning. This is probably best. Thanks, though."

Charlie stretches out his arm behind Selby and touches my shoulder. I turn the corner out of the neighborhood.

We decide to take Northshore Road, which runs along the lake. We figure that despite our ease in getting into town, the 15 out through Arizona and up into Utah would probably be either too jammed up, or else too obvious a target. As it happens, we don't encounter any traffic right away. We really do seem to be the only people left on Earth.

By the time we make it to the lake, the sun is beginning to rise.

"That's really pretty," I say.

"It's because of the smoke," Selby says. "That's what gives it all the color. Not to be a downer or anything."

"It's still pretty," I say. "Smart-ass."

Selby looks pleased with herself.

"So how do you think we can track him down?" I ask Charlie.

"We're not the only survivors," Charlie says. "I think Sells is right about that. We'll find people and start asking. That's pretty much it. And if—"

"Headlights," Selby says.

She's right. We're on a straightaway, and several miles down the road, two distant white orbs are rolling nearer.

"Should we stop?" I ask.

Charlie's eyebrows are furrowed tight. "I don't know. If they're friendly, we can get information. If they're not . . ."

No one bothers to finish his statement.

"Let's stop and see what they do," I say, and take my foot off the gas.

The old Chevy immediately begins to slow. The timing is such that we are only rolling at about twenty miles an hour when the other car slows down. I ease on the brake and finally stop. The other car—it looks like a civilian Hummer—stops about ten yards away, staying in the opposite lane.

"I only see a driver," Charlie says. "We sure we want to do this?"

"Information's crucial," I say. "I think we have to."

He nods and gets out, holding one of our knives behind his back. He stays behind the open passenger door and raises his left hand.

The driver of the Hummer hops out. He is not too tall, but is laden with what looks like military gear. But he doesn't have a military bearing—he strikes me as someone who's taken on the persona of a soldier, but is not an actual one.

But his rifle looks real enough.

I tighten up. The driver, wearing a camouflage cap and black sunglasses, has the weapon strapped around his chest already. He doesn't raise it, but keeps a hand on the handle and near the trigger. I notice he keeps his shooting finger straight, like I've seen on cop shows. So he's not totally untrained, anyway. He has a thick, full beard and mustache, brown peppered with pure white.

"Where you headed?" the driver barks. "And show me both your hands."

"We're aiming for Cedar City," Charlie calls back. "I'll show you both my hands when you let go of that gun."

"Not a chance, motherfucker," the driver shouts.

"Okay," Selby says. "I think we're done here."

"Yeah," I say. "Charlie?"

Before Charlie can respond, the driver keeps going. "And what the hell you headed to Cedar for?"

"Look, I'm just trying to find my dad," Charlie says, but edges a bit nearer the doorjamb. "We only stopped to ask if you had any information, okay?"

"Cedar's fucked," the driver says. He makes no offensive movement, but doesn't let go of the gun. "The whole world is. I suggest you find a place to hunker down and die in peace, boy."

"Charlie, let's go!" I shout.

The driver looks in my direction. Charlie scoots closer to the door.

Then the driver reaches up and slowly takes off his sunglasses, peering at Charlie. "Oh my God."

Charlie's fingers wrap tight around the knife.

"Charlie?"

The three of us freeze as the driver says his name. Suddenly, he lets go of the gun and whips off his cap.

"Charlie, is that—oh my *God*, son."

"No way," Selby breathes.

It's John Prinn. But it's no John Prinn I've ever met. He is all but unrecognizable. Charlie seems to share my doubt for a moment, but then steps away from the truck, staring at the older man.

"Dad? Is that really . . ."

The driver's entire demeanor changes. He slowly raises his hands and takes a step nearer. "Charlie, it's me. Son, it's me, it's Dad. Look at you."

And with that, Charlie beelines for him.

Just as I scream at him, *"No, wait!"*

Charlie skids on the blacktop, maybe three yards away, and hurriedly backs up. John Prinn stops. He's bigger now than what I remember of him. There's no trace of the scholarly bookworm he used to be. Now he looks like someone on one of those "prepper" shows, like he builds fallout shelters for fun.

Maybe he does. And maybe that's good; maybe that's exactly what we need.

Charlie takes a half step back, angling his body toward Prinn. Like a boxer preparing to strike. "Dad . . . you mind if I check your pulse?"

"You think I'm possessed?"

The question makes Charlie flinch.

"One of the pains?" Prinn goes on. "Or ghosts or whatever they are, those goddamn clouds of evil? I'm not. But sure, go ahead. Take my pulse. Then, if you all don't mind, I'd like to take yours. You know they can only inhabit inanimate material, I take it."

Yeah, we figured that out, I want to say. Prinn drops his arms and raises his chin. Charlie slides closer, cautious, and puts his fingers against his dad's throat. A moment later, he nods. Then he offers his own neck to Prinn.

For one second, I'm sure it's the last thing he'll do, that Prinn is a ghost or a "pain," whatever he called the animators. But instead, Prinn takes Charlie's pulse too, and gives him a nod.

"Okay. So we're all who we say we are. That's a damn good start. For God's sake, can I hug you now?"

He and Charlie embrace, and hold it for a long time. Prinn's eyes squeeze shut. I notice Selby brushing quickly at her eyelashes.

Quietly, I say to her, "Are you sure you don't want to look for your—"

"No. No."

"Okay. Sit tight."

I climb out of the truck and walk over to the two men. Charlie reintroduces me and waves an introduction at Selby in the cab. Then he faces his dad again.

"Dad, how did you know we were coming this way?"

"I didn't! I was on my way to find you and Stephen in LA. I knew he had that camping spot he liked. I was headed there first."

"So you know what's happened."

"Of course I do. The goddamn ark opened. Right?"

"Yeah. That's the short version."

"How'd you first find out about it?"

Charlie and I look at each other.

"Go ahead," I tell him.

So Charlie, as quickly as he can, tells his father the entire story. To my shock, Prinn doesn't seem all that put off that we've opened some kind of gate to Hell.

"And then we found you," Charlie says. "So, now, what do you—"

"Well, let's go close it," Prinn says.

"*What?*" The word comes out of me like a bark. "Just like that? We shut the gates of Hell, la-dee-da?"

"You think those things were . . . you think *that's* Hell? Sweetheart, those are the pawns."

"Dad . . . ," Charlie begins.

"Listen," Prinn says. "They want their world back. They

were here first, and they want the good old days. Their world didn't have skyscrapers and Ford F-150s and 747s. They'll tear down every brick and bit of steel we've put up and make it a Garden of Eden. No humans allowed. Anything you've seen so far? Those goddamn monsters? Those are the first act. These are just the landscapers, getting ready for the permanent residents. Something else will be coming out of that cave, out of that endless pit, when the time is right. And all this . . . all this will be gone."

"Dad, wait. Please. What happened? Can we start there?"

Prinn looks up and down the highway, impatient.

"Yeah, what happened in the cave five years ago?" I say. "What happened to my mom?"

Prinn holds up his hands. "Clock's ticking, so here's the short version. We go into the cave, planning on getting some good footage. Interview our guest, all the usual stuff. We stop to take a break, I go up the tunnel to take a piss. That's when the screams started. Like nothing I've ever heard. I run back, and they're all . . . they're just *dead*."

If Prinn's lying, he's a master. His face has blanched pale.

"I have no idea what happened. So I start to scoot back out the way we came, except then—then I heard them. They were getting up. Do you hear me? They were dead, and they got back up."

I catch myself nodding. We know how it works.

"So I hid. What the Christ was I supposed to do? I hid, and they shuffled off down the cave. That was it. I stayed put for hours before finally getting up and running like hell for the entrance."

"Did you tell the police?" Charlie demands.

"You two know better," Prinn says. "You've seen these things. What was I supposed to tell them? Plus, don't you get it? It's magic. The real thing. Something that's not supposed to exist, and I saw it. I don't know how it works. What if it's following me? What if I'm next? I couldn't go home to you two boys and risk infecting you somehow. So I ran. I ran, and I hid, and I studied, and I waited. Then I got ready. And while I did that, I had to wonder about every murder out there. Was that one of them? Some thirsty pain on his way to find me?"

"Pain—those are the clouds? The black-and-green things?" Charlie says.

"We call them animators," I say.

"That's them. The good news is, evil isn't omniscient. It can't just know where you are or what you're up to. Those creatures are mortal in some fashion. Those, uh—animators, you called them? The Wintu Indians, among others, called them pains. But evil still needs senses. If they have a weakness, it's that. The pains can't hurt you by themselves. They're just bugs. Sensate, cognizant bugs, but still bugs. The rexes, those rhinoceros creatures, they take direction and make big holes, but they can be killed. They're mortal. Those giant flame-throwing bug things, I have no idea what those are. They appear to have corporeal bodies, maybe they can be gunned down. I don't know. But whatever's coming next . . .

I don't think we can plan on taking them out by any conventional means."

"So all this magic stuff, this proves God exists?" I say.

"Oh, one thing at a time, all right? *Magic* exists. Or something so far advanced from us we can only call it 'magic.' There's a place where physics as we know it no longer applies, and that place is in the cave. Now can we please get back on the road and fix this thing? Let's go, hop in."

He moves toward his Hummer.

"Hey, I'm not giving up the truck," I say.

"We're packed pretty well in there," Charlie explains.

Prinn frowns and swings himself into the car. "Fine. Follow me, then."

"Wait, just so we're clear," I say. "You're saying we're going back to the cave?"

"That's right."

"All of us? Selby got stabbed—didn't you hear that part?" With some detachment, it occurs to me that three days ago, I never would have spoken to an adult this way. Now? Fuck it.

"Fine," Prinn says. "You girls skedaddle wherever you need. Go back to your house. Charlie and I will handle this."

Charlie looks about as surprised as I feel at that suggestion. I can feel him being torn between going with his dad and sticking with us. We have been through a lot, after all. Frankly, I hope he won't break up the team.

"Charlie?"

"I'll just ride with him," he says after a moment. Prinn

roars the Hummer's engine to life. "If you need to stop, just flash your lights. Okay?"

I move closer. "I don't like it."

"I know, it's okay. We'll be fine. All of us."

He reaches out and hugs me close. It's not until the hug goes on a bit longer than friendly that I feel Selby's eyes on us, burning hard.

I step back. "Don't let him lose us."

"I won't. Promise."

He goes over to the passenger side of the Hummer and climbs in. I get into the truck, start the engine, and take a wide looping turn to get behind the Hummer as Prinn guns it down the highway.

"You two are awfully chummy," Selby says with acid on her tongue.

For a need for something to say, I go, "It won't happen again."

Selby snorts. "Sure it will. Just drive, okay?"

She reaches out gingerly to try the radio. A good idea, but there's nothing but static. I scrounge in Mrs. Brower's console and come up with a CD, which I quickly jam into the player.

Johnny Cash. *The Man in Black*. It beats silence, at least right up until Johnny sings, "God's gonna cut you down. . . ." We go back to silence after that.

The drive goes fast and it goes slow. We stop once to use the bathroom—or, rather, the bushes. With each roll of the tires, we are getting closer to the place that unleashed this hell on

Earth. I wait for some malevolent creature to attack us, to put a stop to whatever plan John Prinn has, but the attack doesn't come. Even if he's right and the pains or animators can't be everywhere at once, aren't they smart enough to post a guard or something? Unless, of course, they don't know there's a way to stop them.

The sun, hard as it is to believe, keeps going through the sky. It will be night by the time we get to the cave.

Only a few times do we pass cars, and none of them give any indication of stopping. At first this seems odd and perhaps even intentional, like someone or something is allowing us to go where we are headed. But then I consider just how much time between the initial outburst from the pit to when the electricity went off: not much. And how far does the outage reach? If it's nationwide—or worse, which I can't imagine, but who knows—then people haven't had much time to get good information, or bad information. There hasn't been as much time for rumors to begin and to fester, driving people to go places that aren't actually any safer than their own homes. So by now, most people who have a place to go have probably gone there. Everyone else has boarded up their windows and is awaiting the cavalry.

That's what I tell myself, anyway. The alternative is pretty damn upsetting: that this is all on purpose somehow, and the pains and rexes and dragonfly creatures will all be there waiting for us.

But they're not.

We make it to the cave without a single encounter. Thanks to John Prinn's preparations, we don't have to worry about gas, even: he'd come prepared with plenty of extra. He also said there were ways to get gas out of gas stations without electricity, but wouldn't elaborate.

We park the vehicles by the remnants of the cave entrance. It takes me a minute to talk myself into getting out of the truck. It doesn't seem, for what it's worth, that anything has been here recently. Our surroundings look like they did when we left.

I can't believe we've come back.

In a sudden rush of sound, the petrified planks burst apart at the center, sending shards of rock raining down on us. I didn't even scream. I just hunched down into as small a ball of human as I could and covered my head. My flashlight bounced on the rock, stayed on, and pointed toward the center of that floor, where the explosion had happened.

I saw what caused it a moment later: a giant horn, like that of a rhinoceros, but bigger than an elephant's tusk.

The horn, black and sharp and curved, smashed again through the floor from below. More chunks of petrified wood burst into the air and crashed back down.

From the hole left behind, clouds of black and green appeared. They took on slender forms, vaguely humanoid, rising en masse from the hole and shining with their own inner, unearthly light, like Halloween glow sticks. First, just one came up from the hole and floated. Then another, and a third. By the time those three began floating casually but purposefully toward us, another ten, and what looked to be another hundred behind them, rose from the ark.

Without warning, they collectively issued a horrific shriek. The sound punctured my entire body, a million pinpricks of terror nicking my skin.

They came at us.

Continuing their wicked howls, the clouds flew toward us and up the incline, spectral and translucent. One of them seemed to target me, and sailed right for my face.

The cloud reached me . . . and went through me. I *felt* it go through, a samurai blade slicing through fruit. Ghostly teeth cut cleanly through me like glass.

It didn't leave a mark—I could feel that even in my horror. It didn't break the skin. It simply passed straight through my bone and brain matter.

That's not to say it didn't hurt. It did. Like distinct blades slicing through me, sharp as scalpels.

My breath froze in my lungs and mouth as a lightning spike of ice shot down my spine. Cold. So very, very cold. I dropped to the ground, unable to move, barely able to breathe, still processing the agony in my face and skull where the cloudy spectre had swiped through me. Like my sinus cavities had filled with volcanic ash.

Paralysis set in. Freezing paralysis, like being in a full-body ice cube. I could blink, and I could force air in and out of my mouth, but nothing more. Powerlessness over-whelmed me, making the pain in my head a distant second.

I could not move, at the mercy of the undead thing that had struck me.

The spectres continued to race overhead, up the incline, and out into the cave.

That's the last thing I saw before mercy came to me and I saw nothing more.

Charlie, Dr. Prinn, and I meet at the front end of the Hummer as Selby slowly picks her way out of the truck. She stays close to the door.

"So now what exactly happens when you get in there?" I ask as Prinn starts decking himself out for the hike. Watching Prinn gear up makes me feel, if it is possible, even more ashamed. He has lights, glow sticks, ropes, carabiners, a helmet, and other tools I can't even identify. What had we been thinking, running through those tunnels in gym shoes, holding discount plastic flashlights?

"It needs my blood," Prinn says.

"Blood? Why?"

"You saw yourself. Blood is what opened it. It needs my blood to close it."

"Okay, but *why*?"

"It's all about sacrifice. Sacrifice dates as far back as we can date. We begin to recognize that we are dependent on forces beyond our control. The sun, the rain. It doesn't take long to realize that the things we are dependent on come from *up*. Somewhere 'up there' are the beings who control our crops. Our cycles of birth and death. We need to keep them happy. So we start giving them some of the crops. We say, 'Here! We recognize your generosity, let us give something back to you!' Then a drought happens. Well, obviously, we haven't given enough. So we give more of our crops. And more. Still no rain. What else can we give? What's left? What is left?"

"Our children?" I say, thinking of the maternity ward in Tucson I'd seen attacked.

"Exactly. Maybe that will prove how serious we are in our devotion and gratitude to these beings. You ever hear of Abraham and Isaac?"

"Vaguely."

Selby pipes up. "God told Abraham to sacrifice Isaac. One reason among a bazillion that belief in God is so stupid."

Prinn laughs out loud. The sound strikes me as being laced with something jagged. Maybe insane. I'm not sure I could I blame him.

"God tells Abraham to sacrifice his only son, that's right," Prinn says. "But if you read the text closely, you'll find something a little surprising. God never tells Abraham how to do it. Abraham seems to know already where to go, and how to do the deed. Abraham knows what he's doing."

"That's unsettling," I say as I consider it.

"Yeah, ain't it, though? See, there's 'Oh, I'm readin' the Bible,' and then there's really *reading* it."

"Why *your* blood?" Selby says.

Prinn shrugs. "There's nothing else left. We humans learned a long time ago that blood must be connected to our life somehow. That's what it wants."

"Yeah, but that thing . . . whatever it was in there forced me to gut myself. Why didn't it make Abby's mom do it, or one of the other guys? Where's the logic?"

"That, I don't know. But from what you describe, I'm guessing they were just worker bees. Some power in the ark, held down there all these eons, it could only seep out so much. I think we were the first to get so close to it, honestly. Maybe if we'd chosen another tunnel, we could have dodged its power completely. But it didn't need blood first. It needed to be . . . well, cleaned off."

"That's it?" Selby says. "That's your theory?"

"It's a work in progress," Prinn shoots back. "Sorry there's not a doctoral thesis on this anywhere, I'll be sure to write one when this is over. Now, are you girls coming?"

"Psh, I'm not," Selby replies immediately.

"Yeah, I don't know if I can go back in there," I say, mostly to Charlie.

"I don't know if I can do it without you," Charlie counters.

"And *I* don't care what you do, but we need to move, now," Prinn says. "Charlie? Let's go, son. We got a long hike and it's already been a long day."

He's right about that. An eight-hour drive is a long haul, even on the best of days.

"Please, Abby," Charlie says softly.

"What about Selby?"

"Oh, don't worry about little old me," Selby says. "I'll keep the home fires burning right up here under the relatively clear albeit smoky sky. Or maybe I'll just drive off with all your shit and find somewhere else to live the rest of my short-ass life."

"That's not funny," I say.

"No, it's not," she snaps.

"You're not serious, are you?"

"Probably not."

"Sells—"

"Just go," she says. "I'll be right here. But I swear to God—perish the thought—I swear to God, if you all aren't back out here by tomorrow afternoon, I'm out. I'm gone."

I reach into my hip pocket and dangle Mrs. Brower's keys in front of my face. Selby's expression sours.

"Well, shit. Maybe I didn't exactly think that one through. Fuckin' Girl Scout."

I walk back to her and hand the keys over.

"It's okay," I tell her. "It's fair. You can't go down there with a hole in your gut. Wait as long as you can, and if something shows up to come in after us, then go. Fast."

Selby closes her fingers over the keys, then looks at me like she can't believe I mean it. But I do. She seems on the verge of saying something, then simply nods once.

I nod back, and, since there's no reason not to, I lead the way into the cave.

If she shares a moment with Charlie, I don't see it, because I don't look. And I don't look because I don't want to know.

We make good time, the three of us. It's easier now because it's not my first time, and Prinn's extra equipment makes some of the more difficult places easier. But being back in the dark again, after everything we've seen . . . I can't help imagining the body of my father waiting around the next turn, the pulverized face of Dr. Riley peeking from some black crevice, or Mom's dried, mummified corpse skittering toward us. In reality—there's that word again—the only thing I recognize as we hike is the crushed plastic bottle Selby had emptied and left behind.

We reach the steep hill leading into the pit. Into an ark where some force once locked up creatures that had no place on this Earth, and which I had unlocked.

"All right," Prinn says, taking off his backpack. "This will do."

"Good," I say. "Because I don't think I could go any far—"

His gloved fist smashes square into my nose. I fly back several feet and land on the ground, barely breaking my fall with my hands. Exquisite pain forces water from my eyes and my spine to lock straight.

"Dad, *what*—!" Charlie screeches, then grunts.

I force myself to roll onto my backside. Prinn has unsheathed a wicked knife, serrated on one side, and is trying to drive it into Charlie. Into his son. Charlie has caught Prinn's wrist with both hands and is trying to steer the weapon away.

"Sorry, son," Prinn grunts, sliding a little on the gravel floor. "It wants my blood. You're my blood. You and Stephen."

The knife inches nearer. Charlie's eyes are wide and sickly in the glow of Prinn's headlamp and Charlie's dropped flashlight. Both men strain against each other. Prinn is stronger.

"I would have taken him. He's the firstborn. But you showed up on the road. Dumb luck that was. God told Abraham to sacrifice Isaac. Now he wants my son. I'm sorry."

"*Dad . . .* ," Charlie wheezes, but the blade comes closer. The tip is now hidden behind a fold in Charlie's shirt.

I'm beside the smashed boulder we found when we first climbed out from the pit. The boulder, crushed to rubble. I find a large stone that fits in my hand, slide to my feet . . . and hurl it as hard as I can at Dr. John Prinn.

The rock thunks him on the side of the head. A serious blow, if not for his helmet. But the impact is enough to rattle him, and he drops his arms away from Charlie. Without thinking, I scream and lurch at him, shoving both hands out. He makes an attempt at cutting me, and the blade slices across my left forearm.

Then he's gone. His arms pinwheel and his legs scratch for purchase, then he's falling backward into the darkness, screaming. A scant few seconds later, and the light from his headlamp is swallowed. His screams echo, but fade.

Fade . . .

And end. Not abruptly, but slowly, like turning down a volume knob. How long will he fall? I don't know.

I crash to the ground, weak and sick, gripping my cut arm tightly with my right hand. Charlie has backed up against the rock wall, staring down toward the ark.

Something must happen.

That's the only thought I can manage to string together with any coherence. Something must be about to happen: a dragon comes flying from the pit, or we're engulfed in green flame, or some tentacled thing comes and wraps us up and takes us down to wherever the immeasurable darkness leads.

But it doesn't. None of it. I have no idea how much time passes, but absolutely nothing comes up from the ark. What's possibly more frightening is that the darkness doesn't bother me quite so much anymore.

"You're bleeding."

Charlie's voice is raw and vacant.

"It's not bad." I stand up, shaky. "Charlie, I'm so—"

"No. Just don't. Let's get out of here."

He picks up his father's bag, and together, we begin the arduous hike back out of the cave once again.

We don't talk. Not even *Watch your step* or *Careful right there*. A disquieting sense of familiarity takes over, like how you can find your way to the bathroom in the middle of the night when you're at home.

Home. Where exactly is that now?

I'm sure the truck will be gone when we stumble out of the cave, but there's Selby, in the cab, reclining against the driver's-side door. Seeing us, she starts to hurry out, then slows as her injury reminds her of its existence.

"Just the two of you?" she says. She doesn't seem surprised.

I nod, and Charlie and I sit on the ground near the truck.

"So now what?" It's the first thing I've said to him in hours.

"I don't know."

"How did he find us?"

"He said it was dumb luck."

"After everything we've seen, are you willing to believe that? What are the odds we'd just run into each other like that?"

Charlie doesn't answer. Maybe there isn't an answer to be had.

"He was the threat to them," I say. "At my house, my dad . . . the animator had you there, but it didn't attack you. You were never the threat to them. Maybe it's over now, somehow."

"Yeah, maybe. Maybe not."

"Want to take the Hummer?" I say.

"Fuck that thing," he says, not sounding like Charlie at all. But I wonder if I'd recognize me, either. Then Charlie adds, "But we should totally take all of his shit."

So we totally take all of his shit. It's tight, but we're able to tie down the whole load with a tarp and elastic cords. Since everything's quiet, we decide to eat a small meal, sitting in a circle with one another and studying our food much more closely than is really necessary to avoid looking at one another.

"The army will probably wipe them all up," Selby says at last.

"Uh-huh," I say. I don't believe it. Neither does Selby.

"Where do we go?" Charlie says. "Riley's? It's close. It's known territory."

"No," I say. "Let's see if we can find a . . . a line in the sand, a front line of some kind. Maybe the army's been able to hold them somewhere. Maybe that's New Mexico, or maybe that's Boston, I don't know. But I say we go that direction."

Charlie and Selby agree. There doesn't seem to be much point in arguing, anyway.

We climb back into the truck together, but this time, I let Charlie drive. I get the sense he needs something to control right now. Selby sandwiches in between us, wincing.

"How you holding up?" I ask her.

"Still hurts. But maybe not as bad. Hard to tell."

"Can I take a look before we go?"

"No, no. I'm fine. I want to get out of here."

So we go. When we get to the highway, Charlie surprises me by saying, "You should've let him kill me."

Selby looks between us, then sinks a little in the seat, not wanting to get involved. She knows she'll get the story eventually.

"Something put those things in the pit," I say. "Now I don't know if that was God or Godzilla. But something put them all in there once before. That means there's a way to do it again. We'll find it."

"This whole thing might be over right now if you'd just let him—"

"No. How could a violent act end violent acts? People have

been trying it for thousands of years and it's never worked. I don't see that this would've been any different."

"Abby—"

"Listen to me, Charlie. Any god or gods who demand we go around killing each other are welcome to destroy this world if they want, because I won't bow to them. Not if those are their rules."

"Amen," Selby mutters.

"All right?" I say to Charlie.

He considers it for a while, then nods once, stiffly.

A few minutes later, the sun kisses the tops of the mountains behind us. It will be dark again soon. So, so soon. I hope wherever we end up, there will be light. Lots of it.

"Remember that whole riding-into-the-sunset thing?" I ask them.

"Yeah, sure," Selby says.

"Do you guys know what it's from?"

"It's a Hollywood thing," Charlie says, checking the mirrors. "From old Westerns. You know, John Wayne and cowboys and stuff. They beat the bad guys, and at the end of the movie, the good guys ride their horses into the sunset."

"Have you ever seen a movie where they did that?"

"I think maybe one of the Indiana Jones movies. Why?"

I gaze into the mirror, reflecting a golden red sunset. "We're going east."

"So the good guys lost?" Selby says. "Nice. Very inspiring."

"Or maybe the story's not over."

Take courage, mortal,
death
cannot banish you
from the universe.

—Benjamin Franklin

"Oh," Selby says. "Okay, or that. Girl Scout."

The last bit of sunlight disappears behind us.

We keep driving into the darkness.

We drive into the darkness together.